ID0984190

MISS
MELVILLE
RETURNS

ALSO BY EVELYN E. SMITH

MISS MELVILLE REGRETS

MISS MELVILLE RETURNS

A NOVEL BY
EVELYN E. SMITH

DIF

DONALD I. FINE, INC.
New York

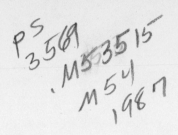

To Christopher

I

"HE'S DEAD!" Miss Melville cried before she could stop herself.

Everybody turned to look at her. Jill Turkel took firm hold of her client's arm. "Don't be ridiculous, Susan. He just passed out."

Susan Melville could see now, as Rafael Hoffmann's burly form was borne past her on "Concupiscent Toad Crushed by Passion"—an artwork admirably adapted to serve as a stretcher—that the artist was not only breathing, but that there was a smile on his bearded face.

"Sorry," she murmured, "it—it must have been the shock of seeing him fall like that."

Jill gave her arm a comforting squeeze. "Everybody understands, Susan. You're not used to this kind of thing."

Indeed I'm not, Miss Melville thought. Usually when I see them drop like that they're definitely dead. *Saw*, she reminded herself, *saw*. Her lethal days were behind her; she must take care not to let her memories of them become fond ones.

"I might have known something like this would happen to spoil my opening," Roland DeMarnay wailed.

"Don't take it personally, Roland," Jill advised him. "At least he didn't get into a fight with any of the guests—which was what probably would have happened if he hadn't passed out."

"I'll bet you were looking forward to it," Alex Tabor suggested.

Jill smiled and didn't reply.

"What do we do with him?" one of the two decorative young men staggering under the weight of the unconscious artist asked.

Since he was wearing dark glasses, unusual at an art exhibit, particularly when worn by a member of the gallery staff, Miss Melville deduced him to be the unfortunate Damian, whom Rafael had assaulted earlier in the evening. "We can't just stand here like live exhibits, slowly developing ruptures."

"Don't be a fool, Damian," Roland said. "Put him on the couch in my office. But first take off his shoes so he doesn't mark the upholstery."

The two youths trudged off. The musicians started playing again. The guests milled around and chattered. Damian and his colleague circulated bearing trays of champagne glasses; other young men went around with hors d'oeuvres and canapes. Nobody looked at the artworks. It was just another opening of another art gallery. Still Susan couldn't help feeling uneasy.

There had been a time, not too many years before, when nobody would have thought of inviting Susan Melville to speak at a gallery opening. There had been a time, too, when she would not have agreed to speak even if she had been asked. However, on this occasion Roland had asked her to speak and she had accepted and, she thought, done rather well. The guests were still applauding as she left the dais at the back of the gallery.

"Good show," Roland said, as he passed her on his way to introduce the artist. Roland was a small, youngish man, good-looking in a blurry sort of way, with a British accent so thick as to seem improbable. His original request, conveyed through Alex, was to have a Susan Melville exhibit to open his gallery, but, "There are over eight hundred art galleries in New York City alone," Jill had declared, "and there are at least seven hundred and ninety–nine I would take Susan's work to before Roland's." She'd glared at Alex. "I think you have a hell of a nerve suggesting such a thing, even if you are her half brother." If he had been Susan's full brother, her tone suggested, things might be different.

Susan wondered what Jill would think if she knew that Alex was not her brother even fractionally, that their relationship was a fictional one, hastily, almost accidentally, devised to obscure the fact that they had once been partners in crime. He'd been a professional assassin, she an unsuccessful artist. They had run into one another after she had on impulse killed an individual whom he had been assigned to dispose of. Recognizing talent when he saw it, Alex had recruited the genteel, middle-aged lady into the organization for which he worked, and she had embarked on a successful new career—with the stipulation that she would kill only those she found truly deserving of that fate.

The identity of her employer had been kept from her as a matter of company policy. Originally she had agreed to work for him with the proviso that he take one of her paintings each time she made a hit. This was to explain her sudden modest affluence to the Internal Revenue Service, for she would never have dreamed of failing to pay taxes on her gains, no matter how ill-gotten. As she'd had no reason to suppose that her employer knew or cared anything about art, she had supposed that her paintings must be mouldering away in some dank basement, preserved only because he had established a corporation to take care of the payments and he too would be accountable to the IRS.

Only after his death did she learn that not only had he treasured her paintings, but he had enshrined them in a room of their own as the jewels of his collection. As soon as the news was out her work was in immediate demand. Now, little more than two years after her employer's death, when Roland had introduced her to the gallery guests as "one of the brightest lights of the contemporary art scene," he spoke no more than what had come to be the truth.

As for Alex, by this time she had come to think of him as truly her brother. Since he had married the daughter of a long-time friend of hers, thus becoming inextricably enmeshed in her circle, it would have been difficult for her to repudiate him even if she had wanted to. Naturally, as a relative, he was going to seek favors for his friends. "All I did was ask if Roland could open his gallery with a Melville exhibit," he said. "I didn't try to exert any pressure on you, Susan, did I?" Which was true. Clearly he couldn't understand why Jill was making such a fuss.

9

Susan, of course, could. She knew that Jill was right. By speaking at the gallery opening, Susan was, in a sense, giving her approval to both Rafael's work and Roland's gallery, neither of which deserved it. When she had refused to let her work be exhibited there, she'd unthinkingly agreed to speak as a graceful social gesture of atonement; and, by the time she realized it would seem like far more than that, it was too late to back out.

"You're letting the whole lot of them use you as an advertisement," Jill grumbled. "You're making a speech for Roland. You're wearing Baltasar's dress. God knows what else you're doing for them that you haven't told me about."

As Susan Melville's artist's representative, Jill felt she should be consulted on all of her professional decisions. No argument with that; but Jill's definition of "professional" seemed to be all-inclusive.

In Susan's youth, artists had always been represented by the galleries that showed their work. Today, however, some artists, like actors and writers, had representatives, but their field of operations was much wider in scope than literary or theatrical agents'. In addition to serving as dealers, artist's reps could also be press representatives, managers, investment advisers, guides, counsellors, and/or friends. So Hal Courtenay had told Susan, and, as Director of the Museum of American Art, he ought to know.

It was Hal who had introduced Jill to Susan. Even though she had great respect and even admiration for him, she did not take to Jill right away. Jill seemed more like a human dynamo than a normal, civilized young woman of thirty-three—which was the age Jill claimed, although she looked and acted much younger. She was aggressive, in fact, downright pushy, which at first put Susan off—unreasonable of her, she realized. A good business-woman, a good agent, had to be pushy, if only to compensate for her client's deficiencies in that respect. Moreover, Susan was so beset by dealers anxious to represent her, and friends and acquaintances anxious to push the claims of favorite dealers, that the strain was growing unbearable. When Mimi Hunyadi (formerly Carruthers) took it upon herself to warn Susan against Jill—alleging that the girl was a vulgar little red-headed upstart who knew nothing about art—that did it. Susan signed with Jill.

Not out of spite. Spitefulness was a petty emotion, unworthy of a Melville. Even Black Buck Melville, her pirate ancestor, although charged by his enemies with every sin imaginable, had never been accused of spite. But, once she had decided to go with Jill, she could allow herself to take pleasure in the knowledge that it annoyed Mimi. It would be a long time before Susan could forgive Mimi for her despicable behavior when, as chairman and loudest member of the MAA's Board of Trustees, she had been the moving spirit in selling out the Melville Wing.

Hal himself had had nothing to do with this, he assured Susan later. He had been in Europe at the time, tracking down some elusive Cassatts. "Otherwise, I would have done my best to stop it." Not, of course, that a curator, even a chief curator, as he had been then, would have had that much clout. Hal had been Director of the MAA for only the past year, ever since the previous director had expired among the statuary, so peacefully that it was some time before it was discovered that he was not part of the collection.

Before joining the Museum, half a dozen or so years earlier, Hal had been a free-lance art expert and critic, teaching at various schools and contributing to most of the significant art journals. He also did an occasional piece for popular periodicals—all in all, a typical member of the city's resident *intelligentsia*. Not at all the sort of person Susan would have expected to be a friend of Jill's, but then art made strange bedfellows these days.

From the purely practical viewpoint, Susan seemed to have made a wise choice in going with Jill. Under Jill's aegis, the prices for her paintings quadrupled immediately and were still on their way up.

Susan had wondered whether whoever arranged for a speaker at an occasion like a gallery opening got some sort of commission or finder's fee. If so, Alex must be getting it, which might account for

Jill's bad temper. However, Susan had a feeling it was something more, some personal animosity toward Roland. It couldn't be a question of money. The girl had to be doing very well, not only as Susan's rep, but also as representative of the late Darius Moffatt's estate—and possibly of other artists as well, for she was evasive when Susan tried to find out who Jill's other were.

When Susan asked Hal about it, he explained that an artist's rep whose clients were very high-priced usually handled only one or two in order to give them the personal attention they deserved. Susan sometimes felt she could do with a lot less personal attention. One thing you could say in a gallery's favor; it didn't keep breathing down your neck at every turn.

As for a commission, if anything like that were involved in getting Susan to speak gratis, it was less likely to take the shape of money than of a favor repaid or anticipated. And she certainly didn't begrudge it to Alex. Through Roland, he had made other arrangements as well. The Baltasar original she was wearing was worth thousands of dollars and there was no question of payment.

When Baltasar's offer had been made, she'd been reluctant to accept, not out of high-mindedness but because she was afraid she might be obligating herself to wear a dress that she wouldn't be caught in dead while she was still alive. She had never heard of Baltasar. His reputation had been achieved chiefly south of the border and in Madrid, and the stories about him she had read in the press convinced her only that he must have an excellent press agent.

Mimi assured her that the ladies she knew in Spain spoke very highly of his gowns and even more highly of his aristocratic connections. "His wife is a *condesa* and he himself is related to the dukes of Asturga—on the wrong side of the blanket, of course, but who cares about that these days?"

"I don't care if he's related to the Duke of Plaza Toro," Susan said. "All I care about is whether I've committed myself to wearing a dress that'll make me want to hide in the ladies' room all evening." But the dress turned out to be beautiful, a heavy dark gray silk shot with gold, that gave her the timeless elegance of a nineteenth-century portrait. So what if Baltasar was using her to help make a name for himself in New York. He deserved to have a name in New York.

Baltasar himself, a tall thin dark man who did indeed look like a Spanish grandee, came up to her now and kissed her hand, to Jill's undisguised disapproval. "My dear Susan," he said, "your speech was truly an inspiration. And the dress looks divine. All the ladies are asking, 'Who created that glorious gown for the glorious Miss Melville?' This is an evening of triumph, not only for Roland and Rafael, but also for me."

"Shhh," Jill whispered, "Roland's speaking." Maybe she thought Baltasar should have designed a dress for her too.

If the speech with which Roland had introduced Susan had seemed excessive to her, his introduction of Rafael Hoffmann was positively fulsome. But Susan Melville was merely a drawing card. Rafael Hoffmann was money in the pot, although, according to Jill, the ante in this case wasn't very high. "Even if Roland couldn't get you, I would still have thought he could do better than Rafael Hoffmann for his opening show," she'd said, looking at Rafael's work with disgust.

Rafael Hoffmann was a multimedia artist. His *oeuvre* combined painting, sculpture, and various crafts, with bits of photography, and, Susan supposed, mechanics or electronics, for some of the pieces moved in curious ways. Some even uttered remarks, most in bad taste, in the artist's own guttural accents whenever the unwary viewer got within a certain distance. There was one chair-shaped object ("Sitting Duck Incarnate") that made a rude noise if somebody was foolish enough to try to sit down on it.

How times had changed. When Susan had gone to the Hudson School—a world-famous institution that had finally cashed in its chips during the 1970s, after a glorious late-nineteenth-century, an eminent early-twentieth-century, and a respectable mid-twentieth-century past—a student would have been expelled for pulling something like that. Today they put it on exhibit.

Rafael himself, however, was a type that had been common

enough when she went to art school, a type that had been common ever since art schools came into being; and before that probably there had been at least one in every old master's *atelier*. He was a huge, hairy young man—hard to judge his age because of the beard but she would place him in the mid-thirties—who looked like an ape and had manners that would have aroused comment among a tribe of baboons.

Not that she blamed him for having mistaken her for Alex's mother rather than his sister when they were introduced. After all, she was old enough to be Alex's mother, and had often considered herself lucky that fate had chosen to pass him off as her father's child (illegitimate) rather than her own. However, she resented Rafael's probing questions into how the disparity in age— and, indeed, in name—came to be.

He kept asking questions about Father," she told Alex, "almost as if he . . . suspected something. You don't think he does, do you? After all, he's been working in Mexico, but, according to the catalogue, he comes from somewhere in South America." The biographical essay in the front of the catalogue was oddly vague about his exact place of birth; and South America was where Buckley Melville had vanished after absconding with millions of dollars, most of them not his own, and where the man Susan loved had had a very unpleasant experience with a tribe of savages. She had been hypersensitive to that part of the world ever since.

"Pay no attention to Rafael," Alex advised. "He seems to have cultivated offensiveness into an art form. If there were awards for it, he'd take first prize."

Roland had stopped speaking and was about to introduce Rafael with a flourish—except that Rafael wasn't there. Roland's young men scattered to all points of the gallery in search of the artist. At last he was brought forth from behind a door (which Jill had discovered led to the washrooms and to another door marked "Private," that opened onto a stairway) and pushed onto the dais. He started to speak. Although his English was good enough, his accent was so thick it was sometimes difficult to understand what he was saying. He seemed to be telling the assembled guests how wonderful he was. "... After years of degradation and neglect, at last I have the chance to reveal my genius in its true light. The world will recognize me as one of the greatest geniuses who has ever lived..."

"Do stop snorting like that, Jill," Susan whispered. "They can hear you all the way out in the foyer."

II

AS SOON as Rafael was well launched, Roland came over to where Alex, Susan, and the ubiquitous Jill were standing. Everything seems to be going well. "Don't you think everything's going very well, Alex? Susan, I can't thank you enough for agreeing to speak. Everybody who matters came, and I know I owe it all to you."

Roland was wrong. Not everyone who mattered had come. Although Hal Courtenay had naturally been invited to the opening of the DeMarnay Gallery, he had not shown up. Perhaps it was too much to have expected him to dignify the occasion with his presence. But Susan couldn't help feeling disappointed. She'd looked forward to seeing him and hoped that this time they could manage to ditch Jill and go somewhere together afterward.

Baltasar's wife, the *condesa*, had not shown up either, although she had been expected. "She was very sorry that she was unable to come," Baltasar explained, "but the doctor has ordered her to rest. She has a tendency to—how do you put it?—overdo things. But I promise you she will be at the Grand Drug Ball and Gala."

"Promise Mimi Hunyadi, not me," Roland said sulkily. Mimi was presiding genius of the Grand Art against Drug Abuse Gala and Ball that the Van Horn Foundation (Mimi had been born a Van Horn) was sponsoring in conjunction with the MAA and several large corporations. It was expected to be *the* event of the coming season, and she had succeeded in roping Susan into serving on one of the committees. Usually Susan avoided that sort of thing, but this time she could not refuse; the cause was too worthwhile. She was annoyed with Jill for saying approvingly, "It'll add at least ten thousand dollars to your going price, more if you can possibly manage to be witty and charming so you'll be asked to serve on other committees."

"But I don't want to serve on other committees. One's enough."

"It isn't a question of what you want," Jill said sternly. "You can't live for pleasure alone. Getting the right people to see you in the right places is what's important. Don't forget to be especially nice to Brooke Astor, and maybe you'll get a one-woman show at the library."

"What do you think of Rafael's work?" Roland whispered to Susan.

"If you try hard enough you can always find something nice to say without having to resort to a lie," Susan's mother always used to say. Susan tried hard to find something nice to say about Rafael's work. "He has great technical facility. That cat rubbing itself against 'Hall Tree of Life' looks almost real."

In keeping with what seemed to be Rafael's prevailing theme, "Hall Tree of Life" had plastic replicas of women's breasts hanging on it instead of hats. However, in this instance Rafael had overreached himself. Susan had never before realized how much a woman's breast looks like a pink pith helmet. The cat was black and without obvious symbolic significance, unless its gold collar, ornamented with what appeared to be green glass jewels, stood for something.

"The cat *is* real," Roland exclaimed indignantly. "Baltasar, I told you to keep that animal shut up!"

"I'm sorry, someone must have left the door open." Baltasar picked up the cat and gave her into the charge of a middle-aged woman whom Susan had met previously at the fitting of her gown. Sanchia Guttierez had looked sad before. Now, wearing a couture gown in which she was obviously ill at ease, she looked miserable. "Would you take Esmeralda upstairs and make sure she doesn't get out again?"

"Si, Señor Baltasar," the woman said, "but I am sure I locked the door. Someone must have let her out." She carried the cat off in the direction of the stairway. Susan had a feeling that she was glad to have an excuse to escape from the festivities.

"Pity it wasn't a dog," Jill murmured. "That would have been really appropriate."

Roland gave her a chilly look.

Rafael droned on and on. His accent was growing impenetrable, not that it mattered much because by this time no one was even pretending to listen to him. He also seemed to be unsteady on his feet. Nervousness? Susan wouldn't have thought he had a nervous bone in his body. She was always one to overlook the obvious. It was Jill who pointed out the truth. "Rafael's loaded to the gun-wales, Roland. You should have kept him away from the bar."

"I tried," Roland whined. "I did the best I could, but I couldn't be everywhere at once, could I? I told Damian and Paul to keep an eye on him, but he was awful, especially to Damian."

"So that's where Damian got his black eye," Alex said. "When I asked him, he said he'd run into 'On the Horns of a Dilemma at Midnight.' Which seemed entirely plausible," he finished as he surveyed the art work in question, a pink phalluslike object ("Really, Roland," Jill had said, "somebody should tell Rafael that phalluses are passé") with a grandfather's clock painted on it and horns, both zoological and musical, protruding from it at odd angles. "Which reminds me—" Alex glanced at the Gold Rolex on his slim olive wrist "—fascinating as Roland's speech is, I'm afraid I must tear myself away. I promised Tinsley I would be back early, and in her condition her every whim is my command. Since she has to keep up such a brave front at the office during the day, she feels she's entitled to go all Victorian of an evening." For Tinsley was determined to work until the bitter end, less out of feminism, Susan thought, than because she did not quite trust Alex to keep his eye to the helm without her.

"Do make my apologies to anyone who's interested, Roland. I'll stop at the buffet and pick up some pickles. Do you provide dog-gie bags?"

"Pity your charming sister-in-law couldn't make it," Roland observed, after Alex had gone, "but naturally she would want to avoid crushes."

"Of course it would be the ultimate act of creativity if she came to the opening and gave birth right here," Jill said.

Roland tittered. "That might do for the East Village perhaps but hardly for Madison Avenue."

In point of fact, the DeMarnay Galleries were just off Madison, in one of the most opulent sections of this most opulent of cities, on the first floor of an elegant white limestone townhouse that Roland shared with Baltasar, who was about to establish a New York presence. "It must be costing them both a fortune," Jill had observed earlier, "even if they're only renting. I understand Baltasar's a well-established couturier abroad, and he must be well fixed, but Roland's just a third-rate dealer, minor old masters, major modern disasters. Where would he get that kind of bread?"

"Maybe somebody's backing him," Susan suggested, hoping it wasn't Alex, although he'd hardly be able to do that without Tinsley's knowledge, and Tinsley would know better than to invest their own or their clients' money in so dubious a venture. But what did Susan herself know about such things? Art was big business these days; possibly Roland's gallery was a sound investment. The location was good and the gallery itself a handsome showcase for any kind of art.

On the other hand, Roland himself did not impress her as a sound investment at all. I shouldn't let his appearance prejudice me, she told herself. Many of our most successful entrepreneurs look equally sleazy.

"More likely he borrowed the money from some sucker," Jill said. "Or—"

"Or what?" Susan asked.

"Oh, I don't know. Took out a bank loan, maybe."

But Susan felt sure that wasn't what she had started to say.

Rafael had begun chanting in a language that Susan couldn't identify. Perhaps it was Indian; she'd heard Rafael had Aztec or

Incan or something like that blood. If Peter had been there, she reflected, he would have been able to identify the language and to tell them more about it than anyone wanted to hear; so perhaps it was just as well that he was away in Canada, teaching at the University of Saskatchewan, the only post he'd been able to get after his return from that ordeal in South America. Not that there was anything wrong with the University of Saskatchewan, an excellent institution, but that he would have preferred somewhere closer to New York. And so would she. On the other hand, in Saskatchewan he couldn't be much further from the Indian tribe he'd been studying unless he went to the North Pole.

That suited him perfectly. For months after his return, he had awakened night after night screaming in a strange language, causing Susan distress and loss of sleep. She hoped that once he had settled down in his job he would not attempt to go out in the field again, this time wanting to turn his anthropological attentions to the Eskimos. She believed they had harpoons and would not hesitate to use them.

"Far be it from me to tell you your business, Roland," Jill said, "but don't you think you'd better turn Rafael off? People are beginning to laugh and once they start laughing at an artist it's only a matter of time before they start laughing at his work."

"You simply don't understand, Jill," Roland said. "His work is intended to be witty and amusing, even a trifle cheeky, but it is true, Rafael has spoken long enough."

He started for the platform. But, before he could reach the artist, Rafael stopped in mid-chant and crumpled to the carpet with a thud that seemed to shake the entire gallery.

III

ALTHOUGH THE ambiance had lightened with Rafael's removal from the scene, the party had improved only by omission. Susan found herself growing bored, and so apparently did Jill. "Well, now that the fun is over, time for us to fade into the sunset. Speaking of which, the evening is still young. Why don't I gather up Charlie or somebody and we can go on a club crawl. Unless you want to stay and circulate?"

It was clear that if Susan elected to stay and circulate, Jill felt it was her duty to stay and circulate with her.

"My only complaint," Susan had told Hal, a few months after she'd signed with Jill, "is that she seems to think she's my nursemaid as well as my rep. I can't seem to go anywhere without having her dogging my footsteps."

To which Hal had smiled and said, "She probably thinks you're so . . . unworldly you need looking after."

Unworldly, indeed! How surprised both Jill and Hal would be if they knew how she had been making her living for the past few years. No, they wouldn't be surprised. They simply wouldn't believe it.

"Perhaps Jill is a bit overprotective," Hal conceded. "You need a chance to . . . er . . . spread your wings and fly on your own."

She'd fancied he was about to suggest a trial flight in his company, but she never knew, because just then Jill had interrupted, as she always interrupted—deliberately, Susan sometimes thought. But why? To protect Susan from Hal? To protect Hal from Susan? Or was it simply that she had the instincts of a mother hen?

She was doing her mother-hen bit now. "Thanks for the invitation," Susan said, "but I feel a little tired. I think I'll just go home."

Jill nodded with an excess of understanding. "I know. It must have been a rough day for you."

Susan wasn't in the least tired; she was just bored. However, the prospect of being hauled by Jill and one of her young men from one disco to another seemed even more boring. Shortly after she'd become Jill's client, Peter had been called to a job interview in the South, leaving Susan tickets to an art film they had planned to see together. She went with Jill. She'd been under the impression that it was going to be an art film about chimpanzees. Instead, it was a film about chimpanzee art—all the arts, including music and the dance. The chimpanzees beat on hollow logs; they screamed; they stomped. Jill was enchanted. "They'd go great at the Palladium," she said.

Susan had agreed. Only Jill had meant her observation as a compliment. Susan had not.

So she left the gallery at the same time as Jill, but not with her. She half expected Roland to make a fuss when they made their farewells; however, although he expressed polite regret at her early departure (and none at all about Jill's), he made no effort to persuade her to stay. Rafael's collapse might have enlivened the party for everyone else, but it had spoiled it for Roland.

As she left, Susan couldn't help but gaze wistfully at the floral arrangements. Even if she stayed to the end, though, she had been forbidden to make off with them. "That's tacky," Jill had said when she caught Susan taking a bunch of bouquets at the conclusion of an earlier festivity. "Even Eloise Charpentier doesn't stoop to that. If you want flowers, why, for heaven's sake, don't you just go out and buy them? At seventy-five thou and up per picture, depending on size and subject, you certainly can afford it." Susan was well aware that she could afford all the floral arrangements she wanted—or needed, rather, for she was primarily a painter of flowers although she had expanded in new directions ever since changing her professional outlook. It was just that she appreciated them more if she picked them up herself.

Eloise Charpentier came out of the gallery right after them. "Anybody going my way?" she asked brightly. One of the richest women in the world, she never paid for a taxi—or anything else —if she could help it.

"I'm going uptown," Susan said, "but I'm walking."

"I'm going downtown," Jill said, "and I'm taking the subway."

Eloise looked disappointed. "Oh, I'm going—er—east," she said, "so I'll bid you ladies good night."

"I'm surprised that you didn't take a cab especially so you could give her a lift."

"Normally I would," Jill said, "but it's been a rough night."

The phone rang so early the next morning Susan thought it must be Peter having worked out the time differential incorrectly again. However, it was Alex with news. "Rafael went into a coma last night and died before they could get him to a hospital. Roland called me up at the crack of dawn to tell me about it. He was positively gibbering—seems to take it as a personal affront."

"Did somebody poison him?"

"Somebody's certainly going to do something drastic to him if he keeps carrying on like this... Oh, you mean Rafael?" Alex laughed. "Of course not, it was a perfectly natural death—a perfectly natural accidental death, anyhow. Apparently Rafael drank a couple of gallons or so of whiskey, and then shot himself up with heroin, which would have killed a moose, except that a moose would have more sense than to mix drugs and drink."

"Was Rafael a drug addict?"

"I haven't the least idea. Why do you ask? Why do you care? I've always felt you needed a hobby, but I didn't expect you to start making an avocation out of sudden death. Death is like sex, you know. To kill is one thing, but to be a voyeur of death quite another. I never figured you for a voyeuse, Susan."

"Don't be silly, Alex. I can't help being interested. After all, I was there."

"So was I. So were a lot of other people. I'm sure they're all talking about nothing else. So far as I can tell, and I've read the morning papers, nobody so much has hinted it was murder—which is what you seem to have in mind."

"Somebody could have deliberately injected him with heroin."

"Why is it so hard for you to believe that he didn't inject himself?"

There was no reason at all why Rafael should not have injected himself. Not with suicidal intent—he'd been too boorishly triumphant in his gloating over glories to come—but without realizing that he was taking too much of everything. Many people had died of overdoses of heroin. Hadn't the artist Darius Moffatt died of a heroin overdose back in the seventies? Or had it been cocaine? No, cocaine hadn't been that potent then.

When Susan had been a hit woman, she'd never employed poison herself. The nature of her work had required immediate public recognition of the fact that each death was brought about by design and with lofty moral purpose. However, she had often thought that if one's aim was simply to get rid of someone without making a statement, poison would be quiet, efficient, and, providing you didn't go in for one of the imported alkaloids, economical. And, of course, a lethal dose of a narcotic would be poison: a lethal dose of anything would be poison.

She remained curious enough to follow the news accounts of Rafael's death. The post-mortem showed that the heroin Rafael had used was "black tar," an unusually potent type from Mexico that had been sweeping the United States and had caused numerous fatalities, even among hardened addicts. The drug came from Mexico and Rafael came from Mexico; at any rate, he had been living and working there. Everything seemed to fit together. As for whether or not Rafael was a habitual drug user, there was no way of knowing. According to the newspapers, his arms were so covered with the nicks and scratches that were the normal accompaniment of the various crafts he used in his art that needlemarks might not have shown.

There seemed to be no ground at all for her suspicions. Even the most unlovable of us, she reminded herself, generally die of natural or accidental causes. Just because Rafael Hoffmann had been murder-worthy did not mean he had been murdered.

The death was officially posted as an accident and the city health commissioner took the opportunity to make a speech before a local civic organization warning against the dangers of drug use by the city's artists and artisans, although he was handicapped by the universal awareness that cocaine was currently the drug of choice among the members of the city's creative community. People weren't taking the drug problem seriously enough, he said.

"Obviously he hasn't heard about our Grand Gala," Mimi Hunyadi said afterward, and put him on her mailing list.

Susan was browbeaten into attending Rafael's funeral along with Alex, Roland, and Jill. There weren't too many mourners besides them: some of the young men from the gallery, Baltasar, Sanchia Guttierez, and a melancholy man with a drooping moustache who was introduced as her husband and seemed to speak no English. It snowed a little, as if Nature had started to add a touch of pathos to a scene deficient in that quality and gave up without really trying. Some of the flowers looked suspiciously like the bouquets Susan had passed up at the opening.

The DeMarnay Gallery closed for a week out of respect for the artist. When it reopened with what was now termed "The Rafael Hoffmann Memorial Exhibit," everything sold immediately, which was to have been expected. Since the artist could work no more, his works automatically became more desirable. What was surprising was the amount of money they fetched.

"If you ask me," Jill said, "Roland didn't delay the opening out of respect for Rafael; he did it so he could go around and jack up all the prices."

But wasn't that more or less what Jill had done with the second Darius Moffatt show, when she'd owned that little gallery in Soho? The Lord knew where she'd gotten the money to start it. She'd been fresh out of City College, she'd told Susan, and without assets or experience. She must have borrowed, it, Susan thought, or been backed by a boyfriend.

The situation wasn't quite the same because Moffatt had been dead for some time when the first show opened, but, after its success, Jill had doubled—or was it tripled?—the prices for the second. It was simply a matter of sound economics, and just went to show that Roland was a better businessman than he looked.

"Well, at least there will be a nice little sum for the widow," he said.

Susan was surprised to hear that there was a widow. The biographical essay had made no mention of a spouse. The bereaved Mrs. Hoffmann, Roland said, lived in Mexico and had never been out of it in her life.

"I wanted to fly Lupe to New York for the opening, but Rafael said no. He said she would feel out of place here, that she was just a simple peasant woman unaccustomed to the sophisticated life of the metropolis. I'm afraid he was ashamed of her."

"Ashamed of her!" Jill exploded. "*He* had the gall to—!"

"Now, now, *de mortuis* and all that. I know it seems ridiculous that a . . . a rough diamond like Rafael should feel embarrassed by anyone else's behavior, but we all have our little self-deceptions, don't we?" And Roland looked fixedly at Jill, who bit her lip and remained silent.

Susan remained silent too, although there were a number of questions she would have liked to ask. Why had Rafael's body not been sent back to Mexico or his native country for burial? Or at least why hadn't Roland arranged to have Lupe flown up for the funeral, since this time Rafael was in no position to object? It's none of my business, she told herself, resolving to get Alex aside and see if he could find out the answers.

However, Alex professed to know nothing at all about Rafael's private life, in fact very little about Rafael himself. "I knew him only through Roland," he said, "and I don't know Roland all that well. We got acquainted because he used to sell pictures to the General from time to time. But we never really . . . palled around

—is that the right expression? I like girls and he likes boys, and never the twain shall meet."

She didn't believe that Alex's acquaintance with Roland was as slight as he professed. Granted that Alex was definitely heterosexual and Roland apparently homosexual, that did not prevent them from being friends, and it certainly did not keep them from having been mixed up in shady deals together. Or unshady deals, but shady seemed more likely. She remembered Hal's once saying that some of General Chomsky's acquisitions had proved to be forgeries, and wondered whether Roland—and possibly Alex, in the days before he had turned respectable—had been involved with them. Not that it mattered. If a collector couldn't tell the real thing from a fake, why waste the real thing on him?

She was surprised to learn that it was Baltasar who had bought the bulk of Rafael's works; she'd thought he had far better taste. However, it seemed that he was already a patron of Rafael's, having purchased some of the artist's works several years before, for his Acapulco salon.

"I felt the harsh aggressiveness of the pieces would provide an effective contrast to the elegant fluidity of my gowns," he told Susan. "Now, after the tragedy, I thought it would be appropriate to place his work in my salon here, as a permanent memorial to a genius that never did achieve its full potential."

But ill luck seemed to follow anything to do with Rafael Hoffmann. His pieces were still in the gallery when a careless workman dropped a cigarette into a can of combustible material and the whole place went up in flames.

Luckily, the fire department was able to put them out before they could spread to Baltasar's part of the building. However, the works of an unfortunate artist whom Roland was planning to feature in his next show were ruined by smoke and water. Although, as Roland (rather cruelly, it seemed to Susan) pointed out, he would get more from the insurance than he could ever have hoped to gain from the sale of his works, he remained inconsolable. As for Rafael's pieces, they were totally destroyed.

IV

SOME WEEKS after these events had taken place, Susan went out to dinner with a former colleague from the European-American Academy. Normally Susan would never have agreed to have dinner with Hortense Pomeroy, who, as a gym teacher (or games mistress as the Academy's brochure had it) had inhabited an entirely different sphere. A drink at most. However, Susan was feeling low. Hal Courtenay had called to cancel a dinner engagement he had with her and Jill for the ostensible purpose of discussing an artists' seminar to be held under the Museum's aegis.

Susan was interested in participating, because, as she told Jill, she felt she ought to become more a part of the comtemporary art world, rather than hold herself aloof as Jill seemed to want her to do. Jill denied any such thing. "You're just paranoid. I am not deliberately trying to keep you away from other artists. Go to Hal's tacky little seminar if you want to. Spoil the image I'm trying to build up for you."

In this particular instance, however, Susan was less interested in making herself a part of the art world than in making herself part of Hal's world. She found herself growing more and more interested in him. Not only was he one of the handsomest men she had ever met, but she had so much more in common with him than with any other man she knew—background, interests, even a bit of shared past; for it turned out that he'd been a classmate of Susan's at the Hudson. She hadn't recognized him when Mimi first introduced them at the Chomsky Memorial Exhibition, and he'd had to remind her. Who would have dreamed that the weedy, rather obnoxious adolescent could have developed into this suave, distinguished-looking scholar, with an accent—apparently acquired during his studies abroad—that was even fruitier than Roland's. He, however, claimed to have recognized her the instant he saw her again. "I could never have forgotten you, Susan, even after twenty years."

"Closer to thirty."

"Ah, well, we were both very young then."

"Do you still paint at all any more?" she asked.

He'd shaken his head with a mournful smile. "I soon discovered that I had a certain technical facility, but no real talent. So I went back to Harvard, took my degrees in art history and became a hanger-on of the art world. Because that's all curators and critics and connoisseurs really are—art groupies. Unable to create, we worship at the muse's feet and sometimes, rendered mean-spirited by our inadequacies, nibble at her toes."

She had an idea that she had read the same words somewhere in one of his magazine pieces. Either that, or she was going to.

Despite the fact that Jill would be there, Susan had looked forward to that dinner. And now Hal said he had to fly to Houston to look at a reputed Whistler that had mysteriously turned up there and had to be inspected in a hurry, because the owner was impatient to sell.

"I'm sure it's a wild goose chase," Hal told Susan over the phone. "What would an unknown Whistler be doing in Houston? But I must go. Part of my job, you know." There was amusement in his voice. Everyone knew museum directors didn't have jobs. They held positions.

Unreasonable of her to feel so disappointed, even after he said, "I'll call you just as soon as I get back and perhaps we could have dinner without Jill; everything doesn't have to include Jill, does it?"

Wasn't that what she'd wanted? Yes, but he's just saying that, she told herself; he doesn't mean it, and even if he does ask me to dinner without Jill, she said to herself severely, I shouldn't accept because of Peter. Not that Peter would mind if she went to dinner with another man. It would never occur to him that Susan could be seriously interested in any man besides himself.

Susan couldn't help wondering about Hal's private life. His public life, of course, was a matter of record. A biography of him had been included in the Museum's Annual Report, together with a pipe-in-mouth picture that made Jill snigger every time she saw it—which might have been the reason why he'd apparently given up smoking.

Susan didn't like to ask questions about Hal. She didn't want anyone to get the idea that she was interested in him personally. Fortunately it took very little encouragement to get Mimi Hunyadi to tell all she knew about everyone who had the slightest connection with the Museum. Unfortunately it took a lot to stop Mimi, so Susan also had to listen to detailed accounts of the lurid (if Mimi were to be believed) lives led by the other members of the Board of Trustees, and in which she didn't take the least interest, although she never would have believed it of Ariel Slocum.

As for Hal, it seemed that he had left the Hudson to marry Cecily Flicker, who must have been at least twenty-five years his senior. She had financed Hal's studies, first at Harvard, then Oxford, and the Sorbonne. When he hit thirty, he became too old for her and she dumped him for a twenty-year-old minimalist. The parting was amicable and the settlement must have been substantial; otherwise, Mimi observed, he would hardly have been able to live as well as he did on a museum director's salary. His handsome apartment on Park Avenue belonged to the MAA, of course, but he also had a house in the Hamptons, a farm in Connecticut, "And a villa somewhere or other—a Greek island, I think, although it might be Italian. One always thinks of the isles of Greece, but there are isles of Italy, too. Any country with a coast is apt to have islands."

"He must be very comfortably off," Susan said, not wanting to use a vulgar word like *rich*.

"Oh, Cissy was always very generous with her ex-husbands. After all, what else did she have to spend her money on?"

Neither Mimi nor the biography mentioned any subsequent wives, but if there had been any in the past, obviously there was none current or she would have been required to appear at Museum and related festivities. Rumor had it that he'd been involved with Peggy Guggenheim at one time, but then who hadn't? Sometimes Susan fancied she saw Eloise Charpentier look at him possessively, but then Eloise looked at everything possessively. When your family owns so much of the world it's easy to forget they don't own all of it.

When Hal had introduced Susan to Jill at an MAA benefit, Susan thought for a fleeting moment from the proprietary way he put his arm around the girl that there might be something between them. Then she decided there couldn't be, or Jill would scarcely have brought one or another of her young men to places where Hal was likely to turn up. She couldn't have been attempting to flaunt them in his face, because they were not the kind of young men to arouse jealousy in even the most insecure bosom. In the roughly two years that Susan had known Jill, the girl had run through at least half a dozen men. "Searching for true love," she had once explained to Susan, on imagining she discerned a raised eyebrow—which was not the case. Jill had merely been projecting the middle-class standards to which she'd been born, not understanding that in Susan's original milieu anything went that didn't frighten the horses. The trouble was that most of Jill's young men would by their appearance alone frighten any horse worthy of his oats. I must not be judgmental, Susan thought. Maybe Jill can't do any better.

Certainly Hal and Jill had known each other for a long time. They had met, she knew, after the first Darius Moffatt show, when Hal's enthusiastic review in *Muse* had launched the artist on a posthumous road to success.

But that must have been nine—no, ten—years ago. Had Jill and Hal become lovers then or later or never? Although curious to the point of nosiness about everyone else's affairs, Jill was reticent about her own past; and Susan was too entrenched in the mores of a more gracious era to do more than give vent to pointed hints, which were ignored with equal pointedness.

Hortense had rung up with her invitation soon after Hal had called to cancel his, and Susan had accepted, perhaps to punish herself for having thought of Hal in a romantic light. Ridiculous, at her age. Not that love and even sex were inappropriate for intelligent adults, but romance was strictly for teen-agers and idiots.

However, the punishment she had inflicted on herself proved to be crueler and more unusual than she had anticipated. Like most gym teachers, Hortense considered herself a physical fitness expert, and, like most physical fitness experts, she was a bore. Susan was bitter, yes, but she had reason to be. Hortense had told Susan they were going to eat at a place called Sprouts 'n Stuff, and said, "My treat," before Susan had a chance to ask for a change of venue. Treat, indeed, Susan thought, as she studied the menu morosely.

Hortense had the athlete's typical disdain of subtlety. Hardly had they finished their zucchini zingers and started on their seaweed and soy lasagne when she started making her pitch. She was organizing a health club for middle-aged women and she wanted Susan's help.

"Seems to me there are plenty of health clubs around already," Susan said, more brusquely than was her wont, but she resented having been put in the position of appearing in public with a lady of mature years and Wagnerian proportions who chose to attire herself in lavender sneakers, baggy purple pantaloons, an oversized greenish yellow shirt-jacket, and a pink beret. The fact that this made Hortense in no way remarkable among the clientele of Sprouts 'n Stuff did nothing to allay Susan's peevishness.

"Yes, but all of these health clubs are aimed at the young or the would-be young, and you know how distressing it is for the average middle-aged woman with the average middle-aged shape to have to work out alongside those skinny young things in their skimpy leotards."

Susan didn't know, since she had never felt the least desire to "work out" herself, stoutly resisting Jill's efforts to make her join in a morning jog. "I myself run," Jill had said, "but I'd gladly slow down to a jog for you."

"But why restrict your club to middle-aged women?" Susan asked. "Isn't that discriminatory? Surely there are middle-aged men equally in need of physical improvement."

Hortense shook her head with a superior smile. She seemed to have more teeth than most people, or perhaps it was that nature had equipped her with a set designed for a horse rather than a member of the human race. "My dear, most middle-aged men who work out at health clubs go there specifically to look at the young girls jiggling around in those skimpy leotards—hopefully more than look at. Men are masters of self-deception. They see the sags and bulges of their wives as disfigurements, but regard their own paunches and protuberances as no more than slight and almost endearing flaws."

Susan remembered that there had been talk around the Academy that in youth Hortense had been crossed in love, her fiancé having run off with a lady mud wrestler. At the time she had dismissed it as part of the bitchery endemic to the cloistered ambiance. Perhaps there had been some truth to the story after all. Not that there wasn't a certain amount of truth in what Hortense was saying. Maybe the fault lies in my own upbringing, Susan thought. I still haven't accepted the idea that now women have acquired some power they can be allowed to age as ungracefully as men.

And, to be fair, men should be allowed to have face lifts without the kind of snide remark Jill had made about Hal. Why shouldn't Hal have had his face lifted if he felt the need? Not that Susan believed he had done any such thing. Some people simply aged better than others. I really must stop thinking of Hal, she thought. At least in that way.

"Anyhow," Hortense was continuing, "women of our age prefer to suffer and sweat in an all-female atmosphere, revealing ourselves in our glory to the opposite sex only after we have achieved our full physical potential."

Hortense apparently felt she had achieved her full physical potential and was revealing herself to the world in all her glory. Susan wondered if Hortense were planning to use herself as an advertisement. If so, she was definitely not going to have anything to do with her health club.

"At first we didn't want to use the term 'middle-aged' in our promotional literature, but we ran up against semantic difficulties. Today 'adult' means dirty, and 'mature' over the hill, so, since we didn't have much choice, we decided to be frank and open about it." Hortense flung open her jacket to reveal a massive bosom draped in a pink T-shirt bearing the slogan, "I'm Glad I'm a Muppie."

"You're glad you're a *what?*"

"A Muppie. Middle-aged Urban Professional. As opposed to Yuppie—Young Urban Professional." Hortense whinnied with laughter. "Don't you think that's darling?"

"No, I do not. And I thought the U in Yuppie stood for—" Susan winced "—upwardly mobile."

"'Upscale' in the case of Muppies, because by that age they'll have moved as far as they're likely to go. And the club certainly isn't going to be cheap. It's a very solid business proposition or I wouldn't have dreamed of bringing it to the attention of a busy professional woman like you."

As if I were a dentist or an account executive, Susan thought, unreasonably irked. "It could be inexpensive and still profitable," she said.

"Now that you're rich, Susan, you can afford to be liberal. But those of us who have to work for a living have to take a more conservative approach."

"I work for a living."

"Oh, well, painting. You can hardly call that work." Hortense went on quickly, in case she had given offense, which she had,

"We have a first-class group of instructors lined up, real pros, and, in addition to the usual aerobics, Nautilus machines, and so on — all geared to the specific requirements of the woman past forty — we're planning to offer some very unusual courses. For instance, Lady Daphne Merriwether has come back after spending years in the Himalayas — you know, where they used to practice polyandry, so a girl really had to be on her toes — with a really effective system of self-defense for ladies. 'Nothing flashy, no threatening gestures or loud cries but simple low-key disablement, and, if need be, dismemberment, with a minimal extrusion of unpleasant body fluids, such as blood.' I'm quoting from the prospectus, of course."

"I rather thought you might be. Does this system have a name?"

"The Merriwether Method. As I've said, there's nothing showy or vulgar about it, and none of that psychological claptrap about releasing one's aggressions. It's completely functional: you hit me; I kill you. You must meet Lady Daphne. I know you'd like her, both of you coming out of the top drawer, as Lady Daphne herself might say."

"I look forward to meeting her," Susan said politely. "However—"

"Since you're in the age group we're appealing to, and since you're doing so well now, I'm sure you'll want to invest in such a worthwhile as well as potentially profitable undertaking. In a way it's your duty." She added temptingly, "As soon as we're well under way, we could extend our range to include those of more modest means, even offer scholarships to the truly deserving. I daresay bag ladies stand as much in need of the Merriwether Method as the more privileged. We could call them the Melville Scholars and have a back door for them to come into the club by."

It's not fair for her to appeal to my sense of duty, Susan thought. For people with her background and upbringing, the word "duty" was like a trumpet to a warhorse. And Hortense knew it. She'd been exposed to enough of the Academy's fund-raising schemes to know how to arouse the guilt feelings in old money, and even though Susan's money was now new, she still had the old-money instincts.

"Here, let me give you some copies of our prospectus. Your friends might also be interested in investing."

She handed Susan a surprisingly bulky envelope.

She whinnied. "Tell your brother, the stockbroker, that, although men can't join the club, we're only too happy to accept their money."

Susan wondered whether, once the club was under way, she might not take a course or two with Lady Daphne. She needed something to take the place of her shooting sessions with Alex. She missed them. Of course there was no longer any need for her to keep in practice, but she felt that once you had a skill you ought to keep it viable. You never knew when it might come in handy again. However, General Chomsky's estate was no longer available to them for target practice. The land had been sold and the art collection removed with all except the choicest items placed in storage while the Museum prepared a permanent home for them —something that, thanks to the General's will, it could now afford.

"The problem," Hal Courtenay had confided in her, as he was giving her a private peep at the Cassatts prior to their public unveiling, "is that our name is the Museum of *American* Art, while a number of the finest pieces in the collection are by foreign artists. The Board hasn't decided whether to try to get a zoning variation, enlarge the entire building, and rename it 'The American Museum of Art' or to put up a separate but connecting building and call it 'The Chomsky Addition to the Museum of American Art,' which would be considerably more expensive and mean we'd have to give up the parking lot. Meanwhile, we're going through the collection and deaccessioning the duds. The General made some very strange purchases as well as—" he smiled at her "—some very perspicacious ones. Your work in particular."

She tried not to simper.

"Some, I fear, are out-and-out fakes."

"The General bought fakes?" She was surprised. Of course she knew General Chomsky hadn't known anything about art, but she would have thought that as a good businessman he would have taken care to have his purchases vetted by someone who did.

"There are bound to be works of questionable authenticity in any major collection. Even experts have been fooled, you know. The Metropolitan has had its share of forgeries—more than its share, some would say," he added with a meaning smile, for he had made no secret of the fact that he did not think much of the direction in which the Met had been going in recent years.

V

EVEN THOUGH Susan and Hortense had dined at six—Hortense being a firm believer in early feeding—night had already fallen by the time Susan finally managed to detach herself. It was a pleasant evening in early spring, and, perhaps subliminally influenced by all Hortense's talk of fitness, Susan chose to walk the dozen or so blocks to her apartment.

Her route brought her past the DeMarnay Gallery, which had been closed to the public for almost a month now. Most of the neighborhood—if you could call so elegant an ambiance by so plebeian a word as neighborhood—shops were closed; most of the residents were presumably still at dinner. For a couple of minutes the street was deserted except for herself and a young man who emerged from the shadows under the front steps of the DeMarnay Gallery, came into the sunken area beyond, and mounted the steps that led to street level. She would have thought nothing of this except that, instead of opening the gate in the iron fence that separated the areaway from the street, he was climbing over it.

He seemed to be taking no particular care to avoid attracting attention, which would have been difficult for him to do, in any case, as he was accompanied by a beagle who was determined not to leave the areaway. Something under the front steps was fascinating him, and he had to be hoisted forcibly over the fence, struggling all the time.

The young man caught Susan's eye and grinned cheerfully. He gestured toward the massive padlock that fastened the gate. "Forgot my key," he said. It was not, Susan thought, an adequate explanation.

The young man set the dog down on the sidewalk. Losing interest in whatever fascinations lay down below, he rushed over to Susan and sniffed her with embarrassing thoroughness. Then, with a short, disappointed woof, he returned to his master.

"Don't let Brucie give you a feeling of rejection," the young man said. "He has very low tastes."

Susan felt she should do something. But what? There were a few people on the street now, but no one had been there to see the young man make so unconventional an exit from the premises. It would be his word against hers, unless he told the truth, which was hardly likely. Anyhow, why should she care if somebody was burglarizing Roland's—or possibly Baltasar's—premises?

In the light of the street lamp, the young man certainly did not look like a burglar. However, these days when law-abiding citizens dressed like riffraff, malefactors might very well choose three-piece suits and ties. He had light hair cut rather short and an attractive, snub-nosed face of the all-American kind that used to prevail among movie leading men before sinister ethnic types became the fashion, and still could be seen in advertising extolling wholesome products like cornflakes and mouthwash.

She looked down into the areaway. In the dimness, she could see boards and lumpy shapes under a tarpaulin, all presumably connected with the workmen who were renovating the place. There was also a grille which, from its size and shape, appeared to have been intended to close off the archway under the steps. However, instead of fulfilling its function, it was leaning against an adjacent wall.

Could the young man have gotten inside the house that way? No, there would be a door under the front steps as well as the grille.

She felt she should say something. "The gallery's closed, you know. There's nobody around."

"So I discovered." He gave her a bright smile. "Do you have any idea when the reopening's planned?"

"No, I'm afraid I don't."

"I understand there was a fire."

"Yes, there was."

"Luckily there doesn't seem to have been any damage—to the exterior anyway. Except for those boarded-up windows, you couldn't tell anything had happened."

As they turned to look at the windows, they saw, through a gap between the boards, a light go on. "I see we were both wrong," the young man said. "Somebody is up there after all."

"Perhaps you'd like to go back in. Only I'd suggest that this time you use the front door."

"Oh, I don't think I'll bother. It's getting late and neither Brucie nor I have had our dinner. Another time perhaps."

A cat emerged from the shadows under the steps. Apparently feeling secure now that man and dog were on the other side of the fence, it came halfway up the steps and hissed at them. The green-studded gold collar identified the animal: Baltasar's Esmeralda.

Brucie barked and attempted to squeeze through the bars back into the areaway. The young man snapped a leash on his collar. "Come along, boy," he said. "Cats are not your game."

He raised his hand to Susan in half salute. "Have a nice evening," he said and strolled off with Brucie, looking like any honest citizen walking his dog.

Susan knew she should do *something*—at least ring the bell and advise whoever was inside of what she had seen. But she didn't know who might be inside. Perhaps this malefactor had left on discovering that the premises were already occupied by another, more dangerous one. It was true that someone who had no right to be there was hardly likely to answer the bell, but in New York anything was possible.

In the end she went home and called Alex for counsel. "I

wouldn't worry," he said. "Roland knows some very peculiar people."

Actually the young man had not looked at all peculiar, which was what made his behavior especially strange.

"Then you don't think I should have called the police and told them about it?"

"You don't want to call the police," he said. And he was right. She didn't. "Anyhow, it's too late for that now. But if it would make you feel better give Roland a ring and tell him about it."

That sounded like an excellent solution. Roland could decide for himself what, if anything, he wanted done about his nocturnal visitor. And, if he couldn't make up his mind, then the burden of indecision would rest upon him. "Where is he staying?" she asked. "What's his phone number?"

"Didn't you know? He has an apartment on one of the upstairs floors of the gallery building."

"But surely it isn't habitable now."

"He told me he's managed to get the place back into livable shape—lucky for him, as he's too broke to afford a hotel. He put everything he had into the gallery."

"But doesn't Baltasar own the building? Why is Roland living there, then?"

"They were both supposed to live there at the beginning. Since the building is zoned for both residential and business use, it seemed like a practical idea. Baltasar has an apartment there, too, on the top floor; there's a sort of penthouse up there, Roland tells me. It was scheduled to be finished by the time the gallery was opened, but apparently it didn't get done in time. So he's still at the Plaza. Lord knows when he'll ever be able to move into the apartment now."

So the light she saw must have been in Roland's apartment—which still didn't explain the mysterious young man.

The gallery's phone rang and rang. She was beginning to think that either she'd been wrong and no one was there, or that Roland had a private number and wasn't answering the listed one.

Finally she heard the sound of the receiver's being picked up, followed by heavy breathing. It's the caller who's supposed to do the heavy breathing, she thought, not the callee.

"Hello," she said.

The only answer was a giggle. It didn't sound like Roland's.

"This is Susan Melville," she said. "I'd like to speak to Roland DeMarnay."

There was the sound of whispering and more giggling. "She wants to speak to Roly Poly," a muffled voice sniggered.

The gigglers and whisperers—there seemed to be several of each—receded. Silence for a minute; then the sound of footsteps approaching, a clattering sound, and a sharp cry as the approacher fell over something. Somebody, not the faller, laughed; and somebody, presumably the faller—this did sound like Roland—swore.

Roland's voice came on the other end of the line, speaking very slowly and carefully. "Shoo—Shoosan Melville. What a delightful shurprise."

He was obviously drunk or on something, and it was none of her concern. "I don't want to worry you," she said, "but I think there's something you ought to know."

She told her story as succinctly as possible, because somebody in close proximity to Roland was making bubbling noises. "I know it's probably nothing," she finished, "but—er—Alex thought I ought to tell you about it."

Roland pulled himself together enough to master most of his consonants. "Oh, it's something. Everything's something. Nothing is nothing."

"Tha's really profound, Rollie," a voice from behind him said.

"That's rollie profound, Really," another voice added. Both voices giggled with glee.

"Are you going to call the police?" she asked.

"Oh, I don't think that's nesh—nesheshary." He took a deep breath and enunciated his words very carefully. "I know it's an imposition, but I would appreciate it if you could come over and show me exactly where you shaw—saw that man come out."

He gave a faint shriek. "Not now, you idiot!" he said in an undertone. "Sorry," he said to Susan. "I don't mean tonight, of course; it's late and I have . . . uh . . . gueshts."

There was a mad outbreak of giggling and one demoniac laugh. His voice became partly muffled, as if he had placed his hand inaccurately over the mouthpiece. "Shut up, you bloody fools; this is important."

Then, to Susan, "Sorry again, I was talking to . . . to . . . " He seemed afflicted by a momentary aphasia.

"Your guests," she finished helpfully.

"Right! If you could posh—possibly come over tomorrow and show me—tell me exactly what you saw—"

"Show and tell!" a voice burbled. "What fun!"

"—I would be most grateful. Perhaps you would allow me to give you lunch. There are some other things I've been meaning to ask your advice about."

"I already have a lunch date with Jill," Susan said, pausing to give him the opportunity to include Jill in his invitation, but all he said was, "Oh."

"The gallery's not much out of our way. I'd be glad to stop off—say around eleven-thirty; Jill likes to eat early—and show you where I saw the man. Or I could come after lunch if that would be more convenient."

"The earlier the merrier," he said. "And now, I'd better go check the door and make sure it's locked."

"By the way," Susan said, before he had a chance to hang up, "does Baltasar know Esmeralda's down there in the areaway?"

"Eshmeralda?" Roland repeated. "Eshmeralda who?"

"Baltasar's cat. He called her Esmeralda or something like that. You remember, she was there at the opening. I recognized her from her collar."

"Oh, yes, his cat," Roland said, as if he had trouble recollecting what a cat was. "I'd better go out and collect her. I wonder how she got out there."

"Maybe he lets her out at night," Susan suggested. Then she remembered that Baltasar wouldn't be there to let Esmeralda out.

"Oh, he'd never do that. Those stones in her collar are real emeralds. First class all the way, that's Baltasar." He didn't explain how it was that the cat was on the premises if Baltasar himself wasn't living there. Perhaps Roland was cat-sitting.

Later that evening Jill called to ask whether Susan would like to go to an auction of contemporary American art at Allardyce's on Wednesday. "To the pre-sale exhibition in the morning; we don't have to go to the auction itself. The *Times* says one of the pictures up for sale is a Darius Moffatt. That's hardly likely, but I feel I should check it out. Interested?"

"Sure, why not." Susan knew the prices that paintings fetched at auctions were important in setting future market prices, and, even though none of her work had or was likely to come up for auction anytime soon, she felt she ought to keep up with these things. "We can make definite arrangements tomorrow at lunch. We're going to have to make a stop first, though. I had a little adventure earlier this evening."

"Met a handsome stranger, did you?"

"As a matter of fact, that's exactly what did happen."

Once more she recounted the evening's events. Jill was a far more receptive audience than Alex, uttering little squeals and cries at appropriate points. "So Roland's up to his old tricks again," she observed after Susan had finished.

"What do you mean? What old tricks?"

"Carrying on with his friends like that," Jill said quickly. "But what do you suppose that guy was doing out there? And you actually spoke to him? Weren't you scared?"

It had never occurred to Susan to be frightened, but, now that Jill mentioned it, the man could have been dangerous. He hadn't looked like a killer, but then, Susan thought, neither do I. "I hardly think a criminal would go skulking about with a dog. Especially not a beagle."

"It doesn't seem likely. A Doberman would fit the picture much better. On the other hand, a Doberman would arouse instant suspicion."

"Maybe he was just a nosy neighbor. I mean the man, not the dog. I hope I haven't alarmed Roland unnecessarily."

"You can't alarm Roland unnecessarily. He needs to be shook up from time to time. Does him good."

"He said he wasn't going to call the police," Susan said.

"And spoil his party! Of course not. Anyhow, the man's gone. Even if Roland does find something missing, he might as well wait until morning. But I doubt that he'll find anything missing that he'd care to report to the police."

"What do you mean?"

"I mean I doubt that he'll find anything missing. Glamour boy was probably just—what's the expression?—casing the joint. What I mean is who the hell cares if Roland was robbed? Serves him right for not asking me to lunch, too. He's a fantastic cook, you know. He should have opened a restaurant, but an art gallery was always his dream."

"You seem to know him quite well," Susan observed.

"Oh, in the art world everybody knows everybody else. Where shall I make our reservations for lunch?"

"Sprouts 'n Stuff," Susan said. "You'll love it."

"Where?"

"Just a joke. We'll go to Leatherstocking's as usual. Wild gymnasts wouldn't drag me to Sprouts 'n Stuff again."

She explained, expecting Jill to jeer at Hortense's project. But she'd forgotten that Jill was something of a health enthusiast herself. She approved of the idea. "It might make a good investment. Health clubs are still very viable, and most of them aren't geared to the geriatric—to middle-aged women. Your friend—what's her name? Hortense?—just might have something there. Want me to look into it?"

"If you want to," Susan said. "I'll bring along the prospectuses tomorrow and you can give the extras to your friends. I'm certainly not going to give them to mine."

When she hung up she got the package of prospectuses with the intention of putting it on the table in her foyer so she'd remember to take it along the next day. The package had seemed unduly squishy. She opened it and saw why. In addition to a goodly supply of brochures, Hortense had enclosed a T-shirt with the "I'm Glad I'm a Muppie" motto. Susan stuffed it back into the envelope. She would give that to Jill, too.

VI

THERE WERE plenty of signs of life about the DeMarnay Gallery next day as Susan and Jill approached. Workmen drifted in and out, carrying boards and pails and obscure implements of renovation. "Hiya, Red!" one called to Jill and made a rude sucking noise with his lips.

She gave him such a dirty look that he advanced his pace from snail to turtle and disappeared into the building after one last languishing glance. The years may come and the years may go, Susan thought, but the American construction worker remains unchanging in his primeval simplicity.

Jill expressed a similar thought aloud. "Slime bag," she said.

The two ladies climbed the short flight of steps that led to the massive front door, now restored to its original turn-of-the-century elegance—or perhaps it had never lost it. Other parts of Manhattan had their ups and downs; the strip between Fifth and Park Avenues from the sixties to the eighties had always been and probably always would be up. It was good to think there were some constants in this ever-changing, usually for the worse, city.

The door stood ajar. From inside came the merry sound of hammering, sawing, general banging, and voices raised in altercation. Jill would have walked right in, but, as the place wasn't officially open, Susan insisted on ringing the bell, even though the disputants were standing in plain view in the foyer.

One was Roland, looking as if he rather than Esmeralda had been the one to be dragged in the night before, the other a handsome young woman with black hair streaming over her sable-clad shoulders. Susan could just imagine the effect she must have had on the workmen. The young woman—although she seemed to be about the same age as Jill, you would never think of calling her a girl—was stamping her booted foot, flashing her eyes, and otherwise exhibiting all the traditional signs of Latin temperament. "I want my money," she was saying, "and I want it now!"

"But, Lupe, that's impossible. There are all sorts of legal formalities . . ."

At the sound of the bell and the sight of Susan and her companion, Roland smiled weakly and yanked at the open collar of his sports shirt, as if by pulling it together he could pull himself together. "Susan, this is Lupe Hoffmann; Lupe, Susan Melville. And Jill Turkel," he add grudgingly.

"Not Lupe Hoffmann," the woman said, "Lupe Montoya." The rage vanished from her face as she turned to the two newcomers, to be replaced by a dazzling smile. "I have never used any of my husbands' names. An artist must retain her own identity, don't you agree?"

"Definitely," Jill said.

Lupe grasped both of Susan's hands in hers. She wore a great number of rings and had a very hearty grip. "Susan Melville, I have heard so much about you. It is an honor and a privilege to meet so distinguished an artist."

"You must be Rafael's wife," Susan said, detaching her hands as sympathetically as possible. "I'm so sorry about what happened to Rafael."

"Pah, he was no good, as an artist and as a man. The world is better off without him."

Although Susan couldn't have agreed with her more, she was a little shocked at the bereaved widow's forthrightness. I'm still the prisoner of my upbringing, she thought.

"But I should have been informed of his death," Lupe said. "I should have been advised of the funeral arrangements. I should not have been left to read about it in the newspapers."

"I certainly do agree," Jill said. "Why didn't you advise Lupe of the funeral arrangements, Roland?"

Roland's pale blue eyes looked waterier than ever. I do hope he's not going to burst into tears, Susan thought. "I sent a telegram to Cancun," he insisted. "You can check with Western Union."

"But I was not in Cancun," she said. "For the last six months I have been in tour in Australia. Everybody knew that."

"Apparently nobody in Cancun did," Roland said, "or the telegram would have been forwarded."

She simmered down a little. "I have been travelling about a good deal. It is possible that it could have missed me," she conceded. "But Baltasar must have known I was not there."

Roland looked guilty. "I don't think I discussed your whereabouts with him. I just told him I was sending you a wire. Everything was in such a state—funeral arrangements and the gallery—and I had to cope with it all by myself."

He looked around him for a sympathetic face and found none. Susan might have felt sorry for him if she hadn't recollected that he had Damian and Paul and other minions to help him cope.

"Rafael died months ago," Jill said. "How come you didn't get here until now?"

"Was Rafael a world-famous artist that the Australian papers should carry an account of his death on their front pages? No, it was not until I got to San Francisco, after cutting short my trip because they did not appreciate my art in Australia—such boors there, I tell you—and I went to pick up Fido and Rover (I had to leave them behind because of those stupid quarantine laws they have there) that I was told what had happened to Rafael."

"I thought you said you read about it in the newspapers," Jill pointed out.

"I never read the newspapers. As an artist, I am above such matters."

There was a whirring sound. A door in the panelling of the wall opened, revealing a small elevator, from which Baltasar emerged, along with a small, bespectacled man carrying a clipboard. Baltasar wore a pullover and slacks that looked as if they had been designed for royalty; the other man was in shirt, vest, and trousers that looked as if he had slept in them. Both looked unhappy. They were followed by Esmeralda. She seemed to be in excellent spirits, weaving in and out of everybody's legs, carrying her tail erect like a flag.

"It is very discouraging, very," Baltasar was saying. "So much work to be done. I'm not sure I can afford it—emotionally, at least. And no amount of insurance could cover the cost of my gowns, and, of course, the Hoffmanns."

"The Hoffmanns?" the little man repeated. "Oh, yes, the art objects. Most regrettable."

Baltasar's expression changed as he caught sight of the group in the foyer. "My dear Susan, Jill, how nice to see you. And Lupe. What a lovely surprise.

He kissed all the ladies' hands. Although he was a tall man, Lupe towered over him. Even if she had not been wearing stilt heels, she would still have topped him. This was a lady who obviously gloried in her physical proportions. Although Susan was beginning to do more and more figure work, Lupe was a subject she would not care to tackle. No matter how she painted her, Lupe was bound to come out looking like Wonder Woman. Leave her to Roy Lichtenstein.

"I was desolated not to see you at the funeral," Baltasar said to Lupe, "but not surprised. I know how things were between you and Rafael."

"It is true that we had not spoken to each other for several years," Lupe acknowledged, "but I hope I know what is correct. No matter what the inconvenience, I would have made every effort to come to Rafael's funeral if I had been informed of it."

Roland's voice rose to a whine. "I didn't know she was in Australia. I wired Cancun. It was a mistake. I'm sorry. What more can I say?"

He was starting to say a good deal more when Baltasar cut in gracefully, "It was in part my fault. There was no reason why I should have assumed that you knew Lupe was in Australia. But, after all, what does it matter? Even if she had been able to come to the funeral it still would not have brought poor Rafael back."

Susan expected Lupe to say something about the undesirability of bringing poor Rafael back, but she was silent. Apparently she was somewhat in awe of Baltasar. Susan could understand that. Although he might claim to be descended only from dukes, there was something definitely regal about him.

The man with the clipboard murmured something and disappeared through another little door in the panelling. Esmeralda stood on her hind legs and prepared to launch an attach on Lupe's boots. Baltasar bent over and picked her up. He turned to Susan. "I must thank you for restoring my little Esmeralda to me. It worried me to have to keep leaving her here at night, but the Plaza does not accept pets. So uncivilized, so different from hotels in other countries. However, I thought she had been locked up securely."

He certainly does have bad luck with his turnkeys, Susan thought, remembering that Esmeralda had made another unauthorized appearance on the night of the gallery opening.

"We had a prowler last night," Roland said. "I told you. I called you right away. Almost right away. This morning, anyhow. Susan—" he motioned toward her, as if by the gesture he was passing on some of the blame "—saw him. He must have let her out."

"What I would like to know," Baltasar said, "was who let him in?"

Roland seemed to take this as an accusation. "Prowlers don't have to be let in. They break in."

"What about the alarm system?"

"The workmen had to disconnect it, so they could paint the grille. They said they wouldn't be able to put it back for a couple of days. I didn't think it mattered since there wasn't anything around now to—to interest a thief."

Baltasar made a sound between his teeth that seemed to be the Spanish equivalent of "Tcha!" "Was there anything to show that anybody had actually broken in? Did you check?"

"Not exactly," Roland admitted. "I had to unlock the door when I went out to take Esmeralda in, so it must have been locked. But I didn't go out and actually look at the outside of the door. It was too dark."

"There is a light under the stairs that can be turned on, I believe."

"I didn't turn it on. I—I wasn't dressed. And I didn't look this morning. I figured I could wait until Susan came and we could look at it together."

"In case something was waiting in the dark underneath the stairs, so it would get her first," Jill put in.

"Jill, I don't think—" Susan tried to interrupt, but Jill continued, "Anyhow, I don't see why you were so insistent that Susan come show you where and how it happened? Couldn't she just have given you the details over the phone? Why make her go to all this trouble?"

"No trouble at all," Susan said. And it was true. Roland was merely an annoyance. It was Jill who was making trouble. "As far as I could tell the man was just prowling. He may not have gotten in at all. Mightn't Esmeralda have sneaked out through an open window or something?"

"That must be it," Roland said eagerly. "I didn't think to look at the windows."

"And you heard nothing?" Baltasar asked.

"I had the stereo on," Roland said weakly.

Baltasar gave him a long look, then turned to Lupe. "My dear, if there is anything I can do to help, please call on me."

"That is what I am about to do. I am as a child when it comes to legal matters. Do you think I have grounds for a suit of law against Roland?" who uttered a protesting noise at this point, "And how do I find out whether there is a life insurance policy?"

Baltasar patted her hand. "Don't worry, Lupita. Leave it to me. I will see that everything is taken care of."

* * *

"Well, shall we go take a look at the scene of the crime?" Susan suggested, adding, "Just a figure of speech," as Roland gave her a reproachful look.

Leaving Baltasar and Lupe, together with Esmeralda, in the foyer, Susan, trailed by Jill, went out with Roland. By this time the workmen had given up all pretense of working and were sitting on the front steps of the gallery, eating and drinking things out of brown paper bags. Several of them made appreciative noises as Jill passed.

"Roland, can't you stop them?" she demanded.

He shook his head. "I don't like it either, but it has something to do with union rules, I think."

"Union rules? Oh, you mean their sitting on the steps. I meant about their passing sexist remarks."

"I wouldn't be surprised if that didn't turn out to have something to do with the union, too."

The workmen laughed coarsely, and one of them made a remark about Jill's physical attributes, that although technically flattering, was of an explicitness that went beyond the boundaries of mere bad taste.

A sandwich was lying on the step next to the offender, tastefully laid out on a paper napkin. Jill walked over, brought up her foot, and stomped it.

The workmen stared at her open-mouthed.

"Next time, Buster, it'll be your hand."

She swaggered back to her companions. She was clearly pleased with herself. Roland wasn't. "Did you have to do that, Jill?" he complained, as he unlocked the gate and they descended into the areaway. "Don't I have enough trouble with the men already?"

Before Jill could say anything, Susan jumped in with, "You wanted to hear about the man I saw last night, didn't you?"

She described the visitor's appearance.

"Doesn't sound like anyone I know," Roland said.

"Sounds like somebody I'd like to know," Jill said, "and, even though I'm not an animal person, I'd even be willing to learn to love the dog."

"Dog? What dog?" Roland yelped. "You didn't say anything about a dog last night, Susan?"

Susan told him about Brucie. "I didn't go into detail last night," she said tactfully, "because you seemed to be busy, but it did seem odd that a prowler should have a dog with him."

Roland's face went ashen. "Would you mind not saying anything about the dog to Baltasar? He—he has a thing about dogs. He can't stand them, and it would make him nervous to know that there'd been a dog anywhere near the place. *Please!*"

The poor man's really going off the deep end, Susan thought. "Of course I won't say anything about the dog to Baltasar if you don't want me to," she said. "And neither will Jill; will you, Jill?"

"Oh, all right," Jill said.

In the daylight, Susan could see the door behind the group of museum-quality garbage cans underneath the front steps, quite a handsome door, considering that it was, in effect, the tradesmen's entrance and would be all but concealed, once the grille (now with a "Wet Paint" sign on it) was put back in place. There were no back doors for tradesmen on the block, because the buildings, like most of the buildings in Manhattan that had originally been designed as private residences, were all attached; no way of reaching the diminutive rear yards from the street.

Roland examined the lock on the door carefully. When he bent over, Susan noticed that, although he had combed his hair carefully to conceal it, he had the beginning of a bald spot. Poor Roland, Susan thought, he'll hate being bald.

"Any chance that your visitor did get inside?" Jill asked.

"The lock doesn't seem to have been tampered with, as far as I can see. But locks can be picked. And this is an old-fashioned one you could pick with a hairpin. I did have a new lock installed on the grille but the workmen took it off when they removed the grille."

"How about the windows?" Susan asked.

They were generously proportioned, easily big enough for a man to get through; however, like all ground-level and below-ground-level windows in New York, they were heavily barred; in this instance, covered with ornamental ironwork that matched both the grille below and the gate above.

"You did check to see that nothing was taken?" Susan asked.

"Nothing was taken, I'm sure."

But he still looked worried. "What's in your basement, Roland?" Jill asked, trying to peer into a window, but the blinds were pulled all the way down to the sill.

"Nothing to interest a thief. Nothing to interest anybody. Just storage space and a workshop."

"Why do you have a workshop?" Jill persisted, in spite of her client's frown. "You've never been good with your hands."

"I can hire people who are, can't I? I was going to use it to unpack and crate exhibits and frame pictures, that sort of thing, maybe even do a spot of restoration in the case of older works. I had such plans for the future. Now—" Roland sighed "—I—I feel the place is under a curse."

"It does look that way, doesn't it?" Jill chirped. "Don't worry, though. They say trouble comes in threes. First Rafael, then the fire; one more disaster and you'll be home free."

"You've always been so supportive, Jill," Roland said.

"Perhaps the handsome prowler could qualify as the third disaster," Jill suggested. "Or Lupe. She looks ready to make trouble."

Roland addressed himself to Susan as if Jill were not there. "It's not that I don't want to give Lupe the money from the sale of Rafael's work, but there are legal formalities to be observed. We're taking it for granted that, as his widow, she must be his heir, but supposing he made a will leaving his money to somebody else."

"The money'll have to be put in escrow until the legal heir or heirs is determined," Jill said.

"Something like that," Roland muttered.

Susan got the impression that the money had not been placed in escrow, that Lupe would be lucky if she ever saw it.

* * *

Roland snapped the padlock on the gate shut behind them as they came out of the areaway. "It's all too much. Sometimes I wish I had never—" he stopped.

"Never what, Roland?" Jill asked. "What do you wish you never had done?"

"Opened that gallery at all. It's a big responsibility, a big responsibility."

Susan tried to think of something reassuring to say to him. Nothing came to mind. Poor man, he was unpleasant, incompetent, and, she suspected, not altogether honest, but she did wish there were some way she could cheer him up.

He smiled faintly. Apparently he had thought of something to cheer himself. "Jill, did you know there's a blob of chopped liver on your shoe? Charles Jourdan, isn't it? Too bad, I wouldn't be surprised if it was completely ruined."

VII

ALTHOUGH SUSAN would have preferred to go directly to Leatherstocking's, Jill insisted that they go back inside the gallery to say goodby to the others. "It's only civil," she said. Susan and Roland exchanged glances. Civility was not one of Jill's long suits. Obviously the girl was up to something.

Once again they ascended the front steps. The workmen had all vanished; probably they were hiding until Jill left. Or perhaps they were on strike. Was it possible that having one's sandwich stepped on by a friend of the management was grounds for a strike? That could be Roland's third disaster, Susan thought.

Roland held her back at the top of the steps while Jill galloped ahead. "I must talk to you alone," he said in a low voice. "I need your advice. It's really quite important. Could we possibly have a drink later this afternoon? Or a spot of tea?"

Oh, dear, Susan thought, he's going to confide in me. People always were confiding in her, asking for advice, bending her ear. They thought that because she listened she was sympathetic, when actually she was merely being polite. Sometimes it paid to be rude. But here too she had been victimized by her upbringing.

"I'm sorry, Roland, but I'm afraid I can't make it tonight," she said. "I'm going to pick Alex up at his office, and then we're going over to his place for a family dinner." Most likely Amy, Tinsley's mother and an old schoolfellow of Susan's, would be there; she was there most of the time now. Susan didn't look forward to an evening of prenatal conversation, but that was what came of acquiring a family.

"How about tomorrow then?" Roland persisted.

It would be unkind to put him off again. Morever, if she pled another engagement, he would simply try to make another date. So difficult to reject someone who didn't expect to be accepted. Better to get it over with.

"I think I could make it tomorrow," she said, "although I'll have to go home and check my calendar just to make sure." She had learned at a very early age always to leave herself an out. "Shall we meet here?"

"That would be very convenient. Or I could come over to your place?"

"No, let's meet here." Much easier for her to leave him than to get rid of him, in case he started telling her the story of his life, she thought.

Super! I'll be working here all day, so how about dropping by around five or so?"

She wondered whether he intended to take her to some neighborhood drinking place or whether he planned to dispense the beverage of her choice on the premises. She felt mildly curious about that apartment of his above the gallery and what Baltasar was doing with his part of the building. Perhaps she could persuade Roland to take her on a tour of the place.

"And you won't tell anybody—anybody at all—that you're going to meet me?"

"I won't tell a soul," she promised, thinking poor, paranoid Roland, making such a big deal out of what was probably nothing, perhaps something as trivial as asking her advice on curtains. But no, Roland would know far more about curtains than she would.

By the time Susan and Roland came back into the foyer, Jill was already distributing copies of Hortense's brochures to Lupe and Baltasar and holding up the T-shirt for their admiration—Lupe's anyway, although it had to be explained to her just what a "Moopie" might be.

Baltasar was looking disgusted. "Why do people wear these silly little over-undershirts with the silly little mottos?" he wanted to know. "Do they enjoy making themselves look ridiculous?"

"It gives them a sense of their identity," Jill said.

Baltasar said something in Spanish. Lupe laughed and Roland gave a feeble titter.

Susan didn't know why she should feel surprised that Roland seemed to speak Spanish. Art dealers often were multilingual. And a lot of people in New York spoke Spanish. She wondered whether Jill did. She was certainly looking angry, but that could just as easily be because she didn't understand what he'd said as because she did.

Susan glanced at her watch. They had spent more time at the gallery than she'd figured on, what with the unexpected arrival of Lupe and Jill's brushes with practically everyone in sight. "Leatherstocking's isn't going to hold our reservations much longer," she reminded Jill. "You know what M. Bumppo is like."

"Like most restaurateurs," Jill said. "You've go to look 'em in the eye and stare them down. It's the only way to deal with them."

But M. Bumppo was not like most restaurateurs. He was worse. A James Fenimore Cooper enthusiast, M. Auguste Benoit had come to the United States fired with the idea of creating a restaurant that would serve food that was both authentically Early American and *haute cuisine*. He called his place Leatherstocking's, after James Fenimore Cooper's tales of the same name; and, although he did not change his own name officially, he liked to be called M. Bumppo after the series' hero. Not Natty, though, that would be carrying democracy too far.

The restaurant was an immediate success, although Leatherstocking himself, and, indeed, James Fenimore Cooper, would not have recognized the food as native cuisine. (Nor would Leatherstocking have been allowed in the place. M. Bumppo enforced a strict dress code, and, although fringed deerskin shirts had come into fashion in Soho, they still were not *comme il faut* at Leatherstocking's, name or no name.) M. Bumppo's *pâté d' élan* (known as "moose mousse" by the irreverent) received rave reviews from all the food critics except Mimi Sheraton, and his *ragout de boufflon avec pissenlits* was the talk of the town.

The place was much favored by such of the uptown art crowd as could afford it, for the prices were as *haute* as the *cuisine*—which meant that it was mostly dealers and museum people and the like who were its patrons (most of the artists whose works were shown in the uptown galleries being dead anyway). Although as a rule Susan tended to shun fashionable watering places when she was off duty, she made an exception of Leatherstocking's. Hal Courtenay often ate there. So, on the other hand, did Mimi Carruthers. As in most aspects of life you had to take the rough (Mimi) with the smooth (Hal).

"Why don't you join us for lunch?" Jill asked, as if the thought had just occurred to her, when, Susan realized, this was what she had been plotting ever since they got there. Why, Susan had no idea. Maybe she hoped to sell Baltasar a picture; maybe she hoped to acquire Lupe as a client. Or maybe she was simply suffering from the same insatiable curiosity that had done the Elephant's Child in.

"I am truly sorry," Baltasar said. "I would have loved to have lunch with you, and so, I am sure would Lupe . . ." Lupe nodded and smiled and was about to speak, but he went on, "Lupita and I are old friends, you know. She was one of my best models before she started her own artistic career. Now that she is here I hope to persuade her to model for me once again, at my fashion show for the charity ball in September."

Lupe started to say something; then apparently thought better of it.

"This affair means such a lot to me. Of course the opportunity to present my work in New York for the first time is a great thing, but even greater is the chance to be able to do something for so splendid a cause."

Jill snorted. She did not believe there was such a thing as disinterested altruism. Maybe she was right, Susan thought, but what was so bad about interested altruism if it got the job done? Of course it was grotesque to hold a Grand Ball and Gala in an art museum as a way of dealing with the growing problem of drug abuse; but if that was the only way of getting the money that was needed out of the people who could afford to give it, then it made sense. Not good sense, but sense.

"Other than holding a gun to somebody's head there's no better way to dig out the money than by throwing a party," Pat Buckley had once said, throwing Susan into momentary panic before she realized that Mrs. Buckley probably had not intended to suggest that she use her extra-artistic talents for fund-raising; although it was not beyond the bounds of probability that Mrs. Buckley would have done so if she had known of their existence. Some society hostesses would stop at nothing in their relentless pursuit of the public weal.

At least there was one thing that could be said about the Grand Art against Drug Abuse Gala and Ball that did not apply to most other charitable events. You were likely to find a number of the individuals for whose particular problem (although not whose particular class) the affair had been arranged sitting at the table as paying guests—something not likely to be true of the homeless, the delinquent, and/or the disabled.

"I only hope I will be able to get a new collection together in time," Baltasar said. "The gowns I had planned to show were ruined by smoke and water. I will have to fly back to Madrid as soon as I can and attempt to recreate them in my *atelier* there. But there is so much to be done here as well. I am torn in all directions."

"Such a misfortune," Lupe said. "But you will rise above it, Baltasar, and create an even more glorious collection, I know. You have never let anything stop you."

"You are too kind, Lupita," he said, kissing her hand. "You give me renewed hope."

Jill was about to snort again, but caught her client's eye and desisted. Maybe charity doesn't begin at home any more, Susan thought, but good public relations still do.

* * *

"Baltasar has some nerve sneering at T-shirts," Jill said, when Susan finally managed to tear her away and get her to the restaurant. M. Bumppo greeted them reproachfully and made it clear that if they had not been especially valued customers ("I always said he had an eye for you, Susan," Jill said), they would have been forced to kick their heels at the bar along with the other sinners. Jill seemed to identify with messaged T-shirts. Perhaps to her they represented the spirit of her generation. As for Susan, she was inclined to agree with Baltasar, but she kept her counsel.

"He talks as if he'd been involved in *haute couture* all his life, when I understand he actually started out in quilted robes, fancy nightgowns, beaded sweaters, that kind of *shmatta*, from the Far East and the Caribbean. Strictly for the bargain basement trade—in the days when there were still bargain basements."

"Don't be such a snob, Jill," Susan said. "The man had to start somewhere."

"All right, all right," Jill said, "but tell me how his gowns got ruined? I thought only Roland's part of the building got hit by the fire."

"Maybe he stored them there because the men were still working on his part. Who cares, anyway? I'm hungry." Susan picked up the menu. "I'm going to start with the *soupe à l'oseille*."

"No sorrel soup for me," Jill said. "We used to eat that in the Bronx, before ethnic became fashionable. It tasted like something that came out of a goldfish bowl then and it still does. I'm going to have the clam chowder."

"*Potage à la palourde* is not—ugh—clam chowder, madame," the waiter said severely. M. Bumppo did not care to have his menu trifled with.

"Whatever," Jill said.

If he was going to poison anybody, Susan thought, and he certainly looked as if he would like to, she hoped he'd be careful to slip it in the *potage* and not the *soupe*. "Why on earth did you ask them to join us?" she asked. "I thought this was supposed to be a business lunch. We were going to discuss the where, when, and what of my next show, remember?"

"And so we shall, Susan, so we shall. We do want to deduct this lunch from our taxes, don't we?"

"Your taxes. We can't both deduct the bill."

"Don't be silly. Of course we can. I am sorry we didn't get a chance to talk to Lupe, though. I have a feeling there's something funny going on. Roland knew damn well she wasn't a simple bare-foot peasant. Did you get a look at those sables she was wearing? She must be doing very well at whatever it is she does."

"Roland was probably just repeating what Rafael told him about her."

"Why would he have told him anything?"

"To explain why she wasn't at the opening perhaps?" But Jill was right: why would Rafael have bothered to give any explanation at all?

"Anyhow, it's just as well they didn't accept my invitation," Jill said. "I wouldn't have had much chance to talk to Lupe with Roland and Baltasar around. And we'd have had to pick up the tab for the whole gang."

"We? You were the one who issued the invitation. You would have had to pick up the tab."

"Don't be so petty, Susan. Probably Baltasar would have insisted on paying. He's of the old school. So is Roland, but a different kind of old school. Incidentally, what did Roland want to talk to you about, anyway? When you two were whispering and giggling in the vestibule?"

Susan had no scruples about lying in a good cause, and thwarting her rep's snoopiness was an excellent cause. "He had a message he wanted me to give Alex. And I may have been talking in a low tone of voice but I was not giggling. I never giggle."

Nor had Roland—although he did giggle on occasion—been giggling at the time, she recalled. He'd acted nervous, almost frightened.

"Something wrong with Roland's phone? Or Alex's?"

"I didn't ask him." Subtlety was wasted on Jill. "I don't pry."

"You must miss out on an awful lot that way." Jill shook a warning finger. "Just be sure you don't go and make any deals without me. Remember, we have a contract." Her tone was joking but she was not.

"I'm well aware that we have a contract," Susan said, wondering, not for the first time, if she might not have made a mistake in signing with Jill so precipitately. On the other hand, thinking of the other people in the art business whom she'd met subsequently, she could have done worse. Her old schoolmate, Dodo Pangborn, for example, was now running an art gallery and most anxious to represent her. However, Dodo had done time in the Bedford Hills Correctional Facility for Women (though for running a house of ill fame under the guise of a religious institution rather than any artistic misdeeds); and, even more of a drawback, her gallery was downtown. The downtown galleries might be currently fashionable, but to Susan there was no art south of Fifty-Seventh Street.

Besides Hal had recommended Jill, Susan reminded herself, so basically the girl must be sound.

"Speaking of contracts," Jill said with a sigh, "I guess we better get down to business. The Europeans are beginning to take an interest in your work and I think our next public showing should be abroad—at one of the international expositions."

"You showed my work at an international exposition last year."

"That was in Chicago. Chicago is in the United States. I was thinking of maybe Zurich. Meanwhile, I don't want you to be overexposed, like those artists who have gallery shows every two or three months. They're not going to last. The public will soon get tired of them; you'll see."

Some of them had lasted for several decades and still seemed to be going strong, Susan thought. However, from the business point of view, Jill was probably right. It wouldn't do to take any chances. Jill was undoubtedly also right when she said that Susan's paintings would fetch higher prices if they were released gradually over a period of time rather than poured out in one great gush of art. Just the same, Susan would have preferred to flood the market and get as much as she could while she was hot. If her popularity had been based on her work itself, she would have been content to take her chances and let her career, however belated, develop naturally; but she had become fashionable by such a freak that she was afraid she would go out of fashion just as suddenly.

"Okay," Jill had told her when she had voiced as many of her fears as she could discreetly, "so you did get to be the rage because it turned out that old General Chomsky had been collecting your paintings secretly—because that way he got them cheap. People are going to keep on buying your stuff because you're good. Didn't Hal write that terrific review of your work before he'd even met you, so you can't say he did it because he likes you, which no reputable critic would do, anyway. Write a good review of an artist's work because he likes her," she added, realizing her words needed clarifying.

That's right, Susan thought, he did write a very favorable piece about me, so he really must think I'm good. He wouldn't have praised my work simply because his museum had just inherited a sizeable collection of my paintings.

"And you would have become popular a lot sooner," Jill went on, "if you hadn't been such a wimp. No matter what you'd promised the General, as soon as you'd sold him a few pictures—so he had an investment in you—you could have let the word leak out."

"I . . . just couldn't," Susan said.

How could she explain to Jill that the General hadn't actually paid her for the paintings at all? He'd paid her to kill, and she'd insisted on giving him a painting each time she disposed of someone, so she could declare her income to the IRS.

Jill patted her hand. "Of course you couldn't. You're too much of a lady. Which is where I come in. In addition, it takes hype to get an artist up into the six-figure bracket, and hype is my specialty."

"I'm not in the six-figure bracket yet," Susan pointed out.

"Do what I tell you and in your next show you will be. I think your next show should be private," Jill said, as the waiter removed the remains of the soup and placed their *canard à la canneberge avec beignets à la citrouille* before them. ("What could be more authentically American than cranberry duck with pumpkin fritters!" M. Bumppo had roared at an unfortunate soul who had ventured to question the authenticity of his menu—after which the offender had been barred from Leatherstocking's for life.)

"It should be by invitation only—and only the extremely well-heeled invited."

Avoiding her client's eye, Jill continued, "That one in your apartment last fall was a great success. Collectors feel they're really getting their money's worth if they see the painters disporting themselves in their native habitat. An apartment on the upper East Side isn't their idea of an authentic artist's studio, though. Pity you don't have a loft in some artistic neighborhood. Soho and the West Village are verging on the passé, though. Maybe the East Village; it's going upscale without becoming too respectable. Visitors can still feel a thrill of danger as they step out of their limos."

"They can feel that anywhere in the city. And I don't want another show in my apartment. One was too much."

That previous apartment show had been preceded by a month of relentless tidying up. Not so much for neatness's sake, although that counted, too, Jill said, but to make sure that the vast output of over two decades was removed from the premises and safely stored. "I've known artists who were prolific, but they pale beside you. For you they're going to have to make up a new word."

Susan felt mildly stung, as if Jill had suggested there was something rather vulgar about being prolific even though she knew Jill had no such thought in mind; and, indeed, would have seen nothing wrong with vulgarity, provided they kept it between themselves, so as not to spoil the image into which she was casting her client.

"If you add up all Darius Moffatt's canvases, I bet it'll turn out that he was more prolific than I am."

"But you're still turning 'em out and he isn't, on account of being dead. That makes the difference. There are going to be a lot more Melvilles unless somebody puts a brake on you. There aren't going to be any more Moffatts ever."

"Unless some more cousins in remote parts of the country turn up with more forgotten Moffatts," Susan suggested.

Jill glanced at her sharply. Susan returned the look with bland composure.

VIII

IF EVER I start feeling sorry for myself, Susan thought, I have only to think of Darius Moffatt and thank my lucky stars. For me it came late but for him it never came at all.

Everybody who could read knew the tragic history of Darius Moffatt. He had died in obscurity ten years before, apparently never having sold a picture in his life. Now he had become almost legendary, hailed by some as one of the most important artists of the twentieth century.

As a youth still in his teens, Darius Moffatt had come to New York to study art, first at the Hudson School and later at the Art Students League. Where he'd gotten the money to pay for his lessons and his keep never became entirely clear. He was not the type to go after scholarships or, if he had been, to win them. But he'd been unable to make a go of life in the city, and so he'd returned to the small New England village he came from to help his twice-widowed mother work the family farm. However, he continued to paint in his spare time, using an abandoned barn as his studio.

Then a real-estate developer had made an offer to Moffatt's mother that she could not refuse. She'd sold him most of the family land, keeping only the house, a couple of acres of land, and the barn. Now she was comfortably off, though by no means wealthy. But her son wasn't happy. Perhaps he missed the land; perhaps he didn't like the idea of living in the midst of a middle-income housing development.

And so he had left the village and drifted across the country, staying with various relatives at their farms, where he helped out in exchange for his keep and a place to paint and enough money to buy the materials with which to do so. They seemed to be an agrarian family. "Very Early American," Jill had put it in one of the early interviews. They also seemed, as it developed later, to be a very large family.

In the 1970s, with most small farms mechanized out of existence, he had drifted back to New York. It was possible that he had heard of the art boom and hoped he might be able to find a place for himself now; more likely he'd had no clear purpose in mind. At any rate, someone had apparently given him a shot of heroin—possibly his first—and he had died of it. His death had passed unremarked by the press. People were always dying of drugs in New York, sometimes from their first shot but always from their last. There might have been a story about him in his native village's paper, if it had one; but Jill, from whom all information about him emanated, steadfastly kept the name of the place a secret. For the same reason she also kept the name Darius's mother had acquired as the result of her second marriage a secret, although that had been her legal name for over thirty years. She was always referred to as Mrs. Moffatt, at least in the beginning; it was only later that the sobriquet an irreverent reporter from the *Daily News* bestowed on her stuck and she became universally known as "Old Mother Moffatt."

"They're very private people up there," Jill had explained in another early interview. "Some of them, especially the older ones, know about Darius and his paintings, of course, but they protect their own. Before Mrs. Moffatt let me handle the pictures, she made me promise never to tell anybody where she lives."

"Sounds more like Appalachia than New England," the mathematics teacher at the European-American Academy, a thin dark girl whose name Susan could not now remember, had said.

"Sounds more like the Twilight Zone," someone else had observed.

Susan had still been teaching at the Academy when Darius

Moffatt's name first came into prominence. They had discussed him in the faculty lounge. As the school's artist-in-residence (which was how the brochure referred, rather embarrassingly, to her), Susan was expected to keep on top of the current art scene. She had not herself seen any great genius in the Moffatt works but was reluctant to admit it for fear of being thought out of step with the times. Fortunately the vocabulary of art appreciation enabled her to discuss the subject at length without ever making it clear what her actual opinion of the paintings was—not that she would have hesitated to lie in order to keep her job but she had found it was better to tell the truth whenever possible; it diminished the risk of being caught in a contradiction.

According to the stories in the press, Moffatt's mother had come down from the little town (or village; the two terms were used interchangeably) where he'd been born and raised to collect her son's body and pick up his meager personal effects from the squalid East Village apartment in which he had passed his last days. She was quite old now, and inflation had cut down her income to minimal adequacy. She was poor. There were a number of canvases in the apartment and Mrs. Moffatt brought a few to Jill Turkel's little Soho gallery for promising artists, to see if she might get something for them.

Susan remembered the mathematics teacher's wondering how an elderly New England widow who had never before set foot in New York had managed to make her way from the East Village to an obscure Soho gallery, carrying a bundle of rather large canvases. Someone suggested that perhaps each gallery that turned her down recommended another one, and so she had trudged across town until she reached Jill's. It was a touching, if somewhat improbable, picture.

Unlike the others, Jill had instantly recognized their genius, she told the press. She gave the artist a one-man show, selected from the best of the canvases. Hal Courtenay, assistant curator of the Museum of American Art at that time an art critic and consultant, had stopped in at the gallery. He always made an effort to look at every art show, no matter how obscure, he said in an interview later. "Most of it's dross, of course, but there's always the hope that one day you'll stumble upon a vein of pure gold to make it all worth while."

This time he seemed to have hit pay dirt. He wrote a long laudatory piece about Moffatt for the *New York Art Journal,* as well as shorter pieces for the *Times* and other popular publications. This brought other reviewers to the Turkel Gallery. Although there were one or two dissenting voices (there always are dissenting voices, sometimes, Susan suspected, just for the sake of dissension) most were as enthusiastic as Hal. A few were even more laudatory; one went so far as to call Moffatt "the greatest genius the second half of the twentieth century has as yet produced."

"Which was, of course, absurd," Hal told Susan at the MAA's second Moffatt Retrospective. "There were several quite good, even if somewhat overrated, artists on the scene already. And, of course, nobody knew about you yet."

And he had looked deeply into her eyes. His were very blue. Why hadn't she noticed back in the old days how blue his eyes were? He'd worn glasses then, she remembered, wire-framed ones. Probably they had obscured the blueness of his eyes. And, since she'd considered him a creep then, she'd had no reason to look deeply into his eyes. He must be wearing contact lenses now.

"Did you remember Darius Moffatt from school?" she asked. "According to the dates, I must have been there around the same times as he was, but I must confess I can't remember him at all."

Hal had shaken his handsome head. "When I first saw the paintings in Jill's gallery his name didn't strike the faintest chord. There was a biography in that first little catalogue, but it was very sketchy. It did mention that he'd gone to the Hudson while he was still in his teens, but it didn't give a birth date so I had no way of knowing when those teens were. Then, later on, when Jill got those photographs from his mother, I began to remember him dimly."

The snapshots, later reproduced in the daily papers, *Time,*

Newsweek, People, and all the art journals, were themselves dim —imperfectly preserved Polaroids of a pale, long-haired, scraggly-bearded, youngish man in work clothes, scowling into the camera. When Susan looked at them with the knowledge that they were of someone she once must have seen at least, perhaps even spoken to, a faint sense of recognition seemed to stir in her mind. But I could simply be projecting, she thought.

The paintings at that first show had sold out immediately. A few months later Jill offered the rest of the paintings that had been in the East Village apartment for sale—at triple the prices of the first batch. This show sold out immediately as well.

And that seemed to be that. The paltry handful of paintings appeared to be all the artist had left behind him. Most of those collectors who had been astute enough to secure one or more of the paintings held on to them, but a few, either overanxious to cash in while he was still in the news, or in need of money, sold theirs. The prices they fetched were fantastic, especially considering that they had sold for a couple of thousand dollars apiece less than a year before.

Almost two years after the second show, great news burst upon the art world. Jill revealed that she had received a letter from old Mrs. Moffatt saying that now she was well along in years she found the big old-fashioned farmhouse too much for her to cope with. She'd decided to sell it and move to a small cottage with all modern conveniences, which she described in detail in her chatty agrarian way. It took two handwritten pages (later reproduced in facsimile in *Art Notes*) before she got to the point. While clearing out the old barn, she'd discovered a number of her son's paintings stored there. Would Jill be interested in handling them?

Jill would, indeed. By this time rising rents had forced her to give up her little Soho gallery, so, acting as the late artist's representative now, she arranged to have them shown at the Stratton Gallery, at prices befitting "one of the great geniuses of the twentieth century." There were twice as many paintings on view as there had been in the previous two shows. Still not an enormous number, but enough to constitute a respectable *oeuvre*, so that his death, as Hal Courtenay pointed out in an article for the *Times Magazine*, seemed less a tragedy for the world of art, if not for the artist himself. All of them equalled and, in some cases, even surpassed the high standards set by the first group. All of them sold at prices ranging from fifty thousand dollars on up. Old Mother Moffatt must be a millionairess. And so must Jill.

The press clamored for interviews with the old lady, or, at the least, with neighbors who had grown up with Darius. Jill remained adamant. She had promised the family that she would protect their privacy. Even though they were no longer her clients, as there were no more pictures to be sold, she was not going to betray them. An aura of quiet dignity and rectitude shone through the interviews, accounting for much of the surprise Susan later felt when she met Jill.

It must have been over a year after Old Mother Moffatt's happy discovery in the barn that one of her brothers died and left her everything he had. Among his effects was another dozen of Darius's paintings. It wasn't clear whether the artist had merely left them behind in the course of his peregrinations or had given them to his uncle, not that it mattered since his mother was the sole heir in either case.

By this time Hal Courtenay had become the MAA's curator of contemporary art. He took the discovery of the new paintings as an occasion for mounting a Moffatt Retrospective. Jill graciously lent the Museum the paintings, prior to their commercial exhibition.

The paintings were never exhibited commercially. The Charpentier Foundation acquired them all at prices that were never disclosed but were reported to be astronomic.

Simultaneously with the exhibition, Hal Courtenay published his monograph *Darius Moffatt, Man and Myth*, which became the definitive work on the artist. Although Hal was in a privileged position, having earned Jill's gratitude for the first rapturous review that put Moffatt on the map, even he was not allowed to interview old Mother Moffatt or even to know her location. All information had to come through Jill. He was, however, allowed access to the Moffatt letters, for Darius had written regularly to his mother. An inarticulate man verbally—though how Jill knew this was never made clear—Darius was not much better on paper.

A typical example of his letters was one he had written while he was staying with his cousins George and Mary (not their real names) who were cousins to each other as well as to him, and man and wife to boot. ("They're a very inbred family," Jill had told an interviewer once, "which may be why they're rather strange.")

Dear Ma,

I am well and hope you are the same. George and Mary and the kids send their love. They are all well except George Junior has the chicken pox but we are sure he will recover (ha ha). I have been painting a lot of pictures now that the crops are all in. Could you send me another half dozen pairs of sox from [name withheld]'s general store? You can't get that kind out here in [location deleted].

Your loving son,
Darry

His other letters were similar—little about his life, even less about his art. The only information the reader derived from them was that Darius had loved his mother. Dr. Joyce Brothers devoted a column in the New York *Post* and, since she was syndicated, other papers, to him.

In the years that followed, it seemed that every few months another group of Moffatt paintings would show up at the home of one or another of his kin. Not only was his family large, but it was scattered all over the country. He seemed to have relatives in every state except Hawaii and Alaska, and he apparently had left paintings with every one of them. As a writer for the *Village Voice* pointed out, rather than drift across the country, Darius must have rushed madly about to have stayed in so many places during the dozen or so years of his wandering.

The fact that the paintings were all beginning to show up, Jill had told that same writer, was not fortuitous. She had asked Old Mother Moffatt to write to every relative she could think of, asking whether they happened to have any of Darius's paintings. "I wanted her to Xerox a form letter which she could just send around, but she said no; that wasn't proper. She insisted on sending a personal handwritten letter to each one, asking them to look in their closets and cellars and barns, and that's why it's taking so long to find them all, especially since her memory isn't what it was, and she keeps remembering third and fourth cousins she overlooked."

Jill shook her head sadly, as the press duly noted. "Lord knows how many paintings will never turn up, that are still mouldering somewhere or were just tossed in the garbage like so much junk."

You could almost hear the readers' collective gasps of horror.

"Don't the relatives ever claim that the paintings belong to them?" a reporter from the *Post* asked, his nose twitching for scandal. "That Darius *gave* them the paintings?"

"Even if that were true, it would be hard to prove," Jill said. "If they took her to court, they might lose everything. This way Mrs. Moffatt gives them a share of what she gets. Besides, they don't sue their own kind. They're not that type of people."

But of course, the public had only Jill's word for that. And, as Susan began to realize later, for everything else concerning Darius Moffatt as well.

IX

"TOO BAD you don't have a barn or some place like that to store your paintings," Jill had said, two years before, as she looked over her new client's total *oeuvre* for the first time. Canvases were stacked in every available part of the apartment, filling the rooms Susan didn't use—for it was a spacious pre-war apartment—and threatening to make those she lived in unlivable.

"Anyhow, you're going to have to store them somewhere and just release a few at a time. If so much as a hint escapes of how many there are already in existence, your prices are going to tumble, in spite of all the hoopla."

"Shouldn't a painting's value be based on its inherent worth rather than its rarity?" Peter, who was in residence at the time, had asked.

"Worth has nothing to do with a painting's price," Jill told him. "Price depends on fashion, rarity, and good PR." Here she patted her chest. "Worth—well—there isn't any objective way of determining the inherent worth of a work of art, so why bother to try?"

"Critical approval?" Susan suggested without conviction.

"Among the Oupi," Peter began, and embarked on a long anthropological narrative that neither of his companions paid any attention to.

Jill opened the door to a closet and closed it again just in time to escape being buried by an avalanche of art. Susan supposed the girl didn't know any better than to open other people's closets, but she couldn't help feeling annoyed. "Well, I think you get the general idea," she said, steering Jill back into the studio, which having originally been the living room of the apartment, was not equipped with closets. "I don't suppose you want to look at them one by one."

"Not right now," Jill said, subsiding into a chair, "although I guess I'll have to eventually. Not that I'm not looking forward to it," she added quickly. This was early in their relationship and she was still wary of offending her client.

"Yes, thank you, I would like something to drink," she replied to Susan's offer of refreshment. "And I hope it's stronger than tea."

She seemed surprised to find that Susan not only had a well-stocked bar but that she joined Jill in a bourbon and soda. For some reason I seem to look the tea type to her, Susan thought. She should look at my paintings instead of at me.

"You know you have enough pictures here to make you a multi-millionaire without you ever lifting a brush again—providing they're carefully marketed. Which, of course, they will be."

"But I want to keep on painting," Susan protested. "I paint because I want to, not because I want to be an artist."

Jill gave her a pitying smile.

"I don't know why you find that so hard to understand," Susan persisted. "Darius Moffatt obviously liked to paint or he wouldn't have kept on painting."

"Who knows what motivated Darius Moffatt, what compulsions moved him to keep on painting, even though he had no reason to expect anybody—except maybe his family—would ever see his work?" Jill asked. She was, whether consciously or not, quoting from *Darius Moffatt, Man and Myth*. "But he was a throwback. Art for art's sake is pretty much obsolete these days, if it ever did hold good. Artists don't like art. Collectors like art. Artists paint so they can sell their pictures to collectors. The only painters who enjoy their work are chimpanzees, like in that movie you took me to, and what do they do with their paintings? They eat them."

She was bitter, Susan thought. She must have had some really rough clients. "I'm not sure I know what motivates *me*. It certainly hasn't been money because I didn't make any up until a few years ago."

"But you hoped to, didn't you?"

"Well, I'd hoped to be able to support myself by painting," Susan said. "I never expected to make money, in the real sense, from it."

"That's because you were born to money. The idea that you yourself could become rich through your own efforts probably never even occurred to you."

Susan's pride was piqued. "The family fortunes were founded by a man who most definitely made his own money."

Jill laughed. "You mean old Black Buck, the pirate? Oh, he's great PR, no mistake about it. But there are at least eight generations between you and him. There isn't much of his blood running in your veins, Susan. I can't see you making anyone walk the plank."

Looking back later, Susan was to wish she had made Jill walk the plank then and there. But everybody makes mistakes, and there was no use crying over unspilt blood—metaphorically speaking, of course.

"All right, keep on painting if it makes you happy," Jill said. "A happy client is a . . . er . . . a happy client. But you can't keep the paintings here. It's not safe."

"Are you suggesting that I should hire a barn? Like Darius Moffatt?"

"He didn't hire a barn; he had a barn, which is a whole other thing. You have to be born to a barn. You're not the barn type. And barns aren't safe, anyway. The family vault, maybe."

"Even in the most elegant of circles," Susan told her, "to which you mistakenly seem to think I belong, it is not customary to store anything but bodies in the family vault."

"Vaults are fireproof," Jill said, apparently confusing funeral vaults with bank vaults. "Sometimes I wake up in a cold sweat, imagining what could've happened to the Moffatt barn over the years. It could have been struck by lightning. Vandals could've set it on fire. The country could have been invaded by—by—"

"Giant fireflies perhaps? In any of those events you'd never even have known the pictures existed, so why worry now over what might have happened. Worry about what's to come."

Jill looked agitated. "What do you mean? Are you expecting any kind of trouble? You've got to tell me now."

Susan was a little disconcerted by such an emotional response. "No, it's only that man is born to trouble as the sparks fly upward. All this talk of fire made me think of it," she apologized.

"Please don't quote the Bible at me," Jill said. "I'm an atheist. It makes me nervous. But we are going to have to store your pictures somewhere fireproof. And get them insured."

Susan's once-a-week maid, now pensioned off ("How feudal," Jill had sneered), had always worried about fire, but Susan hadn't paid much attention, since she hadn't had the money to put her paintings in storage, especially since they hadn't been worth anything to anyone but herself. Now that they had become so valuable, it made sense to take proper precautions; and so the paintings were duly removed to a fireproof warehouse in Long Island City, where Jill was already renting space for purposes she did not explain.

After Susan's apartment had been emptied of extraneous canvases, it was thoroughly cleaned by a crew of uniformed professionals, and somewhat refurbished, although not refurnished—Susan drew an emphatic line there. "All right, slipcovers, if you must," she told Jill, "although I personally think they're a little—" she searched for a tactful word "—dowdy, but no new furniture. It isn't a question of expense; it's a question of personal comfort."

However, she joined Jill in persuading Peter to give up the loin cloth which he favored as informal attire and have his hair trimmed. Jill also said he had to choose between growing a beard and moustache in time for the exhibit or shaving. "The Don Johnson look might do for Hollywood or Miami, but it's definitely uncool in New York," she'd pointed out. Thank heaven she didn't tell him it was "uncool" for a man his age, Susan had thought, for, although he prided himself on being a detached social scientist, Peter was not without his share of male self-delusion.

"I do not like being treated like an exhibit," he had said.

"Then stop acting like one," Jill had retorted. They had not gotten on at all well. They were both difficult people. It's unfair, Susan thought. I'm the artist; I should be the one with the temperament instead of the peacemaker, the moderator, the patsy. No wonder so few people with her background ever achieved success in the arts. True artistry requires passion while true social grace requires that passion, or at least its outward manifestation, be bred out of you.

The exhibit had been a success from the financial point of view. All the paintings on display had been sold for handsome sums— more, Jill confessed afterward, than she had dreamed of getting. "I pushed the prices up because I know how rich people love to dicker. I didn't expect them to pay what I asked, practically without a murmur, or I would have asked more." And she shook her head sadly.

The experience of being forced to act as a hostess combined with the despoliation of her apartment had been unnerving for Susan. It took a while before she could get back to painting in this suddenly alien environment. And her style of painting changed.

She did allow Jill to bring up individual clients from time to time, and tried to be gracious even to the really obnoxious ones, like Eloise Charpentier, who couldn't understand why Susan had chosen to convert her "drawing room" into a studio, instead of using one of the smaller rooms. "It's the only room with a north light," Susan had tried to explain.

"Well, can't you have a north light put in one of the bedrooms? Where do you entertain?"

"I don't do any large-scale entertaining," Susan had said. She'd had enough of festivity during her days as party crasher cum hit woman; and even then she hadn't had to *give* the parties, just provide the surprise endings.

"Oh, you poor thing," Eloise said, and invited Susan to lunch at the Quilted Giraffe, leaving Susan to pick up the check afterward. However, the Charpentier Foundation subsequently bought a million dollars' worth of Susan's paintings (for eight hundred thousand dollars; "The Charpentiers always expect a discount," Jill said), so she supposed it was time and money well spent. But she refused to let another full-scale exhibit be mounted in her apartment, in spite of all Jill's attempts to persuade her to repeat the event.

Today, however, Jill didn't press her. Susan would have liked to think that this was because she had learned that her client could be pushed just so far; however, she had a feeling that the girl had something else in mind from the start, and was just using Susan's apartment as a stalking horse.

And she was right. "That charming Mrs. Hunyadi offered to exhibit your work in her apartment," Jill suggested, casually spooning her *coupe iroquoise* onto the tablecloth, instead of her mouth. She was nervous. She was plotting something.

"Mimi Hunyadi is a bitch," Susan said.

"Of course she is. She also is a member of the board of directors of the MAA, the Van Horn of the Van Horn Foundation, a celebrated patron of the arts, your best girlhood chum, and filthy rich."

"She's all of that," Susan agreed, "but—"

"What's more, she knows all the right people. We can't let just anybody buy your paintings."

"They're available to anyone who can afford to pay the price," Susan said coldly. "In fact—"

"You weren't thinking of offering them at reduced prices to people below a certain income level, were you?"

"Better than offering them at reduced prices to people who can well afford to pay full price."

Jill shook her head. "Susan, Susan, where would you be without me?"

Susan had been beginning to wonder about that herself. "I suppose you think I shouldn't have agreed to let Mimi have a painting to be auctioned off at that confounded anti-drug ball of hers."

"On the contrary, that's good publicity, as well as being a worthy cause," she added, for, as she kept pointing out to her client, Jill was not heartless; she believed in charity as long as it benefitted the giver more than the receiver.

"I, too, appreciate the value of publicity," Susan said, "so I want my next show to be in a public gallery." She knew why Jill wanted to avoid gallery shows. It would mean she would have to split her commissions. "The show last fall at the Stratton went very well, I thought."

It had gone better, in fact, than Jill knew. "Why are you letting this snippet who knows nothing about art handle your work, Susan?" Gil Stratton had asked. "This new-fangled idea of agents for artists won't last. It's galleries who should be handling them, the way they've always done. Come with me, Susan, we'll give you terms you wouldn't believe."

"I have a contract with Jill."

"Contract, shmontract. Think it over and, by the way, while you're thinking, you won't mention my little suggestion to Jill, will you? I wouldn't like to upset her."

I'll bet you wouldn't, Susan thought. You'd never get another Melville show—or another Moffatt show, if any more distant relatives of Darius's show up with pictures. And you might get a brick through your window to boot.

She had never told Jill about Stratton's offer, and, although the temptation was strong, she didn't tell her now. "If my paintings are shown in a public gallery, at least the general public will be able to see them, even if they can't afford to buy them."

"Susan, the general public isn't interested in your paintings—as paintings, that is. Oh, they'll come to see them because you're in the news and because they hear they're going for astronomical sums, but not for love of art. They'd never have come in the days when you were an unknown."

"You don't know that. When I was unknown, there was no way they could see my paintings because they weren't on view anywhere. I suppose if I had brought my pictures to your gallery, you wouldn't have shown them either."

"I don't know what I would have done," Jill said, "For Pete's sake, Susan, that was a long time ago. Just between ourselves, I might not have accepted Darius Moffatt's paintings if I hadn't been desperate right then..."

"Desperate?" Susan asked. "Come on! Gallery owners may be desperate for money to pay the rent. They may be desperate for collectors to come and buy their pictures. But they are never desperate for artists."

Jill swallowed. "I guess I should have told you about it before, only I was ashamed. I wasn't running that gallery all by myself. Even though it was only a hole in the wall, I couldn't have afforded it. I had a partner. His name wasn't on the gallery because he'd gotten into trouble not too long before. It might have started us off on the wrong foot if people knew he had anything to do with the place." She took a deep breath. "It was Roland. He was my partner."

"Roland!" For some time Susan had realized that there was some connection between the two, but it had never occurred to her that they might once have been business partners. No wonder they hated each other.

"How is it that he can open a gallery under his own name now, if he had such a bad reputation then?"

Jill looked annoyed, as if Susan had been supposed to sympathize, not ask questions. "Oh, all that happened over ten years ago," she said vaguely. "People forget over the years, and he'd been working a lot outside the country. I guess he re-established himself abroad."

"So that's how he got to know Baltasar?"

"Must've been," Jill said.

"What kind of trouble had Roland gotten into?" Susan asked,

wondering whether Baltasar had been charitable enough to over-look Roland's murky past or simply unaware of it.

Jill looked uncomfortable. "As you may have gathered, I'm not exactly a friend of Roland's. Just the same, I don't think I ought to snitch on the little prick."

Susan remembered that Roland had sold paintings to General Chomsky. She remembered that fakes had turned up in the General's collection. "Forged paintings, was that it?"

"You're a good guesser," Jill said, after a pause. "Or has somebody said something to you about it?"

Susan shrugged in an omniscient way and made a mental note to grill Alex on the subject at the earliest possible opportunity. He must have known all this and hadn't seen fit to tell her. What kind of a fake brother was he, anyway? But if he had told her, she wouldn't have agreed to make a speech at Roland's opening exhibit. He's still manipulating me, she thought.

"You're right; it was forged paintings," Jill said. "He swore he hadn't known the paintings were fakes. I believed him, because they were very good fakes. Of course it's easy to fake modern paintings; even experts have a hard time telling. There's no real craftsmanship to speak of, and the forger can get hold of the same type of paint and canvas the artist used. And, after the paintings have had a chance to dry, you can't tell whether a picture was painted five years or fifty years ago. So, when he said he'd bought them in good faith, I believed him."

She stopped for breath. For some reason she was looking pleased with herself. "But then when we opened our little gallery, after a while he started getting up to his old tricks again. I didn't want to expose him and have him maybe go to jail, but I couldn't keep on working with him. It would ruin my reputation before I'd even made one. So I borrowed money, and I bought him out. But that left me without an exhibit."

"And that was when Mrs. Moffatt turned up with her son's paintings?"

"Right. I grabbed them, figuring I'd show them for a few weeks, until I could line up another artist. But before I had a chance to start looking, Hal Courtenay stopped in and—" she gave a weak laugh "—the rest is art history."

"I don't imagine Roland was too happy with the turn of events," Susan said.

"He was spitting mad. Kept saying I had signed up Moffatt's mother *before* I bought him out, but that's ridiculous. For one thing, who could have imagined Moffatt's stuff was going to take off like that?"

That at least had the ring of truth. Why then was there something about the rest of the girl's story that didn't quite ring true?

I must have a very suspicious nature, Susan thought. Still, she would have liked to hear Roland's side of the story. And perhaps tomorrow she would hear it. She began to look forward to the coming rendezvous.

X

JILL'S TONE changed. "Well, look who's here!'" Lupe Montoya was standing at the entrace to the restaurant, looking over the clientele. The clientele was looking her over with equal interest, some of the male customers going so far as to get out of their chairs on the pretext of summoning their waiters, so that they could get a better view. *"Saperlipopette!"* M. Bumppo exclaimed, and was about to brush aside the maitre d' in order to welcome her personally, when Jill stood up and waved. "Over here, Lupe!" she called.

"How did a bimbo like that ever team up with a jerk like Rafael Hoffmann?" Jill muttered in an undertone as Lupe strode magnificently to their table and flung herself into a chair.

"I have decided to join you after all," she said.

"We've almost finished," Susan said, "but we'd be happy to wait while you eat."

Lupe shook her head. "I never eat lunch. For me it is very important to keep the figure."

She pushed her sables over the back of her chair and leaned forward, as if to display to the fullest advantage the figure she was so anxious to keep. Her dress was very tight and her décolletage very low for lunchtime.

The waiter who had rushed up to take her order nearly burst into tears when he found out coffee was all she was having. "Another time I will come back and have dinner here, I promise you," she told him.

As the waiter drooped off, the youngest of three men who had been lunching at a nearby table got up and came over. "Would you ladies—?"

"Beat it, Buster," Jill said. "This is a business lunch. And not funny business either." Did it disturb her, Susan wondered, that her own entrance had aroused only respectful admiration?

"What an interesting restaurant," Lupe said, looking around, "so very American. And such charming murals: pictures of Indians and—what do you call those people in the hats with tails—backwardsmen?"

"Backwoodsmen," Susan said. "The murals are supposed to be illustrations to the works of James Fenimore Cooper. *Leatherstocking Tales.*"

"Ah," Lupe said, "I have heard of these Leatherstocking places, and I admit I was surprised that someone like you, Susan, should go to one. But this is not at all what I expected. There are no masks, no whips, not even a chain, except on the *sommelier*." The *sommelier*, hearing himself designated, started to spring forward but was waved back.

Susan tried to explain that James Fenimore Cooper was not an Early American pornographer but an author, a classic, read by generation after generation of children ("No, not child abuse, Lupe.") Interesting that Lupe apparently would not have been surprised that Jill should frequent the sort of establishment she had fancied this to be—and flattering to neither Jill nor Susan.

"But I have not come to talk about literature," Lupe said. "I have come to talk about life; that is, death—Rafael's death. I need to talk to somebody who was there when he died, yet who was not—" she groped for the right word, "—concerned with him personally. Rafael meant nothing to you, yes?" she demanded of Susan.

"Nothing," Susan said, "except as a fellow artist, of course."

Jill closed her eyes and said something under her breath.

"Or you?" Lupe looked at Jill. "You were not a friend of his either?"

Jill shook her head. "I'd never even heard of him before the show."

"Then I will tell you, both of you, what I think. I think there was something very fishlike about the way Rafael died. I think he was—" she paused for maximum effect—I think he was *murdered*."

Susan tried to look appropriately surprised and shocked but could not help feeling gratified that someone else, someone who was in a position to know, shared her earlier suspicions.

Jill looked surprised and shocked enough for two. "He couldn't have been murdered. It was a drug overdose—combined with alcohol. Didn't Baltasar tell you?"

"That is as may be," Lupe said darkly. "I will not deny that Rafael took drugs once in a while like everybody else. But always cocaine, never heroin. And he would never, never drink at the same time. He was very careful of his health. He—can you believe this?—actually worked out, lifted the weights, the whole *manojo*. If he had died of a vitamin overdose, that I would have believed. But drugs, never. Somebody must have given it to him without his knowing."

"Ridiculous," Jill said. "You don't understand. In New York people die of drug overdoses all the time. It's like getting run over or mugged in the park. It's normal."

"You think so? Well, perhaps you are right. Maybe I am over-reactionary. You think I should do nothing about it then? Good, I will do nothing."

"Maybe you should tell the police your suspicions," Susan said. She didn't particularly like the idea, as the police might then interview everybody who'd been on the scene at the time of Rafael's death. However, it was the right thing to do and she owed it to Lupe, and to herself, to tell her that. If Lupe chose not to follow up on her suggestion, then the responsibility would be Lupe's.

"I wouldn't go talk to the police if I were you," Jill advised. "They wouldn't take you seriously without anything to back you up. And they can be pretty rough with foreigners, especially Spanish-speaking foreigners."

Lupe nodded. "That is what I thought. And Rafael was a most unpleasant man and a bad artist, so why should I worry even if someone did kill him, eh? All that should concern me is the money that is coming to me. Baltasar has very kindly given me the name of a lawyer to consult in the matter of my inheritance."

"Maybe you should talk to the lawyer about your suspicions," Susan said. Neither Jill nor Lupe seemed to think this was a good idea.

The coffee arrived. Susan and Jill each had another cup to keep Lupe company. "You and Baltasar seem to have known each other a long time," Jill said.

Lupe looked coy. "Once we were very close, and we are still good friends."

"That was before he married the *condesa,* was it?"

Lupe opened her eyes very wide. To Susan's surprise, they were not the black or brown she would have expected but blue. "Of course, before. He is the most honorable of men."

"What's the *condesa* like?" Jill asked.

Lupe shrugged. "Most people say she is very beautiful, but they always say that if a woman has a title and is passable-looking."

As for Lupe herself, she had been married to Rafael for six years, she told them, in response to Jill's questioning. Most of this time they had spent apart, partly for professional reasons, but mostly because they couldn't stand each other. "Sometimes I find myself blaming Baltasar for having introduced him to me, but I know that is silly. Baltasar did not force me to marry Rafael, and, if he gave me away at the wedding, it was as a favor to me, not because he wanted to."

Susan would have liked to ask why she had married Rafael in the first place but was too well bred to put such a question. Jill wasn't.

"He seemed so—so macho. I was very young then." Susan could see Jill counting on her fingers and then shrug. "But that is all water over the bridgework."

She took a deep breath. "What I do blame Baltasar for is disappointing me now. Since he has the whole top of this fine building which he is not using, I had hoped that he would let me keep little Rover and Fido there for a time. But he said no: I could stay there myself for a while, if I did not mind the discommodity, but the law did not permit wolves to be kept in the city. And he could not let me do it secretly, because of the howling. They are very sweet and good, but I must admit they do make a lot of noise."

"Anyhow, Baltasar doesn't like dogs," Jill said.

"Baltasar not like dogs; wherever did you get such an idea! Baltasar loves dogs. Back in his hacienda he has dozens of big dogs and in his castle he has dozens of little dogs. Also he has cats. He takes this Esmeralda of his everywhere he goes, can you believe it?" She rolled her eyes. "But Fido and Rover are not dogs. They are wolves. You must meet them. They are adorable."

"Roland says Baltasar hates dogs; that's why Susan wasn't supposed to tell him that the man she saw climbing over the fence had a dog with him," Jill said, all in one breath.

"Jill, we promised—"

"We promised not to tell Baltasar, not Lupe."

"I think that this Roland is *loco;* that is what I think," Lupe declared.

"All the things that have been happening at the gallery are enough to upset anyone," Susan said, wondering why she felt impelled to defend Roland. She didn't even like him. But then nobody seemed to. Perhaps that was it—Susan Melville, champion of the underdog. Or maybe it was underwolf. Why were they talking about animals anyway?

"Pah, Roland was always a little crazy," Lupe said. "That is to say, so Baltasar tells me. I do not understand why he chooses to—to let such a man share his building. But then, it is none of my concern."

Susan had been wondering the same thing, wondering, too, if Lupe had any explanation to offer out of her knowledge of Baltasar. Obviously, she didn't or wasn't going to share it with them if she did. She took out a compact that looked like solid gold and examined her face in its mirror; then, satisfied that it could not be improved upon, snapped it shut.

"I don't suppose either of you ladies could provide accommodation for Rover and Fido? They are very good and almost housebroken."

"It would be against the law even more for me than for Baltasar," Susan said, "since I live in an apartment."

"I do, too," Jill said quickly. "They don't even allow children in my house. You need someone with a house in the country."

"Baltasar has an assistant, a lady who has worked for him for years," Lupe said. "She is living in a house in a place called Johnson Heights. That is in the country, no?"

"If you mean Jackson Heights," Jill said, "it's in Queens, which is part of the city. I doubt that you'd be allowed to keep wolves even there, although, judging by the things that keep happening there, it does look as if anything goes in that borough."

"Well, I could ask her anyway," Lupe said optimistically. "It is in a Spanish neighborhood, Baltasar tells me, so they will not notice the howling."

Susan wondered why Lupe had chosen to confide her suspicions about Rafael's death to a couple of strangers, even if they had been in at the death, so to speak. It's always easier to confide in strangers, true, but that's when you expect never to see them again. If Lupe stayed in New York, they were more than likely to run into her.

Susan had a feeling that Lupe was trying to ask for help of some kind. Possibly finding a temporary home for Rover and Fido really was all she wanted, but that didn't seem like enough to account for her intensity. Maybe she was just an intense person. Maybe, it was just her way of trying to make friends, although trying to foist off a pair of wolves on a new acquaintance is not the best way of making friends.

"Have you told Baltasar of your suspicions about Roland's death?" she asked.

"Well, no, there were so many people around."

But there are more people around now, Susan thought, than there had been at the gallery. Was it possible Lupe suspected Roland of having killed her husband?

Of course, it would have been easy enough for him to have injected Rafael with a lethal dose of heroin while they were moving a statue or something. If Rafael had had enough to drink by that time, he probably wouldn't even have noticed it. But why? Could Rafael have been blackmailing Roland? If so, Roland must have committed other and possibly darker misdeeds than those they knew about, because his former ones were apparently no secret. Perhaps Roland had chosen Rafael's work for his opening exhibit because Rafael had blackmailed him into doing it. Perhaps blackmail was a regular way for an artist to get his work shown; certainly it could account for some of the exhibits she had seen in other galleries.

She was a little sorry now that she had put Roland off when she could as easily have told Alex and Tinsley she would skip the before-dinner drinks. Was it too late to change her mind? Roland must have other plans by this time. Besides, she'd feel a fool if it turned out all he wanted was to borrow money or something like that. I can wait until tomorrow, she told herself.

XI

"BUT WHAT is it Lupe does, exactly?" Alex asked, when Susan came to the offices of Tabor, Tinsley & Tabor to pick him up for dinner. Otherwise, he would dilly-dally and leave her to have drinks with Tinsley and Amy, only turning up when they were halfway through the soup. Impending fatherhood was getting to him.

Although the firm's offices occupied only one floor of the state-of-the-art midtown skyscraper in which it paid top-of-the-market rents—for the firm was young yet—those offices were sumptuously appointed and equipped with the fine art collection without which no self-respecting concern would be found even moribund in these days. A number of the paintings hung on the walls were Melvilles—a few the property of the firm, but most on loan from the painter herself. Jill had acceded to this, albeit grudgingly, because, "A lot of their customers are likely to be or become collectors. Not that you need any advertisement; still, it doesn't hurt to be seen hanging in the right places. Just make sure you have Alex sign papers to show they belong to you and weren't a gift." But Susan had already taken care of that. She might be naive in commercial terms, but she was not a fool.

She found her fictive brother sitting behind a desk piled high with papers, keening to himself, as he so often did these days. He attempted to express courteous interest in what she had to tell him, although it was plain that he had little concern for anything at the moment except his private woes. What a shame to see the once charming rogue reduced to a quivering lump of domesticity.

"What sort of performance does this Lupe put on then?" he asked drearily.

"She described it to us in detail, and I must say I'm dying to see it. First, she says, the performance area—stage or whatever is available—is totally dark. The howling of wolves is heard."

"Recorded, I assume?"

"In Australia, yes, owing to the bigoted—her word—quarantine laws in force there. However, when she's in the western hemisphere, she travels with Rover and Fido, and they howl along with the records. Sometimes, she says, if the audience is really 'heap'—I think she means 'hip'—they howl along, too."

"Rover and Fido are her dogs?"

"Actually, they're wolves, but, she says, it saves trouble, even when she travels in places where there are no bigoted quarantine laws, if they have dog names, because people tend to assume they're dogs, which saves a lot of fuss."

"Is that all there is—a lot of howling?"

"No, indeed. Photographs of larger-than-life wolves flash or flicker—she couldn't decide which word she preferred—on and off. Strobe lights, I would guess. This is accompanied by more howling and music that she composed herself."

"She's a musician then?"

"Among other things. She's a multimedia artist, though not in the same way Rafael was."

"Good," Alex said.

"Most of the music is on tape, although sometimes she has live musicians playing drums and other instruments, depending on what's available locally and whether union rules prevail. The lights come up on a giant figure of a wolf, 'semi-abstract but menacing' —her words, not mine—also created by herself."

"She's a sculptress then?" He sighed, as if he had hoped for something more interesting.

"I suppose you could call her that also," Susan said, "but those are only two of her talents."

"Carrying the statue from place to place must present a problem," he said, "but I'm sure she has solved it, so there's no need to give me the details. If she should ever give a performance in town we must all go see it. Get up a little family party—you and Tinsley and I and Tinsley's mother, maybe even the twins if it takes her that long to get a booking. But, for the present—"

"She calls it a construct not a statue and there's no problem transporting it because it's made of papier mâché, although she could probably handle it if it were solid granite. She's built along the lines of a Norse goddess and she doesn't need wolves—four-legged ones, anyway—to get howls. The men in the restaurant were on their hind legs yammering at the sight of her."

Alex began to look interested. "I must really meet her. Only right I should express my condolences," he explained.

"The construct comes apart. Piece by piece is slowly removed. At first she had Rover and Fido do the removing, when they were available, but they tended to slobber on the mâché which softened it and spoiled the fit. So now she does it herself."

Alex looked even more interested. "She's inside the statue—the construct—is she?"

"Eventually all the pieces are stripped away, leaving Lupe wearing a wolf mask and, I gather, nothing else."

"Ah," Alex said, "and what happens then?"

"Like all true performance art, hers is participatory. She sings and does a dance in which she gets as many of the audience as she can to dance along with her after they get rid of their wolf's clothing—i.e., the trappings of civilization—and get down to bare essentials. She and selected male members of the audience then proceed to demonstrate other aspects of natural behavior—with females free to participate ad lib. It is at this point that the performance, especially in less progressive areas, is often cut short by the arrival of the police."

"When I was a boy they didn't use to call that sort of thing performance art," Alex said pensively. "I shall look forward to attending her next appearance in New York, though not, I think, in a family party. She should be a howling success."

He gave a melancholy laugh. Susan smiled. Expectant fathers had to be humored.

* * *

Alex got up and went over to the fashionably inoperative window (those who wanted to commit suicide had to go up to the roof) and stared out at the splendid Manhattan panorama below that added so much to the firm's rent. "Another two months," he said, pressing his forehead against the glass. "I don't know how I'm going to be able to stand it."

Susan refused to let the subject of the conversation be changed. "But I haven't told you the important thing, which is that Lupe thinks there's something fishy about Rafael's death. Remember, I thought there was, too?"

"Two fishies do not make a fact."

"She said Rafael always used cocaine, never heroin, and always in extreme moderation."

"But you said she'd been out of touch with him for years. People change. Anyhow, if he had been murdered, she'd be the chief suspect, wouldn't she? Spouses always are."

"Except that she wasn't around to murder him."

"Oh, who cares if Rafael was murdered or not!" Alex said passionately. "You know what the doctor told Tinsley? From now on she has to stay home all the time until the babies come."

Susan already knew, having received a full account from Tinsley's mother, but she let Alex have the pleasure of telling it to her all over again. "He said: 'You've really been overdoing it, Mrs. Tabor. You aren't a superwoman after all.' But I married her in the belief that she *was* a superwoman. Only a superwoman could cope with all this paperwork." And he swept his hand across the desk, knocking a pile of bonds to the floor.

"Alex, why didn't you tell me Roland had gotten into trouble over some forged paintings?"

"What art dealer hasn't gotten into trouble over a forged painting at one time or another? And I don't see why it should matter to you."

"Jill tells me because of that he couldn't open a gallery under his own name, but had to use her as a front."

"But he has opened a gallery under his own name."

"No, no, the one he ran with her—eight or nine years ago."

"I didn't even know they'd ever had a gallery together. But then I didn't know Jill until you turned up with her."

He looked thoughtful. "Come to think of it, I did meet her with Hal Courtenay years ago at some Chomp House jamboree. She wore her hair long then and kept her mouth shut; that's why I didn't remember until now."

Susan was astounded. A Chomp House jamboree did not seem like Hal Courtenay's milieu at all. "What on earth was Hal doing there?"

"I thought you knew: he used to vet pictures for the General on a pretty regular basis until that big blowup over the fake Picasso Roland sold the old man."

"Then the big trouble Jill was talking about was with the General?"

"Might have been, or it might have been some other forged paintings. I haven't really been following Roland's career."

Was he as uninterested as he sounded? She knew him as well as anyone, she supposed, and yet she couldn't be sure.

Bending over, he picked up the bonds and stacked them neatly on the desk. "Well, shall we be on our way?"

They were out in the main corridor, waiting for the elevator when he said, "Incidentally, I was talking to a fellow I know over at National Underwriters. He says they're not completely satisfied that the fire at Roland's Gallery was accidental. It's just a rumor, so I wouldn't mention it to anyone, if I were you. But I just thought you'd be interested."

XII

WHEN SUSAN joined Jill at Allardyce's Auction Galleries next morning, Jill told her she'd already heard the rumor and hadn't taken much stock in it. "People always say there's something suspicious whenever there's a fire in New York. That doesn't mean anything. After all, who could possibly stand to gain? Roland? All he'll get is enough—maybe not even enough—to pay for repairs; that artist—whatshisname—will get most of the insurance."

"Maybe it was whatshisname who set fire to the place," Susan suggested.

"Naaah, if you expect to set the world on fire with your paintings, you don't set fire to the gallery that's going to show 'em."

"Baltasar?"

But that seemed even more unlikely. A businessman might arrange to have his premises set on fire if his business were failing, but Baltasar's business hadn't even started yet. He lost a lot more than he could possibly gain—irreplaceable artworks (and, no matter what she thought of them personally, she had to admit he would never be able to find their like again); gowns, which could be re-created only after a lot of trouble; furniture . . . but he hadn't moved in yet, so there couldn't have been any furniture. Besides, the fire had been limited to Roland's part of the building.

"They said it was an accident," Jill reminded her. "A careless workman. You've seen their workmen. I rest my case."

She fanned herself vigorously with her catalogue. "Gosh, they certainly keep this place hot, don't they?" She pulled off the three-quarter-length mink coat that she wore no matter what the occasion, sometimes no matter what the season. It was the first fur coat she had ever owned; for Jill, as she was fond of saying, had been reared in humble circumstances (". . . and if you tell me once more that's a small village outside Pittsburgh, I shall be forced to resort to unpleasantness," Susan had said). Actually Jill had come from the Bronx. She'd told Susan this with an air of defiance, which Susan found inexplicable. People came from all sorts of weird places.

Now, with the money Jill must have been making, first as Darius Moffatt's rep and then as Susan's, she should be able to afford several fur coats if she wanted them. And she did. Greed had shone in her eyes the day before as she stared at Lupe's sables. "If you like it so much, why don't you get yourself a coat like it?" Susan asked after Lupe had gone.

"Sable isn't practical," Jill said. "It sheds. Look, Lupe's left hairs all over her chair."

Susan herself had had fur coats when she was young and unenlightened, but now she saw no reason to decorate her body with the bodies of dead animals. She did not have a similar prejudice against leather, though, and when she saw what Jill was wearing underneath her coat, she felt like skinning the girl alive.

"Jill, put your coat back on immediately!"

"But it's so hot in here. What's wrong?" She looked at Susan with wide green eyes, like grapes. Someday I'm going to paint her as a fruit salad, Susan thought. With wax fruit.

For the upper part of Jill's body was clad in the pink T-shirt with the message "I'm Glad I'm a Muppie" emblazoned across her chest, which might more appropriately have been inscribed "I'm Glad I'm a Mammal."

"I'm wearing your gift. I thought you'd be pleased."

"You know perfectly well I didn't expect you to wear it; I meant it as a joke. Especially not in Allardyce's. People are looking at us—at you."

"I like people to look at me," Jill said complacently. "But if you think the shirt makes me too conspicuous, I'll take it off. Only, I should warn you, I don't have anything on under it."

Which was all too obvious.

"You worry too much about appearances, Susan," Jill said.

"You're the one who's always talking about image."

"Image is one thing, appearances another."

"You're not entitled to wear the shirt," Susan said desperately. "You're not a bona fide Muppie."

"But I will be one day—not too far off either," Jill mourned. "Only the other morning I found a gray hair."

Susan refused to be diverted. "Hortense may not like your jumping the gun like that. Giving away her ideas before she's even gotten started."

"Oh, if that's all you're worrying about... I called her last night and she said she'd be delighted to have me wear it, and she'd be happy to give me a further supply of her brochures to hand out to anybody who asked. She was even more delighted to hear that you were planning to invest in her health club, and hopes to see you there as a patron as well as an investor. At reduced rates, natch?"

"Natch?"

"Little archaic expression which I hoped would strike a chord."

"It strikes something, but not a chord. I haven't made up my mind whether or not I'm going to invest in her club, but I am sure that I am not going to patronize it."

"How about if she called it a spa?"

"I still wouldn't patronize it."

"It looks like a good investment to me," Jill said. "As a matter of fact, I'm thinking of taking a piece of the action myself." That did impress Susan, for she knew how careful Jill was of her own money.

"Who else do you think I can interest?" Jill went on. "Baltasar? Roland? Alex? Hortense promised me a commission on any other investors I can bring in. You don't count because she already worked on you herself. Besides, since I represent you, it might not be ethical. I wonder whether Lupe would care to invest her widow's mite? She seemed interested."

"Just Old World courtesy," Susan said. Isn't Jill making enough money as my representative, she wondered; why does she have to hustle like that? "Remember," she said aloud, "we came here to look at the Moffatt."

"Alleged Moffatt. Alleged Darius Moffatt, that is. It could be another Moffatt entirely, or maybe even a Muffett, painting a tuffet."

But the catalogue clearly said, "Darius Moffatt, Portrait of Emmy." The centerfold showed a small black-and-white photograph that gave no clear idea of the original.

"'Property of an individual collector,'" Jill read. "I wonder just who that 'individual collector' might be."

"Can't you tell from the name of the picture who the original buyer was?"

"He was always doing portraits of Emmy; that is, if Emmy and Emma and Emily and Emilia and Em were the same person. You can't tell from the pictures themselves. They're not exactly representational."

You couldn't tell, indeed. Not only were the pictures not exactly representational, they were not exactly abstract either. In fact, they seemed to be a mélange of the most egregious aspects of contemporary painting. The only thing worthy of remark was the skill with which they combined such seemingly disparate styles as neoexpressionism and minimalism with occasional sorties into pop art and constructivism; and, in what seemed to be his later pictures—for his work could be dated only by inference—an occasional flirtation with conceptualism. But the female forms which sometimes appeared in various degrees of fragmentation were too far removed from realism to give any idea of the original human Emmy (or Emma or Emilia or Emily).

"Who was Emmy?" Hal Courtenay had written, "A real woman, a figment of the artist's imagination, or a combination of both, a woman whom he had once known and perhaps loved, and who came to represent his ideal of womanhood?"

Obviously, most if not all of the pictures must have been done from memory or imagination, because Darius could hardly have towed Emmy all across the country without exciting remark from his agrarian and probably Puritanical relatives.

"I'm afraid I can't remember which I sold to whom," Jill confessed. "Especially in the early days when I didn't care who bought the paintings as long as their checks were good. I'll bet it's one of the first ones that went for next to nothing, and now it's estimated at—" she gave a low howl "—a hundred to a hundred and fifty thousand dollars."

"More than I'd be estimated at," Susan said.

"That's because you're still alive. Imagine what your paintings will fetch after you're dead."

"Don't look so happy at the thought," Susan said. "You don't own any of my pictures and the contract between us automatically terminates on my death."

"I have faith in you, Susan. You're going to live forever like Louise Nevelson."

I really must make out a new will, Susan thought. She still hadn't gotten around to changing her old one, which had been made out in favor of her distant cousin Sophie von Eulenberg, who was by this time very old and very mad. She supposed she would leave her money to Peter, and perhaps some to Alex (it would look odd, otherwise), but it would have to be tied up in a trust. She would trust neither with the principal, especially since the bulk of her assets was still in the form of paintings. She would need to appoint someone knowledgeable about art to look after her estate. Dare she ask Hal Courtenay to act as a trustee, she wondered.

"Portrait of Emmy" looked to Susan like most of the other Moffatts she'd seen, but Jill declared, "I've never seen this one before. I'm sure of it."

"It could be one that was never sold through you at all," Susan suggested. "He might have sold it himself. I know his mother told you he'd never sold a picture in his life, but how could she be sure with him wandering all over the country like that? Besides, she's old; her memory might be going."

"Sharp as a tack," Jill said.

"He might have given the picture to somebody—perhaps Emmy herself."

"That's not likely!" And, when Susan wanted to know why, Jill snapped, "Because I say so, that's why."

Susan had an idea of why Jill was so sure, and she was surprised that no one else seemed to have had any suspicions; but then they probably hadn't heard Jill expatiate on the subject of careful marketing and timed release. Darius Moffatt must have left some paintings in his East Village apartment, and his mother probably had brought them to the Turkel Gallery to see if they were worth anything. All the rest of them had been in the barn on the Moffatt place, although whether his mother had come upon them, as the press releases said, or had known they were there all along was a matter for conjecture.

To have disclosed their existence at the time would have been to reveal the whole body of work at once, no chance for the timed release that would step up the artist's prices each time a new group of pictures was put on the market—and which would come about naturally in the case of a still-living and still-painting artist. Susan was almost sure that Jill had fabricated the story of Darius's wanderings—and the relatives with whom he had left his paintings—to make sure that prices would rise in a steady progression.

If there were any remaining from the original store in the barn, no doubt they were cached in that Long Island City warehouse, along with Susan's paintings. Someday, Susan thought, there would be a brass plate on the building that said: "Susan Melville's and Darius Moffatt's paintings were stored here." That is, if the building hadn't been turned into condominiums in the interval.

But there must have been a friend to whom Darius actually had given a painting. And now that friend had decided to cash in, without benefit of Jill. Good for him or her or it, Susan thought.

Jill glared at a small boy who was staring at her chest. "And what are *you* looking at?"

"Which Muppet are you, lady?" he asked. "Are you Miss Piggy?"

Jill stuck her tongue out at him and put her coat back on, to Susan's immense relief.

The boy put an instrument to his lips that Susan, after a moment of memory-searching, identified as a kazoo, and blew a mighty blast. A woman in a purple fur coat appeared and, after an angry glance at Jill, dragged the child away.

"Why don't we go look at the other pictures," Susan suggested.

"I don't want to go look at the other pictures," Jill said. She took another look at the Moffatt. "I'm going to find out the name of this individual collector. I'm going to insist that whoever's in charge here tell me exactly who that anonymous turd is!"

And she stomped off, leaving Susan standing in front of "Portrait of Emmy."

XIII

"YOUR FRIEND seems to have quite a temper," a voice behind her said. "Goes with the hair. Do you suppose there's some genetic basis or is it simply a self-fulfilling prophecy?"

Susan turned. The young man whom she had met climbing out of Roland's areaway the evening before last grinned at her. "Remember me?"

"Indeed I do."

"I'm afraid I didn't have a chance to introduce myself. I'm Andy Mackay."

He handed her a card. It said, "Andrew Mackay, Investigations." It also gave a phone number—nothing else, not even a post office box number.

"No need to tell me who you are," he added, although she hadn't had the slightest intention of introducing herself, "the famous 'Susan Melville, Late Bloomer,' as *Time*, or was it *Newsweek*, put it."

"What are you investigating?" she asked coldly.

"All sorts of things. You'd be surprised how much there is that needs to be investigated."

"And on whose behalf are you conducting these investigations?"

"Forgive me, but I can't tell you that. Privileged information, you know."

"Do you usually carry out your investigations accompanied by your dog?"

"Brucie isn't my dog. I was taking care of him for a friend. He's back home now. But I'm sure he would have sent his love, if he'd known I was going to run into you."

He looked at "Portrait of Emmy." "I know this is going to give you a very poor opinion of me, but I'm afraid I just can't seem to appreciate that kind of thing. The most I can say for it is that at least it doesn't have things sticking out of it. Now, your pictures I like. You can understand what they're supposed to be—flowers and things. Although lately you've been going heavier on the things and lighter on the flowers, haven't you?"

She tried to keep herself from warming toward him. Reputable private investigators, she told himself, no matter how excellent their taste in art, do not climb over locked gates. Nor do they break and enter—or whatever the legal term for picking locks is—because she was as sure as if she had seen him open the door underneath the stairs and come out, that he had been inside the DeMarnay Gallery the other night.

All he had shown her was his card, not his license, she reminded herself. Anyone could have a card printed up, even with raised letters. He might not even be a disreputable private investigator; he might not be an investigator at all.

Jill came back, looking angrier than before. "They say that the consignor wishes to keep his identity private. When I insisted, they said they had no authority to give me his name. They were so fucking polite I wanted to knock their fucking teeth down their fucking throats!"

"Jill," Susan said, "I'd like you to meet Andrew Mackay. Mr. Mackay, this is Jill Turkel."

Jill started to snap out a surly acknowledgement of the introduction. Then she stopped. She looked at Andrew Mackay. He looked at her. He smiled at her. She smiled back.

Oh, Lord, Susan thought, all it needs is a burst of Tschaikowsky to make the moment complete.

As if in answer to her thought, there was a discordant squawk practically in her ear. The inquisitive urchin had crept up unobserved and was serenading them on his kazoo.

A member of the gallery staff rushed up, along with the lady in purple fur. "Madam," he said to her, "kazoos are not permitted in Allardyce's. I suggest you try Sotheby's."

"I will," she said. "All you have here is junk, anyway." And she swept out, to kazoo accompaniment.

"Well, really," the Allardyce man said.

"Mr. Mackay was Roland's late-night visitor," Susan told Jill. "The one with the dog."

"Merely passing by," Mr. Mackay said. "Brucie saw their cat in the yard and went after her and I went after Brucie."

"Sounds reasonable to me," Jill said.

"Mr. Mackay says he's a private investigator."

"Oh, and what is he investigating?"

"I've already asked him that. He won't say."

Both ladies looked inquiringly at Mr. Mackay who, in harmony with his surroundings, gave them a Mona Lisa smile.

"Did you manage to get inside?" Jill asked bluntly.

Mackay looked shocked. "Of course not. Why would I have done such a thing? Besides, it would have been illegal."

"Does the fact that you're talking to us have anything to do with your investigation?" Jill demanded.

He bowed with such elegance Susan couldn't help being impressed. "Let us say that I'm combining business with pleasure."

Jill didn't say anything. She stood there, looking at him with an expression on her face that was impossible, for Susan at least, to read. Susan took her by the arm and led her from the young man's immediate vicinity. "Well, now that you've seen the picture, shall we go?"

"I think I'd like to stick around and watch the auction after all," Jill said. "It might be interesting to see how much it goes for. How about going out and having lunch and then coming back afterward?"

"Do you really want me to come back here with you," Susan asked, "or would you rather be alone with the charming Mr. Mackay—whom I warn you against. Whatever he's investigating, he's up to no good." Or, if he's up to good, maybe you're not, she thought.

"Don't be silly, Susan," Jill said, "of course I want you to come to the auction with me. And we don't know that he is going to be at the auction, do we? He must have other cases."

Susan was startled. She hadn't thought of herself as part of a case. Jill looked back over her shoulder at Mackay who was standing in front of the Moffatt, as if he were testing Marcel Duchamp's dictum that anything becomes beautiful if you look at it long enough.

"He *would* have to be a detective," she said.

"I'd be happy to come to lunch with you," Susan said, "and go to the auction, as long as I can get out by four-thirty."

"Oh, the picture ought to come up long before that."

Since there wasn't time to make reservations at a posh restaurant, they repaired to a nearby coffee shop. All the way there, Jill kept looking over her shoulder, but Mackay neither attempted to follow them or accompany them. Susan was relieved. It would be most unwise of Jill to get involved with him in any way; and it was no use telling her that because she was obviously aware of it. Pity though; he seemed so much more personable than Jill's general run of young men.

They settled into a booth. "Why do you have to be out by four-thirty?" Jill asked. "Date?"

"Yes."

"Anyone I know?"

"I'll have the chicken salad on rye toast," Susan told the waitress. "No mayonnaise."

"I'll have a cheeseburger, medium rare, with a double helping of fries and cole slaw and a Coke. No gourmet food for me today!"

"All our food is gourmet," the waitress said huffily. "The cole slaw is subtly seasoned with fresh herbs and the cheese on the all-lean-beef hamburger is New York State Cheddar, aged to a mellow ripeness."

"I know it's none of my business," Jill said, when they finally got rid of the waitress (but not before she told them how the potatoes had been flown in from Idaho by gentle jet), "but your date isn't with Hal Courtenay, by any chance, is it?"

"Hal said he was going out of town and wouldn't be back until the middle of the week. I told you. If he's back already, he hasn't gotten in touch with me. There wouldn't have been any reason."

"All right, all right," Jill said, "I was just making conversation, not innuendos. Even if I am your rep, I don't have to know everyone you know, keep tabs on you wherever you go—although that might be a good idea. You never know when there might be a sudden call for your work."

"Also, you're nosy."

"Also, as you say, I'm nosy."

"If I were nosy," Susan said, trying to sound casual, "I would ask whether there's anything between you and Hal."

"And, being frank and open, I'd tell you that there was once, a long time ago, but he decided I was too young and uncouth for him and I decided he was too old and stuffy for me—so the field is clear for you."

"Don't be silly, Jill."

"I'm not being silly," Jill said. "He's been making a play for you; you must have noticed. But, if you'll take my advice, and I know you won't, you'll steer clear of him."

"Mind telling me why?"

"Because he's a lying, cheating, stinking snake-in-the-grass, that's why," Jill said.

She stopped and gave Susan a forced smile. "As you can see, we do have our little differences. Nothing serious, of course. But I do think you owe it to Peter to stay away from Hal."

"Since when have you been so concerned for Peter?"

"Maybe I don't show it, but I have always had the utmost respect for Peter. Are you going to have dessert? I'm going to have a banana split with hot fudge sauce, full steam ahead and damn the calories. I'm full of conflicting emotions and when my emotions are in conflict I eat."

* * *

When they returned to the auction room, Mackay was there, to Jill's pleasure and Susan's regret. However, they had reason to be thankful to him, for he had saved them a couple of choice seats up front; otherwise they might not have gotten seats at all. The place was packed.

Jill looked around. "I'm surprised not to see Roland here."

"Why should he be here?" Susan asked.

"This is an important auction," Jill explained. "Most of the other dealers are here. And collectors. Look, there's Baltasar. I wonder why he's here."

"Maybe he wants to buy some pictures," Mackay suggested humbly.

"I know he did buy some of Rafael's pieces to decorate his place in Acapulco," Jill said, "but I didn't know he was a collector. This stuff is too expensive for mere decoration. Still, it's possible. Who knows what he has in his hacienda? Or his castle? Besides dogs, of course, and probably horses. People who live in castles always have horses."

"That sounds like a proverb," Susan said.

"In time it will be."

"Do people buy art only because they want to decorate their places or because they're collectors?" Mackay asked. "Don't they ever buy a picture or a statue just because they happen to like it?"

"Not at these prices," Jill said. "I can see you have a lot to learn about art."

"Maybe you could find the time to teach me," he suggested.

"Portrait of Emmy" didn't come up until a quarter to five. It sold for two hundred and fifty thousand dollars and went to one of Gil Stratton's associates.

When the gavel came down for the third time, Jill gave a loud shriek, tore up her catalogue, jumped on it, and was requested to leave by the management. Susan left also, trying to act as if they were not together, that it was just chance that they happened to be leaving at the same time.

This time Mackay did follow them out. Brave man, Susan thought, but probably it's part of his job. He really did seem to like Jill, though.

"How about a drink?" he suggested. "I should think you could use one."

"She has a date," Jill said, "but I certainly could use one. A drink, I mean. Maybe two, if your expense account can stand it."

Susan didn't like the idea of Jill's going off alone with young Mr. Mackay. For a moment she thought of breaking her date with Roland and tagging along, however undesired her presence might be, but she couldn't do that. It wouldn't be fair to Roland. And Jill probably would feel it wasn't fair to her either.

XIV

WHAT ON earth could Roland have to say to her, Susan wondered again as she walked uptown. Was it something she would
want to hear? Did he want her help in some way? Did he want to
warn her against someone? Or had he simply chosen her to be a
repository for his confidences?

And why had he been so insistent that nobody should know that
they had arranged to meet? She felt a vague sense of unease, for
which there was no rational explanation. The likelihood was that
he wanted to tell her something about Jill; and, indeed, she was
beginning to wonder about the girl herself. Yesterday she had
given Susan to understand that Roland had originally gotten into
trouble for dealing in forged paintings—and that she had parted
company with him when she'd caught him "up to his old tricks."

All of which had sounded plausible enough while she was
speaking. Now that Susan had time to think about it, she recalled
that the two had been running a small Soho gallery that dealt in
the work of little-known artists. Why would anyone bother to fake
a painting by a little-known artist?

Could it be a question of stolen rather than fake paintings? If so,
Roland could hardly have expected to exhibit them in the gallery.
Had he gone in for theft as a sideline; and had Jill found out about
it and wanted nothing to do with him? That made sense. But why
hadn't Jill simply told Susan that Roland was thief? Then she remembered that Jill hadn't been the one to suggest that Roland
had been involved with forged paintings. Susan had, herself, and

Jill had agreed. If Susan had suggested that Roland had been caught stealing paintings, perhaps Jill would have agreed to that too.

What was it Roland actually had done? Maybe I'll find out now, she thought, quickening her step.

Earlier the day had been warmish for the time of year, but since then a chilly wind had sprung up. It was quite cold now. Susan pulled the collar of her coat up around her ears.

As she reached the corner of Madison Avenue, she could see from across the street that a crowd had gathered on Roland's block—a quiet crowd rather than a demonstrative one, the kind of crowd that gathers whenever there is either trouble afoot or a film crew at work; that is, a crew making a movie, as distinguished from a television crew, which goes hand in hand with—and sometimes precedes—trouble.

There were cameras from two of the TV networks and one of the local stations and a number of police cars, plus a bunch of what appeared to be reporters, some with microphones, some with tape recorders, one traditionalist with a notebook. An ambulance drew away as she approached. Trouble, maybe even big trouble, but not major trouble, or all the networks would have been there.

She was strongly tempted to turn back. Later she could explain to Roland that she hadn't wanted to push her way through the throng. Provided, of course, that Roland was in a position where he could be explained to. Because the space the police had cleared was directly in front of the DeMarnay gallery, and the uniformed policeman who was shooing passers-by away was standing at the bottom of the DeMarnay Gallery's steps. Another policeman was posted at the top, and she could see several more down in the areaway. Whatever had happened, had happened right there.

The uneasiness inside her stopped being a vague feeling and developed into something very specific. Prudence told her to turn back, go home, and wait until she heard about it, whatever it was, on the news. But prudence had never been one of her strong points.

She approached the steps. Several reporters glanced at her. Fortunately none appeared to be from the fine arts departments of their respective media, or she might have been recognized and pounced upon. "Distinguished artist in front of gallery where [disaster] occurred" would be good for some kind of story even if she were only passing by on her way to the supermarket.

"Move along please, Miss," the policeman said. "There's been an accident. Nobody allowed inside."

"I'm sorry to hear that. I had an appointment with Mr. DeMarnay."

Although she'd kept her voice low, she could see the reporters' ears prick up. From the expression on the policeman's face and the glance he exchanged with the policeman at the head of the stairs, she could tell that Roland was not going to be able to keep their appointment.

"Mr. DeMarnay," the policeman repeated. "Mr. Roland De-Marnay, would that be?"

"Yes, Roland DeMarnay. I do hope he hasn't been hurt or anything?"

But she knew, as surely as if there had been a wreath hanging on the gallery door and a heavenly chorus singing overhead, that Roland was dead. Poor Roland, she couldn't help thinking, he's never going to have to worry about getting bald after all.

One of the reporters took a tentative step in her direction. "Just what was your business with DeMarnay—?" he began, when the policeman cut him off with, "I'm sure Lieutenant Bracco would like to have a word with you, Miss. If you wouldn't mind coming upstairs."

What would he do if I said I did mind, she wondered. Seize me, handcuff me, and drag me up the stairs? But no question of her refusing. It was an honest citizen's duty to cooperate with the law; and, in spite of having committed some actions in the past that the law in its narrow-mindedness might frown upon, she remained an honest citizen in her own mind and heart, which was what counted.

The first policeman escorted her up the stairs and entrusted her to the second policeman, who opened the door and said to the plainclothesman who appeared, "A lady come to see Mr. DeMarnay," in a manner reminiscent of the Frog Footman.

Inside, boards and buckets and sawhorses were stacked against the walls, but none of the workmen was in sight. No doubt it was the end of the working day; however, it seemed unlikely that they were going to be back any time soon.

"Please wait here, Miss," the detective said, indicating one of the two bronze and leather benches sited on opposite sides of the foyer. He went through the archway that led to the interior of the gallery and was now closed by a barrier, a cross between a curtain and a folding door, made of shining geometric shapes that broke the reflection of his body into fragments and repeated them in almost cubistic fashion, as he pushed one half aside and passed through. The barrier had been there on her previous visits, she recalled, but it had been folded back against the wall on either side, so that she had taken it to be a pair of ornamental pilasters.

A dishevelled-looking Damian and Paul were huddled on the other bench. They appeared to have been weeping. She could think of no tactful way of phrasing her question. "What happened?"

"Oh, Miss Melville," Damian whimpered, "it—it's too terrible to talk about. Paul and I stopped in on our way to lunch to pick up some things we'd left—" here Paul burst into loud sobs "—we've been on hiatus you know, until the redecorating was finished—and we found Roland—squashed to pieces . . . *strewn* all over the basement . . ."

"It was awful," Paul sobbed, "awful. I was sick all over the carpet."

"I was sick, too," Damian said. "I was just as sick as you were, maybe even sicker."

She was not interested in their relative degrees of nausea, particularly as she was beginning to feel a trifle queasy herself. She couldn't help remembering "Concupiscent Toad Crushed by Passion," and envisaging Roland in similar state. "Roland is dead, then?"

"Is he ever," Damian moaned.

"And the carpet is ruined," Paul said.

"Don't be so heartless," Damian admonished him. "Carpets can be cleaned, but nothing will ever bring Rollie back." Damian turned to Susan, "They say he must have been beaten to death after a party, but he never would have had a party without inviting us."

"You never know though, do you?" Paul said. "You think you know somebody utterly, and then they go and do something like this behind your back." He shook his head.

"A party?" Susan repeated.

"We never partied like that," Damian said. "It was just fun and games. I know some people do go in for pain, but it wasn't *our* thing. Besides, Roland had a very low pain threshold."

"All those sinister-looking things he had hanging on the walls and around were just for decoration," Paul said. "That's what he told me when I wanted to—that's what he told me."

"They were valuable antiques. He would never let us so much as touch them, let alone use them."

"But he must have let someone else use them," Paul sobbed. "And they squashed him like a bug in the basement."

"We mustn't speak ill of the dead. Maybe he didn't let someone use the things. Maybe, whoever it was simply took one and—and *bashed* him."

Both of them burst into loud wails. I should try to comfort them, Susan thought, instead of wanting to take a blunt instrument and bash them myself.

The detective returned and, after casting a look at Damian and Paul which of itself was almost enough to lay him open to charges of police brutality, said, "If you'll come this way, Miss—"

She hesitated. "You're not taking me to see the . . . er . . . Mr. DeMarnay, are you?"

He looked shocked. "No, no, of course not. The remains have been removed. Anyhow, the fatality took place in the basement. And that's where most of our people and the forensics people are right now."

"But it's so quiet up here." Surely with all that activity going on they should be able to hear . . . something.

"The basement's soundproofed," he said.

"Of course. How naive of me."

"Lieutenant Bracco is up here in the office on this floor. All very nice and pleasant, except for the artwork and that can't be helped."

"Philistine," either Damian or Paul hissed.

Ignoring this, the detective waved Susan toward the back of the gallery. He pushed half of the shiny closure aside and they entered the alcove that led to Roland's office.

Lieutenant Bracco was sitting at Roland's desk underneath an enormous Italian Renaissance painting with a classical theme. Esmeralda was sitting on the blotter in front of him, washing her face. Each of them pretended that the other wasn't there, Esmeralda rather more successfully than the lieutenant.

On the night of the gallery's opening, the office had been dimly lit. From the brief glimpse Susan had had, she'd thought that the picture over Roland's desk depicted satyrs chasing nymphs. Now she could see the picture was of satyrs chasing other satyrs and, in some instances, catching them. A scene of a very intimate nature was taking place right over the detective's head. From the fact that he never once turned his head in the course of their conversation, it was clear that he was aware of it.

The picture appeared to have suffered no damage from the fire; it hadn't even been darkened by smoke. Or perhaps it had, and Roland had restored it. Pity, she thought.

The lieutenant got up to greet her with the courtesy due an

upper-bracket taxpayer and a lady. "Relative of the deceased?" he asked. He sounded more like an undertaker than a detective.

"No, just a friend."

He looked surprised, either that Roland should have such respectable friends, or that she should have such unrespectable ones.

"A business friend. I'm a painter."

He nodded, as if that made it better, but she still had the feeling that she had let him down somehow. "Please sit down, Mrs.—er—?" he said, sinking back into his seat and indicating a chair on the opposite side of the desk. The plainclothesman remained just outside the door—ready to spring to his chief's aid if she should turn violent, she supposed.

"Melville, Susan Melville. And it's Miss, not Mrs."

Esmeralda started washing her toes meticulously, paying great attention to the spaces in between. There was something hypnotic about the ritual. Susan tore her eyes away with an effort.

"What happened to Mr. DeMarnay?" she asked. "Or can't you tell me?"

"It's a matter of public record, or will be as soon as we've given a statement to the media. Citizens have a right to know. He was battered to death. Looks like your standard sex crime, with things getting out of hand. No evidence of robbery, so far as we can tell."

He hesitated; then went on, "There's a room in the back of the basement, very . . . exotically furnished, and fitted up with all the usual appurtenances—whips, hoods, chains, leather garments, and what forensics tells me are old-fashioned torture instruments—so that sort of thing seems to have been a regular activity."

"Damian and Paul say it wasn't."

"Damian and Paul? Oh, the Bobbsey twins. Well, what would you expect them to say? You know them?"

"I've met them before. They work at the gallery. But of course you know that."

"So they informed me," he said. "Anyhow, that's where it happened. I'm sure you've never been down there."

"No," Susan said, "I never have." And now she probably would never get the chance to, either. "When did he die?" she asked. "Do they know that yet?"

"The fellow from the M.E.'s office says, at a rough estimate, sometime between midnight and three. They'll know more exactly when they get him in the lab. Those two said they found him at noon, and the workmen did see them come in. But they could have done it the night before and come back. On the other hand, that doesn't mean they did it, either. He probably knew other people of that . . . er . . . nature. And the alarm system was off, so it wouldn't have been too hard for anyone to get in, though there weren't any signs of forced entry."

"What was it . . . er . . . done with?"

He seemed disappointed at her unladylike thirst for details, but citizens had a right to know. "The murder weapon was a heavy piece of brass, shaped like—it was a heavy piece of brass that I understand is supposed to be a kind of sculpture. It was wiped clean, so there weren't any fingerprints."

The mere fact that it had been wiped clean did not of itself mean that Roland's death had not been a crime of passion; simply that the killer had come to his senses after the deed was done and set about trying to cover his tracks. But she was already beginning to have doubts that Roland's death was just a simple hit-and-run S-and-M encounter.

"Now, I wonder whether you'd mind telling me what the exact nature of your business with Mr. DeMarnay was," Bracco asked. "Not that it could be connected in any way with the unfortunate event, I'm sure, but we're going to have to ask the same thing of everybody who had the slightest connection with him. Matter of routine."

"Of course. I quite understand. He asked me to come see him, but he didn't tell me why. I had an idea that he might want me to exhibit my pictures in his gallery, which wouldn't, of course, be up to me but to my representative. She handles that kind of thing. I'm afraid I'm not much of a businesswoman." The lieutenant looked approving. As she'd expected.

"But since Roland—Mr. DeMarnay—put it as a personal favor, I didn't like to refuse."

"Personal favor?" The lieutenant looked disapproving.

"He was a friend—an acquaintance—of my brother's." Oh dear, she thought, now she'd brought Alex into it. Well, if they were going to ask questions of anyone who had anything to do with Roland, they were bound to get around to Alex sooner or later. So all she'd done was make it a little sooner.

"They weren't close. His wife—Alex's—is expecting a baby," she added, hoping she'd made her meaning perfectly clear.

The lieutenant seemed satisfied. "I think that's all I need to ask you right now. Unless you know something else that you think might be of help?"

I know that a man died of heroin poisoning here a couple of months ago and that his wife thinks it was murder. I know that there was a fire here a month ago, and the rumor is that it might have been arson. I know Roland was a dealer in forged paintings and God knows what else. It did not occur to her then that Darius Moffatt's death, although it had occurred almost ten years before, could have some connection with the things that had been going on in the gallery, or she might have added it to her mental list.

She shook her head. "I'm afraid I can't think of anything. Really, I hardly knew the man."

Let the police find out all these things and put them together for themselves. That was what they were paid for. Enough that she had thrown Alex to the wolves. She wondered whether Lupe had succeeded in establishing Rover and Fido in Jackson Heights, or whether she was still looking for a home for them. Should she tell the lieutenant about Lupe's arrival? No, let Baltasar. Lupe probably had nothing to do with all this. An unfortunate coincidence that she had happened to turn up yesterday.

"One thing more," the lieutenant said, as Susan was about to get up, "you don't happen to know where we might locate a Mr. Baltasar who has the place upstairs, do you? Those two out there told us he's living at the Plaza, but, although he is registered there, we haven't been able to reach him."

It was almost as if he had been reading her thoughts. "Ordinarily, I wouldn't, because I hardly know him either, but I just came from an auction at Allardyce's. He was there, and he might still be there; the auction wasn't over when I left."

"Thank you, you've been very helpful." The lieutenant picked up the phone and gave instructions to someone at the other end to go to Allardyce's and pick up Baltasar, if he were still there. I hope they're not going to fetch him in a police car with sirens screaming, she thought. He won't like that at all. But then I'm not enjoying myself very much either.

This time she finally did rise, and Bracco rose along with her. "By the way," he said, acknowledging Esmeralda's presence for the first time, "this cat—she does belong to someone in the building, doesn't she?"

Hearing herself mentioned, Esmeralda rolled over and waved her paws in the air as if to show she at least had no secrets. But she has, Susan thought. She must know everything that's been going on here. She probably even knows who killed Roland, might even have seen it happen.

"She belongs to Baltasar upstairs. Her name is Esmeralda."

"Is that Mr. Baltasar or Baltasar something? I mean, is Baltasar his first or last name?"

"It seems to be his only name, at least the only name he goes by. He's a dress designer. They often have only one name."

"I don't suppose he would have participated in the . . . the festivities in the basement."

"I would hardly think so." Although, of course, you never could tell.

"Well, anyway, I'm glad to know the cat belongs here. I'd hate to think a stray got in somehow and we let her stay and leave hairs all over everything and maybe make a mess."

Esmeralda sat up and looked affronted.

"Oh, no, I'm sure Baltasar will be delighted that you're taking such good care of her."

She would have liked to ask whether Esmeralda had been found on the actual scene of the crime or merely wandering about the place. But she had asked too many questions already. She tickled Esmeralda between the ears. Esmeralda purred.

"If you'll just give your name and address and your brother's name and address to Sergeant Collins—" he indicated the detective at the door "—we'll know where to get in touch with you, if it should turn out to be necessary. You will let us know if you're planning to go out of town, won't you?"

"Yes, certainly, but I'm not planning to go anywhere."

"You might as well give him your representative's name and address, too, in case DeMarnay happened to tell her what he wanted to talk to you about."

And if he checks into Roland's past, as he undoubtedly will, and finds out that my representative was once Roland's partner, what will he think then? Especially since it wasn't likely Jill would volunteer the information.

She started to go; then paused at the door. "I've just remembered something. I don't know whether it'll be helpful or not." And she told him about having met Andrew Mackay outside the DeMarnay Gallery, and then again at the auction gallery, behaving suspiciously in both instances. Him she was glad to sacrifice.

The lieutenant seemed a little annoyed. "So they've had this place under surveillance, have they? I do wish they'd let us know what they're up to. I'll have to have a talk with him."

"Who are 'they?'"

He smiled. "Come now, Miss Melville, I've been very frank and open with you, but you must allow us to have some secrets."

"Mr. Mackay went off with my representative," Susan said. "I think I ought to know who he is."

"If she can't take care of herself, she isn't much of a representative, is she? I take it she's young and pretty." Susan nodded. He shrugged. "Well, you know what these private eyes are like."

"So he's a real detective then?"

Bracco considered. "He is an investigator," he said finally. "I suppose you could call him a detective."

"And he does have a license?"

"In a manner of speaking."

She waited, but he offered no explanation. So Mackay was on the right side of the law. Right now she wasn't sure whether that was good or bad.

XV

ALTHOUGH THE light on her answering machine was glowing when she got home, indicating that messages were waiting, they could keep on waiting, she thought, as she sat down to mourn Roland. He was a despicable little man but he deserved to be mourned, especially as she couldn't help feeling that if she had agreed to talk to him the evening before, he might be alive now. On the other hand, she too might be dead. Whatever secret he'd had to impart apparently was worth killing for, unless his death was the crime of passion it appeared to be.

She made herself a drink and turned on the radio. The news reports offered nothing new. Roland had been savagely beaten to death with a bronze statuette of, as the announcer put it, "an erogenous nature," seemingly in the course of an orgy that had gotten out of hand. Such things were happening too often these days, a commentator said. It wasn't clear whether he was referring to orgies or murders.

The phone rang. Alex. "I've been trying to reach you all afternoon," he complained—which, she later discovered, was an exaggeration. There had been only one message from him, although there were so many messages from so many other people (routine these days), it was possible that he had tried her more than once and failed to get through.

"I've been with the police," she said.

"Do they want you to give a course in graffiti appreciation to police cadets, or have you been up to something?"

"In connection with Roland's death. You must have heard about it by now."

"I heard it on the radio," he said. "That's why I've been calling. Very sad about Roland, of course, but why were the police talking to you? You didn't do it, did you?"

She tried to indicate by her tone of voice that she felt this remark was not in the best of taste. "I had an appointment to see Roland this afternoon. Since I had no idea anything had happened, I just walked in on the investigation."

No point in letting him know that she hadn't simply stumbled into the investigation but had seen something was wrong and deliberately walked right into it. And could kick herself now. Otherwise, unless the police got in touch with everybody on Roland's address list, they might never have gotten around to her.

He sounded apprehensive. "An appointment to see Roland! Why on earth would you want to see Roland?"

She explained once again that she hadn't wanted to see Roland. He had wanted to talk to her, and, no, she didn't know why and would probably never know now.

"You should have known better than to go see Roland," Alex said.

"For heaven's sake, I didn't know he was going to be killed, did I?" I went for the same reason I spoke at the opening of his gallery: I didn't want to refuse a request from a friend of yours."

Spluttering sounds came from the telephone. "And I suppose you told the police I was a bosom buddy of Roland's?"

"I told them you were the one who introduced me to him. . . . Well, they wanted to know how I came to know Roland, and that's the truth, isn't it?"

"That doesn't mean you had to go and blab it to the police. You could have said you forgot who introduced you to him. You could have said he introduced himself to you at—at some art thing or other. You could have—"

"Alex, they're undoubtedly going to investigate his background, find out everybody he knew. It would look odd if I'd said I didn't remember who introduced us, when lots of people know he was a friend—all right, an acquaintance—of yours."

"All right, all right. It's just that I hate getting mixed up in something like this when I haven't done anything. In all the years I worked for the General, the police never even knew I existed, except for the odd parking ticket. You really don't have any idea what Roland wanted to talk to you about?"

"None whatsoever. I do have a feeling, though, that he wasn't really beaten to death by a . . . a lover, I suppose you'd call it."

"I'd call it a sex maniac," he said firmly, "and I should think they'd investigate all the sex maniacs of his acquaintance and not bother with anybody else. In fact, it was probably done by a stranger—somebody he just picked up. That's the way most of these sex murders happen."

"You don't really believe that, do you, Alex? After everything else that's happened?"

"It could all have been a series of coincidences."

"And that man I saw coming out of Roland's place that night and thought was a prowler could have been a coincidence, too, only he wasn't a prowler and I doubt that he was a coincidence either. He's a detective or something along that line and his name's Andrew Mackay."

She told Alex what the lieutenant had said, and also not said, about Andrew Mackay. "And why would he have been snooping around the gallery if he hadn't thought something was going on?" she concluded.

"Vice squad, maybe," Alex suggested. "Okay, okay, so they had suspicions about the gallery."

"But who are 'they,' Alex? And what were they suspicious of?"

"Could be the Feds."

"You mean Roland was a spy?" Somehow she couldn't see Roland as a KGB employee. She had more respect for the Russians than that.

"The Federal Government has its fingers in a number of pies— spies, drugs, tobacco, alcohol, firearms, immigration and naturalization, transporting stolen property and/or underage women (or,

in this case, underage men) across state lines. This fellow—
Mackay—didn't give you any clue what he was after?"

"Jill, as far as I could see. The last I saw of him he was going off
with her. I must say he really seemed to like her."

"Probably part of his cover," Alex said. He was not a fan of Jill's.

"What cover? He said he was a detective—an investigator, anyhow. I mean today. He didn't say so when I met him with the dog,
but then he didn't say anything about who he was then."

"Ah, yes, the dog. I was forgetting the dog." Alex sounded very
thoughtful.

"Is there something significant about the dog? He did bark in
the night, you know—although it was at Esmeralda. The cat," she
added, in case Alex had forgotten who Esmeralda was.

"Your guess is as good as mine," Alex said. She knew that evasive note in his voice.

"And you're not going to tell me what your guess is?"

"No, because I could be wrong, and I hope I am."

Sometimes he could be very exasperating. Later she realized
that she had been very dense.

"Has it occurred to you that, if this is something more than a sex
crime, Roland may have been killed to keep him from talking to
you?"

"The thought had occurred to me," she admitted.

Which would mean that the killer would have to be someone
who knew she'd had an appointment with Roland. Roland had
been careful not to let anyone hear what they were saying, but
anyone who was on the premises or even outside in the street
could have seen him draw her aside and talk to her confidentially.
And anyone who had seen them could have passed on his obser-
vations to someone else. So far as knowledge, or at least suspicion,
of their rendezvous was concerned, the field was wide open.

"I don't want to frighten you but you could be in danger," Alex
said.

"If you don't want to frighten me, then don't tell me I could be
in danger. Anyhow if somebody killed Roland to keep him from

talking to me, why should I be in danger? Roland was very effectively stopped from talking to me."

"He might feel Roland had already told you too much."

"But if Roland had told me anything, I could already have passed it on to someone else. Like you, for example. Or he could have talked to other people. Is he—or she—going to batter everyone in Roland's address book to death?"

He laughed. "That would be a tall order. But 'she'? I hardly think a woman would have been able to beat Roland to death."

She didn't agree. So many of today's young women made a fetish of fitness, and often had as much muscular strength as men. And not only young women. Someone like Hortense Pomeroy, for example, could have battered Roland to death without exerting herself. Hortense wouldn't even have needed a brass statuette of an erogenous nature; she could have done it with her bare hands.

"Whatever it was he wanted to say to me might have nothing at all to do with the reason he was killed," Susan said.

"Maybe so, but I still don't think it's a good idea for you to be there alone. Why don't you come stay with us? We have plenty of room and Tinsley would be glad of your company."

Tinsley would be especially glad now. That very morning, her mother, who'd been spending most of her days at the Tabor domicile, had departed for California to visit her younger daughter who was due to give birth any day now. Alex and Tinsley did have a live-in housekeeper, personally selected (and salaried) by Amy herself, but they couldn't impose on her the way they could on a member of the family. No, on the whole Susan would rather take her chances with the murderer.

"It's kind of you to offer, Alex, but I'm sure I'm not in any danger. Besides, I can take care of myself."

"I'm not so sure of that. Remember, you don't have a gun any more."

"There are a couple of guns still left from Father's collection that I think I can lay my hands on."

"But they're old. They might not work. You're out of practice."

"The last one worked very well," she reminded him. "And I'd been out of practice then much longer than I am now."

As soon as she got rid of Alex, she went to the closet shelf where she had stored the remaining guns in a suitcase, locked ever since Peter's return. Not that he was snoopy, but better safe than sorry. They were in excellent condition, which they should have been as she had devoted considerable time to their cleaning and polishing ever since she discovered her affinity for them. She had fresh ammunition for them now. She'd purchased it while she was attending a fine-arts conference at a university in a state with more liberal gun laws than New York's.

Why she'd picked up the ammunition she didn't know exactly, except that she hated things that were incomplete, and a gun without ammunition was like an unfinished canvas. And the conference had been very boring. Of course these guns were nothing like the state-of-the-art models she'd grown accustomed to when she'd been a professional, but they had been the finest obtainable in their day, certainly adequate for emergency use—and easier to explain if she should happen to be caught carrying a concealed weapon. Not that the fact that the gun had belonged to her father would make her possession of it any more legal; just that at least there would be no questions about the gun's provenance.

But she didn't intend to be caught carrying it, she thought, as she loaded the gun.

She got out one of the big handbags that she'd carried in her gun-toting days. After transferring her belongings (always such a nuisance, changing bags) she dropped in the gun. Amazing how much comfort it gave her to know that there was a gun within reach. It wasn't that she didn't believe in strict gun control laws. She knew, through vivid personal experience, how the mere possession of a gun could provoke the mildest of persons into violence. In her case her impulsive behavior had had positive results, both for herself and society, but that was the exception. She had read and heard of too many instances where otherwise upstanding citizens who, piqued by loved ones or fellow motorists, had expressed that pique with a bullet, for her to feel that unrestricted ownership of handguns was a good thing. Some people just could not be trusted with guns. If that's an elitist viewpoint, so be it, she told herself.

Only after she had armed herself was she able to relax and play back the messages on her answering machine. There was one from Hal Courtenay. Was he back in town or had he called her from Houston? His message gave no idea of the time he had called or his reason for calling. It merely said he was sorry to have missed her and would she call him back. Since he gave no number for her to call him, that must mean he was back in New York and had called her immediately upon his return. She would need to find out why he had been so anxious to see her before she could let herself feel flattered.

She phoned the Museum. "I'm afraid Mr. Courtenay is out of town," his secretary said.

"I know he went to Houston, but I thought he might be back."

"Houston?" The secretary sounded puzzled. "I was under the impression he'd gone to Litchfield. He has a farm up there. In any case, he's not expected back until tomorrow."

It was none of her business whether he had gone to Houston or Connecticut. If he'd been out of town, he would have left an out-of-town number for her to call back. No, he must be back in town and simply hadn't checked in at the Museum. No reason why he should if he wasn't due until the next day.

She called his home number. An orchestra played several bars of *Pictures at an Exhibition;* then Hal's mellifluous voice said, "This is Hal Courtenay. I am so sorry not to be here to receive your call. However, if you will be good enough to leave your name, number, and a message, I will be only too happy to call you back, just as soon as I possibly can."

Another few bars of *Pictures at an Exhibition,* followed by a chime—no beep for Hal Courtenay.

She gave her name and number and said, "Returning your call."

That was one of the drawbacks of an answering machine. Two machines could chat back and forth indefinitely without their owners' ever making direct contact.

There were a lot of other messages, but nothing of real interest.

She didn't call any of them back. They could wait until tomorrow, or the next day, or, in the case of one or two, forever.

XVI

CLOSE TO eight o'clock her phone rang. This would be Hal, she thought. On previous occasions the idea of hearing his voice could... well... not cause her heart to skip a beat—her heart didn't go in for that sort of thing—but arouse pleasurable emotions in her. Now she felt only mildly interested in discovering the purpose of his call. Of course Roland's death had put a damper on any pleasurable emotions she might be feeling in any connection. More than that, though, it was hard to believe that the director of a respected museum, someone who should be an arbiter of taste and elegance, would do anything so tacky as to have his answering machine respond with a burst of canned music. Next thing you knew, the elevators in the Museum would be playing Muzak.

She picked up the phone.

It wasn't Hal. It was Jill. She was practically gibbering. "I just heard about what happened to Roland. Did you know? Why didn't you call me?"

It hadn't even occurred to Susan to call Jill. "Calm down, you're hysterical. I knew you were out with Mr. Mackay. I wouldn't have expected you to be back so soon."

"Nor would I," Jill acknowledged. "We had a couple of drinks, and we were getting on very well, or so I thought. Turns out we have a lot in common. He doesn't run but he does play squash. And he likes sushi."

She made it sound as if sushi were some kind of game. Well, in a way when you ate raw fish, you were playing Russian roulette. But she'd already told Jill that a number of times; no use telling her again. And no point. For all she knew Roland had never eaten raw fish and yet, there he was, dead as a mackerel.

"So things were going great," Jill went on, "and there was talk of dinner, but he said he had to call his answering service first. When he came back, he was looking very funny. Something had come up, he said, and he'd have to take a rain check on dinner. Naturally I thought it must be another woman."

She brightened a little. "Maybe somebody told him what had happened to Roland and that was what called him away. Why didn't he tell me, though?"

"A detective's work is confidential, Jill," Susan said, knowing she sounded like a schoolteacher. She hated sounding like a schoolteacher, especially when she was imparting information that she had acquired from watching television rather than some more scholarly pursuit. "Probably there are all sorts of things that come up in the course of his work that have to be attended to right away. It might have had nothing at all to do with Roland."

"Maybe," Jill said, "but I still have a feeling that it did."

So did Susan, but she saw no reason to tell Jill that. Nor did she feel it needful to mention that she had told the police about Mackay's presence at the scene of the crime earlier in the week; and that it was possibly as a result of that disclosure that the young man had received the message that took him away from Jill.

So she had spoiled Jill's date. Someone had spoiled Roland. A life was more important than a date, though possibly not to Jill. Especially not Roland's.

"I went home wondering whether or not I'd been dumped," Jill went on. "Then I turned on the radio, and I heard about Roland. Oh, Susan, I'm so scared; I don't know what to do. Could I come over and stay with you tonight? Please?"

She seemed to be in a panic. Susan couldn't understand why. "What do you have to be frightened about? He was beaten to death in an orgy. It could happen to anyone—anyone who went in for orgies, that is."

"You know that's not true: that it was just a sex murder, I mean. There was too much funny stuff going on at the gallery before."

Since that was precisely what she herself had told Alex, Susan could not in all honesty disagree. "But why should that put you in such a panic, Jill? You haven't had anything to do with Roland for years, have you?"

"Anybody who's ever had anything to do with Roland, in any way, is in danger," Jill insisted, without answering the question directly.

"Ridiculous. That would mean that I'm in danger. Baltasar, Lupe, even the workmen renovating the place are in danger."

"But you especially could be in danger, after the way you and Roland were whispering together on Monday."

Susan was annoyed. Jill was practically accusing her of conspiring with Roland. She wondered to whom else Jill might have been talking in similar vein. "As I've already pointed out, we were not whispering, merely conversing in low tones. And the idea of either you or me being in danger is absurd."

She made her words very firm to overcome the lack of conviction that lay behind them.

"Does that mean you won't let me stay over tonight?"

"Oh, if you're nervous, come over," Susan said grudgingly. "But I don't want to hear one word about how I ought to get new furniture."

"I'm really grateful," Jill said. "You're the best client I've ever had." Since the only other client Jill had apparently been able to hang on to had been dead from the start, the tribute was not as handsome as it might have been. "I'll throw a few things together and be over there as soon as I can. And I promise not to say one word about your furniture, even if it collapses under me."

I hope she understands it's just for tonight, Susan thought. I don't want her moving in here on a permanent basis. My days of poverty are over; I'm certainly not going to start taking in boarders now. And if Jill showed any signs of outstaying her limited welcome, Susan could always tell her Peter had decided to come back home for the spring break, instead of going on that field trip up north. No matter how edgy Jill was, she wouldn't want to stay if Peter were around.

But why is it me she chooses to stay with? Susan wondered. Surely she has people who are closer. Jill's parents, she knew, had retired to a condominium in Florida. Originally Jill hailed from the Bronx. Was there no place in the Bronx where she could find shelter? Well, perhaps seeking refuge in the Bronx was like fleeing the frying pan for the fire. But she must know people in the other boroughs, in the rest of the Metropolitan area, who would take her in.

The likelihood was that she didn't know anyone else who had as much room as Susan did. Spare bedrooms in New York City had gone out with the passenger pigeon. Only the very rich and those who had managed to hold on to the commodious flats of their forebears still had them.

Perhaps this was a ploy by Jill to achieve total possession of Susan by physically encompassing her. Was it possible that Jill might have killed Roland in order to give herself an excuse for moving in on her client? I'm getting to be as crazy as she is, Susan thought.

Suddenly she found herself wishing Peter had come home for the spring break after all. His presence, although maddening at times, was comforting in a way no one else's could be. As soon as all this is cleared up and the weather gets warmer, she thought, I'm going to fly up to Canada and spend some time with him. And maybe we can figure out some way he can come back to New York permanently, some way he can find a job here.

Of course Peter didn't have to work. She could support both of them. He wouldn't object at all to being supported in a style to which he'd had no trouble becoming accustomed. But she didn't like the idea of supporting him, not because she had any old-fashioned ideas about support being a male prerogative, but because that would mean he'd be around the apartment too much of the time. She couldn't count on his spending his days in the library.

Maybe I could establish a small foundation in an appropriate field, she thought, with him as the sole employee. I'll talk to Mimi about it; she knows all about establishing foundations. With the aid of a good accountant, perhaps things could be worked out so that it would cost Susan nothing to set up, even under the new tax laws.

The phone rang again. This time it was Hal. "Susan, I'm so glad I finally reached you," he said warmly. "I suppose you've heard about Roland DeMarnay, although that isn't the reason I called. The first time I tried to get you I hadn't even heard the news yet. Shocking, isn't it?"

"Yes, it's awful," she said. "And sad, too. Such a waste," she added, because she couldn't think of anything else to say.

"The waste of a human life is always sad."

"I see you're back from Texas," she said, wondering whether he'd tell her he'd changed his plans and gone to Connecticut. The secretary could have been wrong, of course. And what if she wasn't? What do I care where he was? In Houston, in Litchfield, or on that confounded Greek or Italian or whatever island of his?

"I got back early this afternoon. I called you from the airport—I was so anxious to hear your voice—but, alas, only your machine answered."

"The machine answers in my voice," she pointed out.

"Ah, yes, but it isn't really the same, is it?"

"I was at Allardyce's."

"Oh, yes, the contemporary art auction. I took a look at the catalogue before I left but there was nothing there we wanted, at least not at their estimates. Ridiculous the prices contemporary art is fetching these days, especially when so much of it is junk, don't you agree?"

She agreed.

"I suppose you and Jill were there about the Moffatt. What did it go for, do you happen to recall?"

"Two hundred and fifty thousand."

He whistled. "That's the highest a Moffatt's gone for yet." For some reason the news seemed to please him; why, she couldn't understand, since to her Moffatt's work seemed a shining example of the junk movement. Of course that meant the value of the Moffatts in the Museum's collection would be increased; maybe he was pleased on the Museum's behalf.

"Pity he couldn't have seen some of the money when he was alive," she observed.

"That's the way it's been with so many artists. They achieve fame and fortune only after they're dead. Only the fame doesn't do them much good and it's their heirs who get the fortune."

"And the collectors and dealers."

"And the collectors and dealers."

"I wonder how much my paintings will sell for after I'm dead."

"You mustn't look at it like that, Susan. One of James Rosenquist's pictures went for over two million dollars recently, and he's still alive. And a Jasper Johns sold for close to four million, and he's alive, too."

"But the paintings were sold at auction by the people who owned them," Susan pointed out. "Neither of the artists gets any of the money."

"That's true," Hal said, "but it certainly will make a difference in the prices they get for their paintings from now on. Listen, Susan, I know this is unpardonably last-minute of me, but I wondered whether you could have dinner with me tonight?"

"I haven't made any plans, but Jill's coming to stay overnight. Roland's death has made her nervous. I don't know why." She made the words clearly a question.

There was a pause before he answered. "I believe she was associated with him in a business way some time ago."

"She told me he was a partner with her in that gallery she was running in Soho."

"She told you about that?" He sounded surprised and not altogether pleased. "I wasn't sure whether she wanted you to know, so I never mentioned it," he added. "But that was such a long time ago, there couldn't be any connection. I'm sure they haven't had anything to do with each other for years. And his death was one of those sadomasochistic things, wasn't it? So why should there be any reason for her to be nervous?"

"I don't know. I just know that she sounded frightened."

She wondered whether Hal knew why the partnership had broken up. But of course he must. He had become Jill's lover afterward, so she was bound to tell him everything. Or was she? I've never told Peter everything. On the other hand, Peter never was all that interested.

There was a harsh cackle.

"What's that?" Hal said sharply.

He's on edge, too, she thought. "The intercom's buzzing. Probably the doorman calling to tell me Jill's here. Why don't you come over, too? I doubt that Jill will be in any mood to go out but we could have dinner sent up."

"Thank you," he said, "but I really wanted to have dinner with you alone. There are a number of things I wanted to talk to you about. Could we make it later this week? Perhaps at my apartment. I have a wonderful cook."

As she waited for Jill to come upstairs, she remembered that Roland had also been insistent on seeing her alone. I'm getting as jumpy as Jill, she thought, suspecting everyone, imagining all sorts of wild things.

She got her handbag and looped the strap over her arm. Let the wild things come on, she thought; I'm ready for them.

XVII

JILL CAME in looking like a wild thing herself, hair flying every which way, even the fur on her mink standing on end. She carried a small overnight case, which she set on the floor, and a large shopping bag with grease spots, which she handed to Susan. "Little hostess gift. I don't know whether you've had dinner or not, but I'm starved, so I brought up some Chinese food. Why are you hanging on to your handbag like that?"

"I thought you might be a delivery boy," Susan said, peering into the shopping bag, from which succulent odors issued. "There's enough here to feed an army. Are you expecting anyone else?"

Jill shuddered. "*No*, I don't want to see anyone else as long as I live. Not until tomorrow, anyway, if I live that long. Anything left over would do for breakfast. Chinese food is good cold. And anything left over after that you can reheat for lunch. Are you expecting a delivery? What are you expecting?"

"Peter always sends me flowers on my birthday."

"I thought your birthday wasn't until September."

"Yes, but Peter's so absent-minded he always gets it mixed up with Ground Hog Day."

"But Ground Hog Day was back in February."

"I must be a little mixed up too." She helped Jill out of her coat. The girl was shivering. Her terror was real enough, whatever else about her might be false.

"I felt eyes upon me all the way here," she said.

"The eyes of admiration, no doubt."

"Not that kind of eyes—creepy, crawly eyes, the kind of eyes that paranoids feel watching them all the time. There are canvases in that closet!" she said, as Susan opened the door to put away her coat. "You're relapsing. You promised me that you would send your stuff to the warehouse as soon as it started spilling out of the studio."

Even fear could not keep her from poking her nose into other people's closets. Susan shut the door firmly. "It's my closet and I'll put what I want in it."

"Even skeletons?"

"I keep my skeletons elsewhere. Now, let's get this food into the kitchen. There's so much of it, it's almost a pity Hal didn't accept my invitation to dinner."

"What invitation?" Jill followed Susan into the big, old-fashioned kitchen. "What Hal? Hal Courtenay? Why did you invite him?"

"He called just after you did. I asked him to join us and we'd have dinner sent up. But he said he was busy."

"He's back in town then?"

"I would hardly have asked him to fly in from Texas to take pot luck."

"When did he get back?"

"Early this afternoon."

"You mean he said he got back early this afternoon?"

"Well, I wasn't waiting for him at the airport. Does it matter when he got back?"

Jill didn't say anything. Why, Susan wondered, as she reached into cabinets and cupboards, was Jill so upset at the knowledge that Hal was back in town somewhat earlier than expected?

Was it possible Jill thought Hal might have something to do with Roland's death? Nonsense, Hal hardly knew the man.

Although knowing someone was hardly a prerequisite for killing him. Quite the opposite sometimes. She herself, for example, would have had great difficulty in killing someone with whom she was personally acquainted, no matter how unspeakably vile that person was; unless, of course, that person had done, or was attempting to do, something unpleasant to her. Other people might be less sensitive—less oversensitive, perhaps.

Come to think of it, she had no idea of the extent of Hal's actual acquaintance with Roland. They might have known each other very well. But that wouldn't account for Jill's fear, even if it was Hal she was afraid of.

"Shall we eat here or in the dining room?" she asked.

"The dining room of course." Even in her current state of emotional dishevelment, Jill seemed shocked at the idea that anyone who had a dining room would even dream of eating in the kitchen. Under other circumstances she would probably expect me to dress for dinner, Susan thought.

"I should think you'd have this place modernized," Jill said, casting a disparaging glance around. "I know—I know—I said I wasn't going to criticize your furniture, but this isn't furniture, it's—it's equipment," she concluded triumphantly. "With the money you're making, you can afford to get it fixed over. You could sell most of the stuff here as antiques, maybe even come out ahead. That stove is a collector's item if ever I saw one. And the sink—"

"Well, then, I'm in fashion. I have an antique kitchen."

"It's not fashionable if that's the way your kitchen has always been. It's fashionable only if you have a modern kitchen to begin with and have all the appliances taken out and the antique ones put in."

"How about if I make believe that's what I did?"

Jill shook her head. "They look as if they belonged there. That's always a dead giveaway."

Fear seemed to have increased rather than impaired Jill's appetite. She consumed prodigious quantities of food, but refused to open her fortune cookie afterward. "It would be tempting fate," she said.

Susan didn't open her cookie either.

"Susan, do you think he really likes me?"

Susan didn't have to ask who "he" was. "Mr. Mackay certainly does seem to be attracted to you, but I wouldn't have thought you'd be attracted to him. He doesn't seem like your type somehow."

"Too clean-cut, you mean? Susan, I'll tell you a secret. Inside every woman, no matter how hip, there's a secret yearning for a man who looks like a toothpaste ad." Giving Susan no time to meditate on this profundity, she patted her stomach. "I do feel much better. It must have been too many drinks and too little food that made me so jittery. You're right, there's no reason to suppose Roland wasn't beaten to death by an ordinary sex maniac, just because a couple of other things happened in the same place."

"I never said Roland was beaten to death by a sex maniac," Susan protested. "It was just that when you said—"

"Forget I ever said anything. I'm not responsible for what I say. I always get the jitters whenever somebody I know gets murdered."

"Look, Jill if you know something that you think could make you a threat to anyone, you'd better tell the police about it. Then you wouldn't be a threat any more."

Unless, she thought, you yourself killed Roland, or had a hand in his killing, in which case I could not in all good conscience advise you to go to the police.

There was a stubborn look on Jill's face. "I don't know anything, so there's nothing to tell. Let's turn on the TV and listen to the terrible things they say about Roland on the news."

Roland's death had been so overwhelming to them, it was almost a shock to realize that it was not the lead story. There had been a failed attempt to assassinate a South American dictator (really they should have hired a professional, Susan thought, as pictures of the mess the unfortunate amateur had made appeared on the screen), several bombings in various parts of the world, and a fresh political scandal in Queens—all of which took precedence over Roland's demise.

The scenes of carnage and calumny were interrupted by the simultaneous buzzing of the intercom and the ringing of the phone. "Jill, would you ask whoever's on the phone to hold on while I answer the buzzer?"

"Gen'lman on his way up," the doorman announced. He was a new man and he still hadn't got it through his head that he was supposed to discover the name of a caller and find out whether he was welcome before letting him up. Susan tried to explain correct procedure to him once again.

"It's a young gen'lman," he said, as if Susan ought to be glad to have such a caller, no matter who it was, no matter what time it was. Not that eleven-twenty was late in absolute terms, just late for an unexpected caller.

"It must be Alex," she said to Jill. "He was worried about me."

"Aha, see, I'm not the only one who's paranoid."

But paranoia implies irrational fears. Susan was afraid that Jill's fears might have a very rational basis. And she began to feel a little afraid herself.

"Who is it on the phone?" she asked.

"Who was it, you mean? He hung up. It was Baltasar. He wouldn't tell me what it was about. He said never mind; it wasn't important. He'd call again. What do you suppose he wanted?"

"I have no idea."

But Susan did have an idea of what he must want—to speak to her alone, like everybody else. Why he wanted to speak to her she didn't know. It was unlikely he would want to weep on her shoulder; he didn't seem the type. Just the same, remembering what had happened to Roland, she resolved to call Baltasar as soon as Alex left. She would sleep easier that way.

The doorbell rang. Susan opened the door. The merry quip about fatherhood she'd had prepared faded on her lips.

Because it wasn't Alex standing outside. It was Andrew Mackay, looking both apologetic and determined.

"Forgive my dropping in on you like this, but I had to talk to you alone."

"Come in, but before you say anything I ought to warn you that I am not alone. Jill is here."

"And why shouldn't Jill be here?" Jill asked, erupting into the foyer. "Oh, it's you."

"Yes, it's me," he said.

They stared at each other. For once Mackay wasn't smiling. This calls for music, too, Susan thought, something tragic this time, about two lovers about to be sundered by cruel fate. There probably was something suitable in *Tristan*. There probably was something suitable in most operas. They wouldn't be operas without it. She couldn't see Jill as an operatic heroine, though, not even in a modern opera.

"Look," Jill said, "if I'm in the way, I can always leave. I'll probably get murdered on my way out, but who cares."

Andrew opened his mouth and shut it. He cares, Susan thought; the more fool, he.

"No need for you to leave, Jill," she said. "If Mr. Mackay wants to talk to me alone in his official capacity...?"

"Professional capacity," he corrected her. "I have no official standing. Call Lieutenant Bracco; he'll tell you the same thing. You don't have to talk to me if you don't want to."

"You heard what he said, Susan. Don't talk to him." Jill clutched her client's arm. "Please, please, don't talk to him. Send him away."

Susan disengaged her arm. "We can go into the library. Jill can amuse herself watching television, or listening to the radio, or throwing a tantrum."

"I could read a good book," Jill said, "but all the books are in the library." Her voice was shaky.

"All right, Mr. Mackay and I can talk in the kitchen."

"You don't have to go that far. I'll be a good girl and wait in the studio. I can always brood."

XVIII

MACKAY TOOK off his coat. Susan did not offer to take it from him, so he carried it over his arm as he followed her into the library, which she used as a sitting room when she had need of one. It was a smallish room by the standards of the rest of the place, good-sized by today's norms, lined with a miscellany of well-read books, the old rare editions and leather-bound sets having fallen under the auctioneer's hammer years before. There was a working fireplace in which a fire was burning. Mackay looked at it suspiciously. Probably thinks I'm burning evidence, Susan thought.

She gestured him to an easy chair covered with dark red leather so worn it had passed beyond the boundaries of comfortable shabbiness and looked as if it were moulting. He looked around him and, finding no better place, threw his coat on the adjacent ottoman, then sat down himself.

She prepared herself for interrogation.

"She's mad at me," he said.

When it came to police matters, she would cooperate with him, but she wasn't going to make things easier when it came to matters of the heart. "Do you blame her?" she asked.

"But she knew I was an investigator from the start. I never tried to hide that from her, so why should she be so upset to find me ...uh..."

"Investigating," she finished for him.

"Yes, investigating."

"Perhaps she didn't think you'd invited her out to investigate her."

"But I didn't. Well, not exactly. Anyhow, we never did get around to talk about—about anything that had to do with anything. We just talked about us. I was open and aboveboard from the start. So why is she acting like this?" He looked honestly bewildered.

Susan resisted the temptation to tell him to write to Dear Abby. It would be unkind as well as unwise. Although he himself might have no official standing—and she didn't really believe that—he was undoubtedly associated with those who did.

"I don't know why I took it for granted you would be home alone," he said. "Probably I should have called first to check."

"Probably you should. Everybody else who wanted to talk to me alone did."

He looked alert; the bloodhound sniffing on the trail. "Who else wanted to talk to you alone?"

Well, maybe it was his business. But she saw no reason to spare his feelings. "Jill to begin with . . ."

"Besides Jill?"

"Hal Courtenay and Baltasar . . ." Should she tell him the names of her other callers? No, they hadn't said they wanted to speak to her alone, only that they wanted to speak to her.

"I know who Baltasar is. Should I know Hal Courtenay?"

"Hal Courtenay's the Director of the Museum of American Art."

He frowned. "I think I remember coming across the name somewhere."

"Hal's quite well known, gets in the papers often, new acquisitions, membership drives, authoritative opinions, articles on art. There was a piece by him in the *New York Times* a couple of months ago and one about him in *Connoisseur* last year. And, of course, he goes to parties a lot—part of his job—so he's often in the society (excuse me, *style*) columns."

He shook his head.

"Perhaps you saw him on TV? He often appears on Channel 13 and sometimes on 31."

"That's not it, either. Tell me, would Courtenay have known DeMarnay?"

"Museum people are bound to know dealers. They buy pictures from them."

"They do!" He looked surprised. Where did he think museums got their pictures from, anyway? The tooth fairy?

"Hal was the one who introduced Jill to me and suggested that I sign up with her," she added.

He appeared to consider this and dismiss it. However, she could see he was thinking about it, even though he went off on a different tack. "Tell me, why did you really go to see DeMarnay this afternoon?"

"Surely Lieutenant Bracco told you."

"He told me what you told him, but..."

"But you don't believe it was the truth?" She arched her eyebrows. Pity they didn't use lorgnettes any more, she thought, or she could have looked at him through hers.

He put out his hand, as if to disclaim any lack of faith in her integrity. "No, no, I'm sure you wouldn't lie to the police. But I had a feeling that you might not have told him ... uh ... the whole truth. In other words—" he gave her a smile that was intended to be disarming, but didn't quite make it "—that you might have been holding out on him."

"You said you had no official standing," she reminded him. "So, if I had been holding out on the lieutenant, which, of course, I wouldn't have dreamed of doing, why wouldn't I hold out on you?"

"You mean you're not going to answer my questions?" He looked disappointed, as if she had failed him somehow.

"I didn't say that. I might answer your questions, if you'll answer mine first."

She doubted that she actually had any concrete information that could be of use either to him or the police in their investigations; all she had were some vague suspicions that she had no intention of passing on in their present nebulous state, but he didn't know that. And she wanted to know what was going on, not simply out of a citizen's right to know, i.e., vulgar curiosity, but because this was her concern. She herself might not be involved, but people she knew were—Jill, for one, and Hal, even Baltasar (although him she hardly knew). And then there was the nagging fear that Alex might be somehow caught up in this.

"My dear Miss Melville—Susan—are you suggesting a deal?"

"I understand bargains are not unheard of even in official police circles, to which, I take it, you don't belong—or do you?"

He didn't answer, but leaned back in the moulting armchair with a sigh, and put his hand in front of his eyes. In the lamplight the lines in his face deepened and he looked older and even handsomer. Poor Jill, she thought.

"I can't promise you anything," he said finally, "but I'll tell you as much as I can. And you'll tell me whatever you know. Promise?"

"I promise."

"Go ahead, ask your questions."

"That night I ran into you outside the gallery, did you actually manage to get inside?"

He took his hand away from his eyes. "You don't really expect me to answer that?"

"Oh, but I do. I know that as a licensed investigator, whether public or private, you had no business being inside; so officially you were not there, even if you were. So there's no reason why you shouldn't tell me about something that you didn't do."

It took him a while to figure this out, or at least to realize that he never would be able to figure it out. "All right. Off the record and strictly between ourselves I did get inside—something which I'll deny even under torture if ever I'm accused of it. But, if you're expecting startling revelations, you'll be disappointed. I didn't get very far inside. It was my bad luck to hit a night when DeMarnay and his friends were having a . . . a . . . "

"Party. That's what Damian called it."

"Damian? Oh, yes, Damian Schwimmer."

She wondered how he knew Damian's last name. But of course,

he was a detective. Detectives knew how to ferret out such arcane bits of information. She wondered what else he might have discovered about other people in Roland's orbit. The idea made her uncomfortable. It would make anyone uncomfortable. Everyone has secrets they don't want out in the open, she thought, but some are more secret than others.

"They were rampaging all over the place," he went on, "so I couldn't get a look around. I was afraid they might catch me and—"

"And prevail upon you to join in?"

He smiled weakly. "That was the least of my worries." She didn't believe him. "Do you want the details or will a broad general outline do?"

She fought back an unworthy desire to ask for details. "I have a pretty good idea of what must have been going on, gained from literature and the news; and, of course, as I told the lieutenant, I spoke to Roland on the phone not long after I saw you, so I heard them."

"I know," he said. "You reported suspicious character leaving premises, or at least you said you did. We have only your word for it that you did tell DeMarnay that you saw me."

He was watching her carefully. Why? What could he possibly suspect her of? At least what could he possibly suspect her of that had any connection with this particular crime or, as she was beginning to think, series of crimes? Why wouldn't she have told Roland? Was Mackay trying to make her nervous so she would say more than she had intended?

"Oh, I'm sure he mentioned to whoever was there with him at the time that a possible intruder had been sighted. And, oh, yes, I remember he told Baltasar the next day, and there were other people around. I'm sure they'll confirm it."

"I'm sure they will, too," he said. "Not, of course, that I doubted your word."

"Nice of you to say so," she said, "but I understand. Of course, you have to doubt everyone's word. Even Jill's."

Hitting below the belt, she knew, but she was observing Merriwether rather than Queensberry rules. I really must meet Lady Daphne, she thought. I could learn a lot from her and who knows, she thought modestly, I might have something to teach her myself.

"How did DeMarnay act when you spoke to him on the phone? Was he sober?"

"He and the others—I could hear them in the background— did seem to be high on something. They didn't sound violent. They sounded . . . affectionate. But it was still early."

"It was later than when I saw them. They were certainly affectionate when I was there. Very affectionate. And also high. But this was the night before he was killed so it isn't really relevant, is it? Just . . . just . . ."

"Indicative of a general pattern," she suggested.

"Indicative of something, anyway. They were running around naked, except for some sort of spicy gook they'd smeared on themselves. One of them had put on so much he left a trail of slime, like a snail. They were drinking wine and snorting coke, which, incidentally, was why I couldn't do anything with Brucie."

"Brucie?" She was surprised. "I didn't know dogs could be such prudes."

Mackay stared at her. "You're serious? You really don't know why I brought Brucie along? I thought that was obvious—or at least would be later, when you'd had time to think about it."

The truth of the matter was that she had been exceedingly obtuse. "You mean Brucie is one of those drug-sniffing dogs?" So that was why Roland had been upset when she'd told him about Brucie's presence on the scene. "I didn't know that the police or Customs or whatever took dogs to parties to sniff out drugs."

"They don't. The dogs are used to sniff out large quantities of drugs, amounts a dealer might have on hand. If they took them to every party in New York where drugs might be used, New York would be the canine capital of the world. Not that it isn't already. I never saw so many dogs in my life as there are here."

So he was from out of town. Washington? She didn't ask because she knew he wouldn't tell her.

"Brucie was trained for quality not quantity. As soon as he sniffs the slightest amount of coke he starts demonstrating. Luckily Roland and his friends were yipping and whining so much themselves, they didn't notice, and we were able to get away, but there was one close call—" He shuddered.

Again she would have liked to hear the details, but she didn't like to ask. And he probably wouldn't tell her anyway. He was a curiously old-fashioned young man. She might have deduced that from his appearance, but she'd been under the impression that it was some sort of disguise.

She still didn't understand why Roland should have been suspected of drug dealing when she'd been given to understand that forged paintings were his line. Not that criminals were necessarily specialists but Roland hadn't looked like someone who could chew gum and walk at the same time, let alone deal in drugs and forged paintings simultaneously. Or even alternately.

Roland had started out as an art dealer, Andrew told her, possibly even an honest dealer. Certainly nothing had been known against him until General Chomsky got upset over that fake Picasso Roland had sold him (the one Alex had told her about). How he'd found out it was a fake wasn't clear. Perhaps Picasso himself had spilled the beans. She tried to remember just when Picasso had died.

Roland had insisted that he'd bought the picture from a private party whose name he refused to divulge, believing it to be genuine, and had sold it in good faith. He'd offered to take it back and make full restitution. The General had accepted and dropped all charges. Technically, Roland's record was still clean. Nevertheless, Mackay said, the General had been angry and he hadn't kept the matter secret. Everybody in the art world knew about it. Mackay seemed to think that this represented a permanent blot on Roland's escutcheon. Susan knew better than that.

Roland hadn't come to the attention of the police again until a few years later, when he and Jill opened their art gallery under her name. Mackay seemed to feel that their suppression of Roland's role was entirely understandable. Susan did not. As far as she could see, there was no reason why they should not have used Roland's name as well as Jill's (granted the lack of euphony that the combination would have involved). Roland had no criminal record and his slightly tarnished reputation was hardly likely to frighten away the kind of artists and collectors that would fall within the gallery's purview. If the gallery had been set up on a grander scale, like the DeMarnay Gallery, it wouldn't have frightened away any kind of artist or collector.

"I gather that the police continued to keep an eye on him," Susan said.

Mackay looked embarrassed for his colleagues. "As a matter of fact, they didn't. It's true there seems to be a lot of hanky-panky going on in the art world, but that's not one of the New York police's prime concerns. Oh, they deal with art crimes when they've been committed, but they don't go around checking artwork and antiques to make sure they're authentic."

He looked disapproving. He wasn't going to criticize the New York police; at least not to a civilian. Neither was he going to give them an A for effort.

XIX

WHAT HAD happened to turn the authorities' attention to the Turkel Gallery, he told her, was that Customs had found cocaine in the frames of some paintings consigned to the gallery by an artist from Colombia.

"I suppose the sniffer dogs detected the drugs?"

"Well, not exactly. Not at first, anyway. Customs is always a little leery of anything that comes from Colombia, and these seemed a little heavy for pictures of that size. So they opened one or two crates. But all they found were pictures, in heavy, old-fashioned frames, the kind I'm told they don't use much any more here, but that could have been what they like in South America."

"So Customs broke open one of the frames?"

He shook his head. "They couldn't do that just on vague suspicions. They re-crated the pictures. But, just as they were about to be taken away, a clumsy workman happened to drop a crate."

"Purely by accident."

"Purely by accident," he said firmly. "The crate broke, and so did one of the frames. The dogs started barking their heads off. That's when they broke open all the frames, and found them loaded with coke."

"Jill told me she bought Roland out when she found he was dealing in forged paintings."

"Did she say that? Maybe she didn't want to tell you what really happened because she was ashamed of being connected with drugs, no matter how innocently."

"How can you be so sure she was innocent?"

There was a long pause before he answered. "I—they couldn't be absolutely sure of anything, of course. But there was nothing to show that either she or the other partner was involved. DeMarnay set up the deal. He handled all the paintings. He did all the paperwork. Jill didn't have much to do with the business end of things. She was a kid, right out of school, not much more than a receptionist, really. Okay, so they named the gallery after her—"

"Wait a minute!" Susan finally managed to break into his monologue. "I thought there were only two partners."

"Both Jill and DeMarnay ran it; that is, he ran it and she—"

"Was actually a glorified receptionist, I know, I know. But tell me about the third partner."

"I forget what his name was. Anyhow, he was a silent partner. All he did was put up most of the money. He had nothing to do with the gallery's operations."

"You're sure of that?"

He seemed surprised at her interest. She was surprised at his apparent lack of it. "There never was anything to show that he even came near the place. Lots of businesses do get started that way. Somebody puts up the money; somebody else supplies the expertise."

"Was this the Turkel Gallery's first show?" she asked.

"I think there were two, maybe three, before. All by local artists. No question of smuggling."

She was curious about those early shows, but he had no further information about them. The authorities had been interested in drugs, not art. If she was really curious, she could always look them up, she thought.

Roland had gotten a clever lawyer, Mackay told her, who managed to keep him from being formally charged. Although the police hadn't had much doubt that he'd been guilty of trying to smuggle drugs, they couldn't prove that the whole thing hadn't been the artist's own idea—especially since he'd paid for the privilege of being exhibited in New York, something which was not an unusual practice, though, Susan felt, highly deplorable.

"If Customs hadn't been so eager, they would have fixed up that first frame, re-crated the picture and waited to see who bought the paintings after they'd been put on exhibit. Because that would have been the fellow they were after—maybe even the guy behind the whole thing."

He shook his head. "They really blew that one."

"Could it have been the silent partner?" Susan asked.

"It could have been anybody. Why pick on him?" He grinned suddenly. "Or even her. There have been lady criminals, you know. If you can be a criminal and a lady at the same time."

"I don't see why not," she said.

Jill and the other partner had bought Roland out; that much at least was true. They then went on to make a success with the Moffatt paintings, while Roland went back to dealing on his own. For the past few years he had been working mostly abroad, south of the border, and in Europe. Although the New York police had dutifully informed their foreign colleagues of Roland's questionable background through Interpol, his record with the local police forces seemed to be clear in all respects. However although Andrew didn't say so outright, Susan gathered that he felt foreign police forces might not be as devoted to duty as their American counterparts.

"He must have met Baltasar while he was dealing abroad," Susan deduced, "and I suppose to Baltasar Roland might have seemed like a reputable dealer."

"Maybe so. And the fact that Baltasar was born in Colombia is probably only a coincidence."

"I thought Baltasar came from Spain, of noble blood."

"His family came from Spain way back. As for noble blood . . ." Mackay shrugged. "He is a Spanish citizen now. But he was born in Colombia."

"Don't you think you're being a bit bigoted? I'm sure most Colombians are honest, decent people."

"I'm sure they are, too," he said. "They also export coffee. And pickpockets."

She refused to dignify that with any comment. "Was Rafael Colombian, too?"

"No, he was born in Argentina. And he'd been working in Mexico."

When Roland came back to New York to open his gallery, Andrew told her, the authorities did take an immediate interest in him. They'd gotten a tip that one of the big international drug dealers they'd been anxious to get their hands on for a long time was planning to send a huge shipment of drugs up from Mexico. Rumor had it that this could be as much as two hundred kilos, a quarter of a ton.

"That's a lot, isn't it?"

"Worth a small fortune." He seemed to figure in his head. "A large fortune, actually. It could come to more than fifteen million dollars wholesale."

She was impressed. She would have liked to ask how much that would be retail, but he might think she was interested in getting into the business, herself.

"DeMarnay's first exhibit was coming from Mexico. A lot of drugs have been coming in from Mexico. It did look as if he might have been playing the same old trick. So we kept an eye on him —and a lot of other people, as well," he added. "There was always the possibility that he was straight." A remote possibility, his tone indicated.

"Wouldn't it have been foolish of him to do something like that for his opening show, when he must have known he'd come under suspicion? Especially since they'd set up such an elaborate installation. Wouldn't it have been wiser to wait?"

"Look," he said, "I can't second-guess them." He got up and walked over to the fireplace and then back. He seemed restless. "Maybe they made a mistake. That's how we catch 'em—by their mistakes or through informants. DeMarnay might have thought the police had forgotten all about him. Or he might not have had a choice."

She considered this. "Blackmail, you mean?"

"That's a possibility, if somebody had proof that he'd done some of the things he'd been accused of." Catching Susan's eye, he said, "Jill couldn't possibly have had anything to do with something like that."

But what if Jill had, Susan wondered. What if, for some reason Susan couldn't imagine, Jill had killed Roland; although, if she had been blackmailing him, it would be much more likely that he would kill her. Would Mackay try to cover up for her? He couldn't be that far gone. Why, he had only met the girl that morning. Love at first sight happened only in books. This was real life.

"More likely, if he was working for a drug dealer, he might simply have to do what he was told. He'd have no choice."

But everyone has a choice, she thought. When she'd worked as an assassin for General Chomsky (only, of course, she hadn't known the identity of her employer), she would never have accepted an assignment unless her target was a thoroughly evil person. On the other hand, maybe Roland had decided that he did have a choice. Maybe he had made that choice . . . and that was why he was dead now.

She wondered whether, if he had not been an acquaintance of hers, she would have accepted him as an assignment. She couldn't make up her mind about that, but she knew that she certainly would have killed his putative employer without a qualm. Drugs were bad medicine.

"Do sit down, you're making me nervous."

Mackay sat, but he kept shifting uneasily in the chair, anxious to be gone, not from the apartment but from the library. "I hope my coming here didn't scare Jill away," he blurted.

"She's here for the night. She's frightened all right, but not of you, as far as I can see. It's Roland's death—it seems to have terrified her."

"Did she say why?"

Susan shook her head. "No, she refused to talk about it. And—"

as he started to get up "—she's even less likely to talk about it to you than to me."

He subsided in the chair, muttering to himself.

"I wonder if Rafael's death had anything to do with all this," Susan mused.

Apparently that point had not occurred to him. "That's right, Hoffmann did die of an overdose on the night the gallery opened. But there wasn't anything suspicious about it. That kind of thing happens every day in New York."

"His wife thinks he was murdered."

He was all attention. "How do you know that?"

"She told me when she was in the gallery yesterday. She'd just come back from Australia."

"Lieutenant Bracco didn't say anything about her to me!"

Susan did a spirited impersonation of someone cudgelling her brains. "I don't remember whether or not I mentioned her to Lieutenant Bracco. He didn't ask me who'd been in the gallery the last time I saw Roland, and I was so shocked I—well—I just couldn't think."

He regarded her with a skeptical eye.

"But surely Lupe—that's her name, Lupe Montoya—told him, herself."

"As far as I know, he doesn't even know she exists. Which he wouldn't, if nobody had told him about her."

"Didn't Baltasar mention her arrival?"

"Apparently not."

"Maybe you spoke to the lieutenant before he spoke to Baltasar."

He shook his head. "After."

"Then he must have been acting like a gallant Spanish gentleman, keeping her out of it, since she didn't seem to have any connection with the murder."

"Maybe so, but that's for the lieutenant to judge. Still," he sighed, "Baltasar's a foreigner." It wasn't clear whether he meant one must make allowances for foreigners or whether foreigners were not to be trusted.

* * *

The authorities had figured Roland might have been stupid enough to try the same trick twice. They made plans to open the frames of the Hoffmann pieces in Customs, but there turned out not to be any frames. "It was all—would you call it sculpture?"

There were a number of things she could have called Rafael Hoffmann's work, but she desisted out of respect for a man who, however despicable, had not only been a fellow artist but was dead. "It's as good a name as any."

"The pieces were very heavy, but sculpture usually is heavy. We couldn't figure out how heavy they should have been because they were made up of all kinds of different stuff—wood, metal, stone, paper, plastic, all mixed together."

His voice held a note of grievance as if he felt the main object of multimedia art was to confound the law. Wouldn't it be interesting, she thought, if that had been the original purpose of that type of art, originated because Customs had grown too sophisticated for sculptors simply to stuff their bronzes with illegal substances. (She wondered whether during the Prohibition Era—but, no, even the most innocent revenue agent would be bound to suspect statues that gurgled.) Then, the style could have caught on with collectors and now be produced for its own sake. Mere speculation, of course, but the theory pleased her. It would explain so much.

"Customs couldn't go ahead and destroy a valuable art collection just on suspicion. What if they'd been wrong? Can you imagine how the Civil Liberties Union would have carried on?"

"The same way they would have carried on if Customs had been right," she said. "What about using Brucie and his colleagues?"

"They tried sniffer dogs, of course, but the cocaine, if it was there, would have been hermetically sealed and then covered by layers of non-porous stuff—metal, fiberglass, various synthetics, God knows what else, with tons of paint and varnish piled on top. Even a superdog couldn't sniff through that."

"How would they get the cocaine out then?"

"The pieces would have to be broken up. Roland and his associates could do it, of course. It was their property."

"You mean Rafael would have gone to all that work just to see his things destroyed?" Little though she thought of Rafael's *oeuvre*, she was shocked. Maybe it didn't represent art in her eyes, but it certainly represented a lot of effort.

Mackay looked at her as if she had started to show signs of mental deficiency. "That's what he would have made them for. And that's what he would have been paid for."

"But he seemed so sincere in thinking he was going to make his reputation as one of the world's greatest artists with this show."

"Maybe he was a good actor."

But she didn't think so. She knew artists. Rafael had been genuinely dedicated to his profession and to himself. He had truly thought he was the greatest thing since Michelangelo. In fact, that was too modest a claim. Shortly before the opening (which was to become his closing) he had confided to her that he had always felt Michelangelo to be highly overrated.

The authorities had been watching the gallery, waiting to see who would take possession of the pieces. That was all they could do. It was entirely possible that the stuff was clean, that Roland had either gone straight—or been smart enough not to try any tricks with his opening exhibit.

And then the gallery caught—or more likely was set—on fire, and the pieces were completely destroyed without ever having left the place. Which made it almost certain that the authorities' suspicions had been correct.

They might have had grounds for a warrant now, but what was the use of searching the place? The drugs were certain to be gone by this time. The pieces would have been broken up and the drugs removed long before the fire; then taken away little by little to a "safe house," where they would be readied for distribution.

Since work was still being done on the top floors of the gallery, there were always people going in and out, carrying things. They could easily have taken away a quarter of a ton, a few pounds at a time—only it would be kilos, of course. Mackay seemed to think the spread of the metric system had some connection with the rise of drug-related crime.

"You should have sneaked in sooner, since you were going to do it anyway."

He looked at her. "Do you think I wouldn't have liked to? The alarm system was always on before. And there were always a couple of tough-looking guards on duty. They never came back after the fire, which made us even more sure that there had been drugs in the statues. We tried to get in before the fire. We sent in men as building inspectors, as meter readers, as people from the EPA looking for radon contamination. The guards followed them wherever they went. We tried to get some of our men in as construction workers, but we ran up against the unions. You'd think people engaged in illegal activities would hire non-union help, but no. It was a closed shop in every sense of the word."

"Why did you bother to sneak in *after* the fire?" she wanted to know.

"When I saw the alarm system was off I thought I'd take a look around to see if there was any evidence that drugs had been there, and also to get the lie of the land. This was too expensive a set-up for a one-shot operation. They had to be planning to use the gallery again."

"It must have occurred to them that if they had to set a fire each time they got in a new shipment, the police would be bound to get suspicious. Not to speak of the fire department."

"I don't know what they had in mind. Maybe next time they were planning to bomb the block, and place the blame on subversives. There's a consulate across the street. Maybe they would have tied it in with that somehow."

But all that didn't explain why Roland had been killed. The drugs had been successfully removed from the artworks; the finger of suspicion had rested on no one; what reason was there to kill Roland?

"Drug dealers are always killing each other. It's an occupational hazard. And it is possible that his death wasn't drug-related. That sex maniac could still have done it."

"Which sex maniac?"

"Any sex maniac. I mean Roland could have been a drug dealer who was killed by an unrelated sex maniac."

"I'm beginning to wonder whether Darius Moffatt's death was really an accident."

"Darius Moffatt!" He seemed startled by this sudden addition to the cast of characters. "Oh, yes, the guy who painted that picture we saw today? Did he die too?"

"Yes, of a shot of heroin. Like Rafael. Except that Rafael was also drunk, and, as far as I know, Darius wasn't."

"When did it happen?"

"About ten years ago, just before Roland and Jill started their gallery. Or just after. I'm not sure which."

He didn't seem struck by the coincidence. She got up and took her copy of *Darius Moffatt, Man and Myth* (autographed, of course) from its shelf. "Here, this will tell you about him."

Andrew got up, too, and took the book without eagerness. He's humoring me, she thought. Well, I'm a taxpayer.

He studied the picture on the back. "I take it that's Moffatt. Good-looking fellow."

"No," she said, "that's a picture of the author. Hal Courtenay. The director of the MAA. There's a picture of Moffatt somewhere inside."

He sighed. "Well, it was all a long time ago, and I think the connection's a little far-fetched, but I'll look into it. You never know."

It was late, he said, and he had to be running along, but first he would go into the studio to say goodnight to Jill. Susan tactfully remained in the library. He came back so soon it appeared that their parting had not been an amicable one, and picked up his coat, brushing more leather crumbs off it before he put it on. It's a nuisance, she thought, but I suppose Jill is right; I will have to get the furniture reupholstered. Or get new furniture. After Roland's murder had been settled. She wouldn't be able to keep her mind on furniture now.

She escorted him into the foyer.

"You understand, I'm going to have to tell Bracco all you've told me—which isn't all that much," he added to make it clear he felt he had given more than he had received. "He'll probably want to talk to you again."

"Maybe it won't be necessary," she said hopefully. "You'll be able to tell him everything I know."

He smiled. She was going to have to see the lieutenant again, she gathered.

"Good night, Susan. I'll be in touch." The door closed behind him.

An instant later the bell rang. She opened the door. "Sorry to bother you again, but this Hal Courtenay—would Hal be short for Henry?

"It usually is," she said, "although he always uses Hal, even on his professional papers."

"I just remembered where I ran across the name before. He was the third partner in the Turkel Gallery."

XX

"I CAN see from your face that he's been telling you things about me," Jill said. "Bad things. Things he had no business telling you, or even knowing."

Her own face was tear-streaked and her mascara had run. She was a sorry sight, but Susan could not feel sorry for her. "He told me things I had a right to know," she said.

"Roland always spoiled everything," Jill said. "If only he hadn't gone and died, nobody would ever have dug up those old stories and you'd never have known about them."

But Mackay had been watching Roland for some time. He must have known about the Turkel Gallery and Jill's connection with Roland long before he had met Jill. It was just that now Roland's death had given that knowledge immediacy. His past would become of interest to the press. They would dig and they would find a rich lode of definite scandal and alleged crime—a veritable embarrassment of riches for the tabloids and a springboard for pontification for the *Times*.

Susan had never really fancied Jill as a candidate for Roland's murderer. However, even if it turned out that she had killed the art dealer, Susan would not necessarily have held that against her. Whoever killed Roland might have had very good reason for the act. But Jill had lied to her. And that Susan could not forgive. Neither could she forgive Hal. He had been the one who introduced Jill to her, and not, she was beginning to suspect, out of disinterested kindness toward either of them.

"If you have some explanation, I'm willing to hear it," she told Jill.

"First tell me what Andy told you—" Jill began; then changed her mind. "I don't want to talk about it. Besides, you wouldn't believe me."

"I believed the other stories you told me. Who knows, maybe I'll swallow this one too. But it's going to have to be a lot better than the other ones because I'm a lot more suspicious."

Jill shook her head. "It's no use. I'm going to bed. Just show me where I'm supposed to sleep. Unless you're throwing me out?"

Once a visitor had been invited to stay, you didn't throw him or her out unless he (or she) did nasty things on the carpet. That was the code by which Susan had been brought up, and she did not intend to violate it. "No, you can stay here tonight." That Jill didn't want to talk, Susan wasn't going to insist. It would save a lot of awkwardness.

"Aren't you afraid I might creep in and kill you or something?" Jill asked bitterly.

"Don't be silly. There's no reason for you to kill me. I don't know anything that the police don't know, and I'm not the one who's frightened out of her wits."

"Does that mean you trust me?"

"Not in the least," Susan said. "It's a long way from not thinking you're a killer to trusting you." Besides, she thought, just in case I'm wrong, I have a gun in my bag. However, there was no point in sharing that information with Jill, and frightening her even more—unless it became necessary to shoot her.

She showed Jill to one of the spare bedrooms that still had a bed in it. "You can sleep here. I'll get some fresh linen."

"That's all right," Jill said. "I can sleep on the floor."

"I can also get you a hair shirt to sleep in, unless you'd like to go get that suitcase of yours out of the foyer. I assume you have nightclothes in it." Perhaps Jill slept in the nude. She'd be sorry if she did. The heat in the apartment tended to go down at night.

Jill made a sound that was a cross between a sob and a grunt.

Susan went to the back of the apartment and got clean linen out of a closet. How worn and thin the sheets had become. It hadn't occurred to her before that she could ever need new ones, that sheets were not forever. But any sheets she bought now—no matter how much she paid for them—would never last as long as the old ones had. Nothing was made to last any more. It was probably because of the atom bomb. Why manufacture sheets that would last for future generations when there was a good chance there weren't going to be any future generations? Might as well buy seconds, she thought.

When she came back with her arms full of sheets and pillow-cases (fragrant with the lavender she always put between them because lavender was what you put between sheets), the door to the bedroom she had allotted to Jill was closed. She could hear Jill inside, fumbling at the lock. "There's no key," she complained, as Susan said, "Here's the linen," and, unable to knock because her arms were full, pushed open the door, and Jill along with it.

"What's the sense of having locks on your doors if there aren't any keys to them?" Jill demanded.

"Do you have a key to your bedroom door?"

"I don't have a separate bedroom. I have a studio apartment—a small, rent-stabilized studio apartment in an ungentrified walk-up," Jill said in what Susan's mother would have described as "a socialist tone of voice."

But Jill had no right to talk like a downtrodden member of the proletariat. She ought to be making plenty of money, more perhaps than Susan, herself, since Jill's commissions from both the Moffatt and the Melville works together, plus any odd jobs she might take on the side, should amount to more than Susan was making. Of course, in spite of Jill's cutting every possible corner as well as a few impossible ones, there were a lot of expenses that had to come out of her share of the take. Nevertheless, she ought to be very comfortably off, and well able to afford a decent if not a luxurious apartment, even at today's outrageous prices.

Susan had never seen Jill's apartment, never been invited there. All she knew was that it was in Brooklyn, but she'd been told that there were some very nice places in Brooklyn. Jill might be lying again. But why?

Susan dumped the linen on the bed. "There must have been keys once, but I can't remember ever seeing any." Her family had been occupying the apartment since before she'd been born. It had been their New York *pied à terre* at first and, after her father had decamped, their principal, and then their sole, residence. Now she owned it. In all that time she had never seen any keys. There had been no need for them. Privacy had been understood.

She remembered an old boarding-school trick. "You can always hook a chair under the doorknob if it makes you feel safer."

"I'm not afraid of you," Jill declared angrily, as if the very idea were absurd. "I just want to be left alone."

"Don't worry. I won't intrude on your privacy." Susan turned at the door. "There's one question I must ask you. Is Hal—?"

"I don't want to discuss the matter. You want to know anything about Hal, you ask him."

"I intend to," Susan said.

Jill gave a choked sob. "He'll say it was all my fault somehow."

"Roland's death, too?"

Jill's only answer was to slam the door.

"Well, goodnight then," Susan called through the door. "Maybe you'll feel different in the morning, after you've had a chance to sleep on it."

What an asinine thing to say. Sleep on what? By morning Jill would have had a chance to think up more lies, and Susan would have had a chance to grow even more suspicious. At least I didn't tell her things were bound to look better in the morning, Susan thought, because, as far as I can see, they're going to look worse.

She went into the studio and turned on the answering machine. If Baltasar called again, he would have to leave a message, and the same went for anyone else who tried to speak to her. But the phone didn't ring again that night, or, if it did, she didn't hear it.

* * *

She went to bed, but she'd known before she lay down that the chances of her getting much sleep were slight. Pieces of a picture began to come together but they did not fit neatly. The edges were ragged, like the parts of Lupe's construct after Rover and Fido had been chewing on it.

If Hal Courtenay had been one of the partners in the Turkel Gallery, it would seem to indicate that Roland had been right, providing Jill had reported his suspicions accurately: they'd had the Darius Moffatt paintings lined up from the start. It had been planned in advance for Hal to give Moffatt an enthusiastic review and set the ball rolling. But who could have envisaged that the ball would roll so fast and so far?

Why would a man like Hal have gotten involved in such a scheme? Possibly the whole thing could have been a joke, Hal's desire to thumb his nose at the art establishment by secretly backing this decidedly inferior artist; then setting him up as a genius. But, no, it was too costly a set-up even for a rich man— and too dangerous for a man in his position. Not only had he been a museum curator (assistant curator, anyhow), but also a distin- guished art historian, critic, and expert with a reputation to uphold. He would hardly have laid that reputation on the line for a joke that a lot of people wouldn't think was funny.

And there would have been nothing to tempt Roland to join in the operation. No, they must have expected to make money out of the gallery, but not more than a modest profit as the pictures were gradually released over the years. Possibly they had planned to do the same thing with other artists as well. If one didn't take off, they'd try another and, little by little, build the gallery up. Why, it was almost legitimate. In fact, except that Hal would be using his status to puff the pictures, it was legitimate.

When Roland's dabblings in the drug world had been found out, the other two (or rather Hal, because Jill obviously had had only a small financial stake, if that, in the venture) had bought him out. They couldn't have been involved in the drug deal themselves or why would they have bothered with the Moffatt scheme? Which would seem to indicate that Hal could not be, as she had half feared, the shadowy figure that loomed behind the whole picture—the international drug dealer whom Mackay had mentioned in connection with the Hoffmann exhibit, and who might have been the same individual who had involved Roland the first time and for whom Roland might have been working ever since.

It was ridiculous, anyway, to think that a man of such culture and distinction, a museum director, no matter how flawed his character, how tacky his answering-machine messages, should be a trafficker in drugs. Yet what better front for an international drug dealer than that of a museum director, travelling all over the world in search of art and artifacts; moreover, an individual with an Italian or Greek island of his very own, perfect headquarters from which to conduct nefarious activities. She recalled that her own ancestor, Black Buck Melville, had owned such an island, although it had been in the Caribbean, a more convenient location for a man in his line of work.

However, the mere fact of owning an island did not automatically make a person suspect of being an international drug dealer, any more than having an apartment in Jackson Heights made a person suspect of being a national one. Jackson Heights . . . What had made her think of Jackson Heights? Where had she heard it mentioned recently? She couldn't recall. It didn't seem relevant.

There was a fourth party involved in the Hal-Jill-Roland relationship. Someone she had been overlooking in her speculations. What about Darius Moffatt himself? Had he been an innocent, or part of the plan to exploit his pictures beyond the bounds of legitimate hype?

Had it been a coincidence that he'd died just before the exhibit opened? Surely, in spite of what she'd told Mackay, his death must have been an accident. Hal and Jill were hardly likely to have killed the goose that could lay more golden—no silver—eggs.

They couldn't have expected that his works would turn into pure gold. But eggs were eggs. Even if you're selling plain goose eggs, you don't make pâté de foie gras out of the goose.

Perhaps they'd been forced to kill him. Perhaps he had refused to go along with the scheme? Not likely. As far as he would be concerned, it would simply seem like a good way of getting his work before the public. To him, as to most unsuccessful or under-successful artists, all critics would seem axiomatically prejudiced, cronyistic, venal, devoid of a genuine appreciation of true art, too ready to pander to fashion and flattery. A rave review, no matter how obtained, would be no more than his just due. No, they wouldn't have killed Moffatt for that reason. He would have been eager to go along with the scheme.

He must simply have died of natural causes. (In New York death from a drug overdose counts as a natural cause.) How had they managed to gain possession of his work after he died? Or had it already been in their possession at the time of his death? The story of Old Mother Moffatt and her barn was, as she had already realized, probably fictitious, the creation of Jill's fertile brain.

So, it was likely, was Old Mother Moffatt herself. Darius might have had a mother; in fact, he must have had a mother, because they hadn't started breeding babies in test tubes until years after his birth. It seemed doubtful, however, that she was getting anything out of this if she were still alive. And that seemed doubtful, too. They must have made sure that the dead artist had no heirs to haunt them, or they would not have embarked on such an elaborate deception, with its chain of paintings, interviews, magazine articles, books, and so on.

What fun they must have had, she thought, a little wistfully. And, provided they hadn't killed Darius himself, and had a legitimate claim to his works, all of it was legal or as near legal as made no difference.

So everything had worked out well, with Darius's paintings dwindling to their inevitable end. And then that painting had turned up at Allardyce's.

Apparently they had made a mistake. Moffatt must have sold a painting during his lifetime or given one away. Possibly there was an heir after all. How frightened Jill and Hal must have been. But Jill hadn't seemed frightened at the auction, just angry. She became frightened only after she'd learned of Roland's death.

Had Roland somehow hung on to one of the Moffatt paintings? Was that why he had been killed? For just one picture? There had been hundreds before, but none before had commanded such a price.

Susan felt as victimized as Roland, though not, of course, as drastically. It was possible that Jill was doing a good job in her capacity as Susan's representative. Nevertheless, Susan didn't like being represented by someone whose only other client was a myth. Would I feel so strongly about it, she wondered, if I didn't feel that I myself am, in a sense, a myth?

XXI

SUSAN FINALLY did fall asleep, but she was awakened after what seemed like only a few hours, by a sound that she could not at first identify. Then she realized what it had been—a door closing somewhere inside the apartment. An intruder? Picking up the handbag with the gun in it, she went to Jill's room.

It was empty. Pinned to the pillow was a sheet of paper torn from one of her sketch pads. On it was scrawled, "I'm not staying where I'm not wanted—Jill . . . P.S. You need some new sheets."

It was the front door she had heard closing, which meant now it was locked only on the snap latch. If I hadn't heard her leave, she thought crossly, any one of the neighbors could have come in with a credit card and killed me.

She thought of calling down to the doorman to tell him to stop Jill, in case Jill hadn't passed him yet. But he could hardly restrain the girl bodily. If he tried, Jill would probably put up a fight. And then both of them would sue Susan.

Let her go, she thought. Why should I care, anyway? But a line from an old song rang in her head: "Let her go, let her go, God bless her . . ."

Saint James Infirmary, that was where the line came from. She thought of Jill's body stretched out "on a long white table, so young, so cold, so fair . . ." and she shuddered. If she had felt Jill deserved it, there was a time when she might have killed the girl herself, but she didn't want her to die as the result of her own inaction.

She was being silly. That was what often happened when you woke up in the small hours of the night and started thinking.

She looked at the clock. Not so small as all that—almost six. By this hour Jill should have no trouble finding a cab—a lot more easily than she would two or three hours later when the streets would be full of strong young men with attaché cases pushing little old ladies aside and grabbing their cabs. Jill would be all right, she told herself.

She tried to go back to sleep, but she couldn't. Suppose someone had really been after Jill, and had been lurking in the street all night waiting for a chance to get at her. Supposing Jill simply got killed by a casual mugger for her fur coat. Supposing she had felt so repentant over past misdeeds, that she had gone and thrown herself into the river—conveniently situated only a few blocks to the east. That was one of the troubles with New York, Susan thought; it had too many rivers and they were all too handy for anyone who didn't mind drowning in a stream of effluvium.

Nonsense, she told herself. Now that it's daylight, Jill has probably realized how groundless her fears were and simply gone home. Except that, and it came back to the beginning again, her fears might not have been groundless.

Susan got up and dressed; then called Jill's number. Jill's machine answered. Perhaps she hadn't had enough time to get home. Or she hadn't gone home but to some other place of refuge—some friend who might be even at that moment engaged in the act of killing her.

Jill might have stopped somewhere for breakfast. She might simply not be answering her phone. "Jill, if you're there I insist that you speak to me," Susan told the machine. "It's urgent. Gil Stratton is trying to get me to be his client."

But the machine went on whirring. Nobody picked it up. Jill was not home.

Hal might know where Jill had gone, but he might also be the one, or one of the ones, of whom she was afraid; in which case

Susan didn't want to let him know that Jill was no longer safely ensconced in her apartment. Besides, even though he was a fraud and possibly a murderer, he didn't know she knew that, so it was too early to call him.

Perhaps Andrew Mackay might have some idea of where Jill might be, or at least could find out. He's a detective, she thought, let's see how well he can detect. Anyhow, it was never too early or too late to call a detective.

She rooted around in the bag she had been carrying the day before until she found Mackay's card. She didn't know whether the number was of his home or his office—or whether, in fact, he had an office (or, for that matter, a home), but she called it. Again, only a machine answered. Am I the only living person left in the city, she wondered. Has everyone else left for another planet, leaving only their machines behind to take messages until their tapes run out?

"Andrew," she said into the phone, "this is Susan Melville. Jill has disappeared."

There, she said to herself with satisfaction, that ought to get him going.

By this time it was seven o'clock, not too early to call Alex, a relative by blood if not by consanguinity. He whistled when she gave him a recap of all that had happened since she had last spoken to him, rather, of all that she'd learned, for in actual fact nothing had happened. It only seemed that way.

"The worms certainly seem to have emerged from the canister with a vengeance," he said. "Whatever possessed you to let her come over? It could have been dangerous."

"Well, she's gone and I haven't come to any harm, so it's all water over the bridgework, as Lupe would say. That's right, I wonder where Lupe fits in in all this, if she fits in at all. Andrew seemed to think she might be connected in some way, but as far as I can see she's just an innocent bystander."

"If you can call a lady who travels with a pack of wolves innocent in any sense of the word. Listen, Susan, why don't you come over to breakfast and then we can talk about it and decide what to do or, better yet, what not to do. Do nothing is my instinctive reaction, but I agree that the matter needs discussion. Oh, by the way, I have the *Times* and the *Wall Street Journal*, of course, but would you mind picking up the *News* on your way? And *Newsday* and the *Post* if they're out. Oh, yes, and a dozen eggs, if you would be so good. The far-from-efficient Mrs. Liebling has slipped up again."

Tinsley was still asleep when Susan arrived, so she and Alex had breakfast alone together, in the Tabors' pleasant breakfast room overlooking Central Park. Tinsley's family counted among the superrich and so their handsome penthouse condominium on Fifth Avenue (a wedding gift from the bride's family), while being up to date in every respect, was well equipped with such relics of a bygone era as both breakfast and dining rooms and "more baths," as Jill had observed, "than you can shake a mahl stick at."

Alex prepared breakfast. The housekeeper didn't come on duty officially until eight, except in case of emergencies—for which she generally exacted a pound of flesh in addition to overtime, so that Tinsley and Alex were wary of seeking any extra services. "It isn't the money," Tinsley said, "it's the martyrdom."

Alex was a much better cook than Mrs. Liebling, anyway, Susan thought, but he nearly spoiled her breakfast by informing her that, while she was on her way over, Lieutenant Bracco had called. "He wanted to come over here to talk to me, but I told him my wife was pregnant and easily upset, so I'd stop down and see him at his office before I went to mine. I figured that would touch a chord. Civil servants have a high regard for motherhood."

"Why don't you consolidate your standing by taking him an apple pie?"

"I'll leave that to you. He said he wanted to 'have another chat' —his words—with you, and that he'd left a message to that effect on your machine; but, if I happened to talk to you before you picked it up, I should let you know. He has a few more questions he wants to put to you."

Even though Mackay had warned her that she was likely to get a call from the lieutenant, she was nonetheless unnerved. "Did you tell him I was coming over here?"

Alex was shocked. "What kind of brother do you take me for? I told him I had no idea of where you might be, but that only the other day you had spoken of longing to paint the sun coming up over the Himalayas, and I wouldn't be surprised if you had packed up your palette and impulsively dashed off to Nepal."

"And what did he say to that?"

"He said he'd told you to let him know if you were planning to leave town and he had no doubt you would have gotten in touch with him if you intended to go to Naples. He seems to have formed a very favorable impression of you. I wouldn't be surprised if you'd made another conquest."

Mrs. Liebling appeared at the breakfast room door, breathing fire, with a touch of brimstone for Susan. "You should have called me," she said. "I would have been only too happy—"

"There was no need to disturb you. I am perfectly capable of making breakfast for my sister and myself."

"It's not right for a man to do the cooking," she said, glaring at Susan.

There were a number of French chefs, including M. Bumppo, who would be interested to hear that, Susan thought, but she held her tongue, not wanting to roil Alex's domestic waters.

"Mrs. Liebling," he began ominously, "I have told you before—"

"At least I can clear away," she said, making a grab for the dishes.

"We haven't finished yet," Alex said. "Why don't you go see if Mrs. Tabor wants anything. I'm not going to apologize for her," he told Susan, after the housekeeper had left with a parting sniff. One of these days I'm going to do a picture of her as a dragon, Susan thought, no, a fire-breathing toad sitting under a canopy of poison ivy leaves. "Amy hired her and Amy is your friend."

"If Amy hadn't been, you wouldn't be where you are now," Susan reminded him.

He hesitated before he said, "All right, I apologize for her. How about putting a bad word for her in my dear mother-in-law's ear? I don't want to seem ungrateful, but you have no reason for gratitude."

Together Alex and Susan scanned the relevant parts of the papers. Because of the other events in the news (plus a small war that had started up during the wee hours), Roland's death got no more than a cover line in the tabloids, plus an inside story on the third page of the *Post* and the fourth of the *News*, while the *Times* relegated it to the Metropolitan Section as if it were merely a routine local event, which she supposed it was to the *Times*. All of the people she had killed, she couldn't help remembering, had hit the front page, even though some had been carried over to Section D (Business and Obituaries).

Otherwise there was nothing in the papers about Roland's demise that she didn't already know. There really hadn't been time for them to do much digging. Tomorrow, especially after the drug angle had been brought out into the open, there would be more background information, and she would learn more about Roland's past from presumably reliable sources.

She wondered how soon and how much of what Mackay had told her about Hal's and Jill's enterprise would get in the papers. If they unearthed Hal's direct connection with the Turkel Gallery, which they might well do, since it was presumably no secret—it was just that there had been no reason before for anyone to take the trouble to look it up—Hal would find himself in a very unenviable position.

As they went through the papers, her attention was caught by a small item in the *Times* and larger ones in the other papers concerning a Lady Daphne Merriwether who, after having been struck by a bicyclist who had not stopped for a red light, had attacked and nearly killed him with her bare hands. The bicyclist, who was nineteen, was in the hospital. Lady Daphne, who was seventy-five, was in police custody. Bully for Lady Daphne, Susan thought, and decided against calling the episode to Alex's attention. He had enough to think about.

Alex seemed genuinely surprised to learn that Hal had been the principal backer of the Turkel Gallery. She'd been half afraid he'd known and hadn't told her. "That's right, Courtenay did stop working for the General about the same time as he gave Roland the boot," Alex said thoughtfully. "Could be they were in the thing together. I'd just started working for the organization then, so I really wasn't in on things. In fact, I didn't have too much to do with the art side until I recruited you. But I wouldn't be at all surprised to find out Courtenay authenticated that Picasso. What does surprise me, though, is to find out Courtenay's apparently a crook. He always seemed so stuffy. But then there's no law saying crooks have to be free spirits. What puzzles me is why this fellow Mackay should be interested in them at all, if he's decided they have nothing to do with the drug aspect of the matter. He seems, from what you tell me, to be some kind of narc."

"Drugs would make him a federal agent, then?" she asked.

"Not necessarily. The city and state police have narcotics divisions. He could even be a private detective. The cops sometimes use private eyes to do things they can't do themselves."

He spoke authoritatively. He had spent most of his adult life and the latter part of his adolescence working against the law. The fact that he had never been caught should give him authority.

"I thought the police resented private detectives."

Alex laughed. "I see you're still keeping up with the television shows."

She hadn't had a chance to watch television, except for the news, in weeks. And she missed it. Fictional crime was always so much more satisfactory than real-life crime, if only because it had to be solved by the end of the hour, while real-life crime often never got solved at all.

* * *

"Do you think Roland could have been blackmailing Jill and Hal?"

"Why would he stick his neck out like that?" Alex said. "He wasn't a courageous man, you know. And, if he had wanted to blackmail them, why now, when he had this big drug deal going?"

"Then why is Jill so afraid?" Susan asked. "And of whom?"

"Good questions," he said. "I only wish I had some equally good answers. The only one I can think of is Hal, and the Moffatt thing doesn't seem like enough to kill for, unless he killed Moffatt. Besides, he doesn't seem the killer type to me. Not that that means anything, of course." He smiled and patted her hand.

She pulled her hand away.

"And, of course, we don't know what else Roland was up to or who he was up to it with. But don't worry about Jill. That's one lady who can take care of herself."

Susan didn't agree. In spite of Jill's tough exterior, she was extremely vulnerable.

Alex got up. "Well, it's time for me to go pay my respects to the lieutenant. Like to come with me and save everybody trouble?"

"No, thanks," she said, "I'll wait until I hear from him directly." Which wouldn't be very soon, if she had any choice in the matter.

XXII

THEY PARTED at the front door of Alex's building. He gave her a searching look. "You're carrying one of those big bags you used to carry when you were doing jobs for the General."

She had not expected him to be so observant. "Waste not, want not," she said. "It's a good bag. Lots of wear left in it."

"You aren't carrying a gun in there, are you?"

She couldn't lie about it. Much too embarrassing later if she should happen to find herself obliged to shoot somebody. She didn't say anything.

"But that's ridiculous. There's no reason for you to carry a gun any more."

"It makes me feel more comfortable. Isn't that reason enough?"

"No, it is not. Do you mean to say you're planning to carry a gun when you go to see Lieutenant Bracco?"

Since she hadn't had any intention of seeing the lieutenant when she set out that morning, she hadn't made any plans with respect to the gun. But she wasn't going to traipse all the way back to her apartment simply to put it away.

"The police are hardly likely to search me. Anyhow, why should you worry? It's one of father's old guns; it has no connection with you."

"But he's my father, too, now," Alex explained patiently, "and you're my sister. How would it look in the papers: 'Stockbroker's sister charged with illegal possession of concealed weapon'?"

"How would it look: 'Well-known artist charged, etcetera'?"

He laughed. "Not nearly as bad from my point of view. You're right, of course, I'm not my sister's keeper. I can't tell you what to do; that is, I can tell you, but I don't have any way of making you do it any more."

And he sighed, no doubt thinking of the past, when he'd been in a position to coerce her into doing his bidding. But even that hadn't always worked, she remembered with pride. She'd been her own woman then—far more than she was now. Part of the price one had to pay for success, she supposed. Had it all been worth it? Although there were some aspects of her new life she could do without, the overall answer was an emphatic yes.

Alex offered to give her a lift in his cab to wherever she was going, but, having no particular destination in mind, she was in no hurry to get there. All she knew was that she didn't want to go home and pick up her messages. The answering machine did have a remote control system whereby messages could, in theory at least, be picked up from any phone, but she never used it; as she explained over and over again to Jill who felt that whenever her client was away from home, her constant concern should be to get to a phone at periodic intervals to pick up messages from her representative. Jill couldn't get it through her head that sometimes one of the reasons Susan left her apartment was just to get away from the phone.

Of course Susan could and sometimes did stay at home and simply not pick up the phone, especially when she was painting and could not be disturbed, letting messages collect until she was in a receptive mode. Or she would listen to them and not answer. But, whenever she did that, she found herself feeling guilty—a hangover from the past of which she had been unable to rid herself. This way she hadn't actually received the lieutenant's message, so she felt no obligation to act upon it.

Why was she so anxious to avoid the lieutenant? He had been perfectly affable at their previous interview. Why would he be less affable now? She had given him all the information he had asked for; and, if she had neglected to give him further information that might have been pertinent, how on earth was she to know what did and did not pertain? Was she a mind reader? Besides, how could she have been expected to think of details in the stress of the moment?

In any case, everything she'd told Mackay should have been readily obtainable elsewhere. In fact, by this time the lieutenant probably had found out all she could tell him from other sources. Probably all he wanted from her was to check out a few things.

In due time she would go home and pick up her messages; then she would call the office and go down and have a chat with the lieutenant, over a cup of tea, perhaps. No, that was the British police. American police served coffee in plastic cups.

Only there were other things she had to do before she went home. Important things. As, for instance, go to see Baltasar. How could she have forgotten how worried she had been about him the night before?

She must check immediately to make sure that he was all right. It was the decent, human, time-consuming thing to do.

She'd go to the nearest telephone and call him. But it was always so difficult to communicate on one of those street phones. Every passerby could hear what you were saying, while you couldn't hear the person on the other end, because a heavy truck or a fire engine or a car with a loud radio invariably went by just as you made your connection. Once she had dropped in a quarter just as a particularly noisy parade had marched down the street. Her money had run out before the person on the other end had been able to hear anything but a brass band playing a medley of folk songs from some unidentified nation.

What she would do was go to the Plaza and call Baltasar on one of the house phones. He would ask her to have breakfast with him, and she'd join him for a cup of coffee—which would not be served in a plastic cup. The Plaza's standards had not deteriorated that far. The police would never think of tracking her down in the Palm Court. After that, she might—yes, she would go to the MAA and beard Hal in his den.

* * *

She decided to stroll down Fifth Avenue to the Plaza. It was a nice day for a walk, brisk and invigorating—so brisk and invigorating it was hard for her to keep her pace down to the stroll necessary if she was not going to reach the hotel too early.

She rang Baltasar's room. There was no answer. He seemed to be an early riser. Not that ten o'clock was so very early, just that she'd been under the impression that natives of Spanish-speaking countries kept late hours, although, she supposed, there was no reason why your mother tongue should affect your circadian rhythm.

Baltasar could be anywhere. How did she know what his haunts might be? However, there was a good chance that he might be at his building. There was a better than good chance that the police might be there, too. Not Lieutenant Bracco, though. He would be at his office, talking to Alex. The likelihood was that they would simply have left a man on guard at the scene of the crime, someone who didn't even know that the lieutenant wanted to see her; or who, even if he did, probably would not be able to identify her by sight.

And what if he did recognize her and inform her that she was being sought for further questioning? So she would go and be questioned further. It isn't as if I were a fugitive or even a material witness, she thought.

There was a policeman stationed outside the gallery. He was standing in front of the gate that led to the basement steps, flapping his arms, although it didn't seem to her the day was all that cold, and muttering to himself. Clearly he didn't like his present post and didn't care who knew it. He glanced at her without apparent interest as she paused in front of the gallery.

She smiled at him. "Could you tell me if Mr. Baltasar is inside?"

"You can ring the bell and ask," he said. "I'm a policeman not a doorman."

He seemed to have a cold in his nose, poor man. Or perhaps he was coming down with the flu. She hoped he was. Bed rest would do him so much good.

* * *

To her surprise, it was Damian Schwimmer who answered the door. The "Schwimmer" seemed to give him a whole new dimension. "Do come in," he said hospitably.

Esmeralda came forward with a cordial meow and twined herself around Susan's legs as she entered. Both Damian and Esmeralda seemed glad to see her. She was touched. She bent over and patted Esmeralda's head. Damian looked as if he would have liked to have his head patted, too, but there she drew the line.

"Baltasar asked us to stay on for a bit and look after things," Damian explained. "We're staying in Rollie's apartment."

It wasn't clear whether he meant himself and Esmeralda or himself and Paul. "Since it wasn't the actual scene of the crime, which is sealed off, not that wild unicorns would drag me down there—" and he shuddered, "—the police had no objection. First they searched the place with frightening thoroughness. All of Rollie's little secrets revealed. Too sickening for him, only, of course, he's in no position to be sickened any more."

He looked sad. She looked sad, too. They shared a moment of respectful silence. I suppose I'll be expected to go to his funeral, she thought. I do hope there aren't going to be any more murders. I hate wearing black.

"Paul and I were absolutely terrified that the police would search us, too. They didn't, though." Damian didn't look terrified, even in retrospect. He looked disappointed.

"Do you know they found a secret room in the sub-basement? More of a secret storage closet than a secret room. A large walk-in type of closet. And not so secret because the police found it right away."

She had never even thought of the sub-basement, but, of course, all those old buildings had sub-basements below ground level—where they had used to keep coal in the old days, before oil heat took over. It would have been a perfect spot for a concealed cache, except that it was one of the first places the police would look. They knew about these old buildings too.

"Did they find anything there?" she asked. "I mean anything that would shed any light on what happened to Roland?"

"It was absolutely empty, not even a skeleton. But, a very sweet boy on the D.A.'s staff told me, one of those little men with microscopes found traces of coke there. They seem to think Rollie was a drug dealer or smuggler or something. Which is ridiculous. He may have used coke once in a while—everybody does—but he couldn't have been trading in it. That would be immoral. I'm sure Rollie didn't have the least idea the room was there. What I think is the previous occupant of the building must have been a drug dealer." He nodded firmly.

Esmeralda butted her head against Susan's legs. Susan obediently bent over and patted her again. Why is this cat making up to me, she wondered. And then she laughed at herself. I'm beginning to suspect everyone of having ulterior motives, even the cat.

"Anyhow I must admit it's a blessing that Baltasar's letting us stay here, because I don't know how Paul and I would have been able to go on paying the rent at our hotel, now Rollie's gone and our jobs with him."

"Well, perhaps whoever takes over the gallery will keep you on," Susan suggested.

Damian shook his sleek head. "I'm afraid Baltasar has other ideas. He's suddenly decided not to have a gallery here at all. Thinks there's a curse on the place or something like that. But if there should be a curse—although, mind you, I don't believe in such things—it would be on anything that set up here, not just an art gallery. So why not leave it as a gallery?"

"Maybe he'll decide to keep it as a gallery once he gets over the shock."

Damian shook his head. "He's set things in motion." Lowering his voice, he said, "He's been going over the place with the strangest lady, who seems to be thinking of renting it. And I'm afraid she has something a lot different from an art gallery in mind."

He made such a face that Susan leaped to erotic and erroneous conclusions. "A brothel, do you mean?"

He laughed. "Oh, no, that would be fun—and there might even be spots for Paul and me. I'd love to work in a brothel. You meet—you must meet such fascinating people there."

Susan felt a little embarrassed at having entertained such an unseemly thought. That was the result of association, however casual, with Dodo Pangborn. No, if she left Jill, she definitely would not become a client of Dodo's. Not that she had ever considered the prospect seriously.

"I'm not sure what Baltasar's prospective tenant is actually planning," Damian said. "That is, I know what it sounds like, but I can't believe my ears. She seems to be—but I hear the elevator. I'd better be discreet, or I won't be kept on even temporarily."

If only Damian had said, "But hark, I hear the elevator," or—better yet—"hark, I hear the lift," it would have sounded like a line from an old melodrama.

XXIII

THE LITTLE door in the woodwork opened and Baltasar came out. This time, instead of being accompanied by the contractor, he handed out—Susan blinked—Hortense Pomeroy, of all people! Today she was dressed for business in a hairy purple and green culotte suit. Atop her head was the pink beret, or perhaps another pink beret; it did look fuzzier than the one she'd worn to Sprouts 'n Stuff. Attached to it by what looked vaguely like a Girl Scout badge was a jaunty lavender feather.

Never had anyone seemed so out of place in an art gallery. No, that wasn't true. She looked like something perpetrated by a pop artist of the sixties. But what was she doing here?

"... Should have taken the stairs," she was saying. "Greatest exercise in the world for man, woman, and child. Beast too. Bet *she* never takes the elevator."

At first Susan thought Hortense was talking about Susan herself. For a moment she wondered what she had done to arouse the physical educator's disapproval. Then she realized it was Esmeralda to whom Hortense referred. Esmeralda stretched sinuously, as if to indicate she needed no physical fitness classes to keep in condition.

There was a look of strain on Baltasar's face—either from too much of Hortense's society or from the series of disasters with which he'd been forced to cope. Somehow she could not feel sorry for him; he was not the sort of person who aroused sympathy. A sort of reverse *noblesse oblige*, she supposed.

"I assure you, Miss Pomeroy—"

"Hortense, please."

"—Hortense, that if Esmeralda were able to open the door and reach the buttons she would be taking the lift more often that any one of us. There is no animal lazier than a cat."

He saw Susan and his dark face seemed to light up. "My dear Susan, how nice to see you. I tried to get in touch with you last night."

"I know, Jill gave me your message. That's why I came over—"

"Susan, I can't begin to thank you enough!" Hortense interrupted. Striding across the foyer, she grasped both of the other woman's hands and pumped them up and down, as if she were trying to start her engine. "I always knew you'd go to bat for an old school chum, but I never thought you'd hit a homer like this."

As if they had gone to school together, instead of merely teaching at the same place. And what was the woman talking about, anyway? "I didn't know you two knew each other," Susan said.

"Never actually met until this morning. Phone chums—" Baltasar winced "—that was all. But we know each other now, thanks to you." She patted Susan on the shoulder with a hand like a slab of meat loaf.

Susan looked inquiringly at Baltasar.

He rubbed the back of his neck with his hand. "After the terrible things that have happened at this place, I felt certain that no art dealer would wish to have a gallery here, nor would any artist want to exhibit his works in such a place."

"I don't see any reason why not," Susan objected. "It's a good space at a good address. I'm sure there are any number of dealers who would jump at the chance to take it over."

Behind Baltasar's back Damian raised a circled thumb and forefinger in encouragement; then, either out of delicacy or boredom, he vanished behind the shiny curtain that still closed off the back regions of the gallery.

Hortense waggled a roguish finger. "Now, now, Susie, don't spoil the good work. Of course no artist who had the least . . . uh

... sensitivity would want to show his work in a place with such a—a dark cloud hanging over it."

"Please call me Susan, not Susie." Sensitivity indeed. What did someone as boorish as Hortense know about sensitivity? And she didn't understand what Hortense was talking about. What was she doing here? And why did Baltasar feel the place could no longer function as an art gallery? Did he think Roland was going to come back and haunt it? Even if he did, that was hardly likely to bother the average art dealer. If Roland's ghost tried to haunt Gil Stratton, for example, Gil would just laugh in its face. As for an artist, he would probably try to tie-dye its sheet.

"Jill—I'm afraid I have forgotten her surname, that charming young representative of yours—gave me one of this lady's brochures the other day," Baltasar explained. "I found it of enormous interest. Such a worthy-sounding enterprise."

"Turkel. Her name's Jill Turkel, and she was acting on her own, not as my representative, when she gave you that brochure."

"Oh, I understood that, of course. I knew you would not personally be involved with so commercial a project."

For some reason Susan couldn't quite put her finger on, she felt vaguely insulted.

"I, too, really must thank Jill," Hortense said. "I tried to get her on the phone this morning, but only her machine answered."

"She's disappeared."

"Oh, well, these artistic people..." Hortense said. Apparently she didn't make Baltasar's distinction between art and commerce. "I tried to call you, too, and only your machine answered. And here you are, so at least *you* haven't disappeared."

"Speaking of disappearances," Baltasar said, "you do not happen to know where Lupe has gotten to, do you, Susan?"

"Lupe!" Susan was startled. "I'd have thought you would know, if anyone did."

He shook his head. "I would have thought so myself, but didn't. She left the gallery the day before yesterday—not long after you and Jill had gone—promising to call and let me know where she would be staying. Since then I have heard not a word from her. I am beginning to feel concerned. I know she seems very . . . very much in possession of herself, but she is a young woman alone in a strange city."

Should she tell him that Lupe had come to Leatherstocking's after she had left the gallery? No reason to bring it up; for some reason Lupe might not want him to know. "Wasn't she supposed to get in touch with your lawyer?"

He looked at her with faint reproach. "That idea did occur to me, of course. But he says he has not heard from her either. Incidentally, while Lupe was here at the gallery, she asked for your address and telephone number and also Jill's. I secured them from poor Roland . . ."

He paused. Susan wondered if they were in for another moment of respectful silence; then Hortense boomed, "Roland, wasn't that the fellow who got bashed?" and the opportunity for such a moment was over.

"I hope you do not mind that I gave Lupe your addresses. It seemed to me a good thing that since she was a stranger in a strange country she should make friends with some nice ladies."

"Of course, I don't mind. I wish she had called me." Or Jill, Susan was about to add, but, for all she knew Lupe *had* called Jill.

"If this lady you're talking about is from out of town, maybe she registered at a hotel," Hortense offered.

Baltasar seemed struck by this suggestion, which, Susan had to admit (grudgingly) to herself, was a sensible one. "She might be at a hotel, yes, and did not call me because she heard about what had happened here, and it made her nervous."

That didn't make sense. If Lupe was nervous, it seemed to Susan the first thing she would do would be to call the only real friend she had in the city. Susan had a suspicion that Baltasar was being less than candid with her, that he knew perfectly well where Lupe was and, for some reason of his own, did not choose to admit it.

* * *

"How would one go about checking the hotels?" Baltasar asked. "There must be a great many of them here. There seems to be a great many of everything here."

"I imagine the police will be doing that for you," Susan told him.

"Ah yes, the police." Baltasar looked as if he had smelled something bad. "They must be demons of efficiency, your police. One of them came to fetch me from Allardyce's yesterday. I cannot imagine how they knew I was there. But I suppose they must have their methods."

"Well," Susan said, glad she had long since gotten over such *gaucheries* as blushing, "they're not called New York's Finest for nothing."

"They questioned me quite extensively at the time, and then this morning, I was called down to their offices at an incredible hour. The lieutenant had found out about Lupe's existence somehow—" Susan tried to keep her face blank "—and he was displeased that I had not thought to inform him about her advent. But what, for Heaven's sake, could she have to do with Roland? She had never so much as set eyes on him before."

"The police undoubtedly want to talk to everyone who had been in the gallery that day," Susan told him. "It's routine."

If he'd been a television watcher, he would have known that. But perhaps Spanish TV was different.

"But, if it was a sex crime, surely there would be no need to question women," Hortense said.

"This morning the lieutenant told me that they are beginning to think that perhaps it was not a sex crime, after all," Baltasar said, "that perhaps some enemy of Roland's killed him in that manner in order to divert suspicion from his real reason."

Baltasar must have learned about the drug angle by this time, Susan thought. However, she could understand his reluctance to mention it in front of Hortense. You don't tell a prospective tenant that she may be taking over a former drug den.

"Ah," Hortense said, "a man like that must have many ene-mies."

"A man like what?" Susan asked.

"Oh, you know," Hortense said.

Susan did know, but she wondered how Hortense did.

"The police were annoyed with me, too, because I hadn't men-tioned Lupe," Susan told Baltasar. "I must admit I was so . . . so upset I'd forgotten about her. But you, as an old friend, couldn't have forgotten—"

"I saw no need to drag her into it. She is a foreigner. It is frightening to be questioned by the authorities when one is not in one's own country. I know; I am a foreigner myself. You cannot imagine the trouble I have had with your building inspectors, your sewer inspectors, and now, your police inspectors. Can you imagine! That detective said I must not leave the city without letting him know where I was going."

That wasn't because you're a foreigner. He told me the same thing."

"That makes it even more insufferable. To think that they would treat you, dear lady, in such a manner; it is almost beyond belief."

"The police always tend to take such an authoritarian approach, Lady Daphne always says, and I suppose you could call her a foreigner. She's British, you know. She's gotten into trouble with them, again. Dear Lady Daphne, always so impetuous. One of our instructors," Hortense explained to Baltasar.

"Lady Daphne? That means she is of the nobility? Good, that will lend prestige to the undertaking."

"I understand your dear wife is also of the nobility. I hope she will lend her name to the undertaking. That will give us even greater prestige."

Baltasar looked taken aback for a moment; then he recovered his aplomb. "If she ever decides to leave Spain and come visit this country, I am sure she will be only too delighted to do whatever she can to help. But she is of rather a retiring nature, like so many Spanish ladies of old family."

That wasn't how the *condesa's* friends had described her, according to Mimi. One of the most celebrated hostesses in Madrid, they'd said. And hadn't she been supposed to come to the opening of the gallery? Even if she hadn't been able to make it, still she had planned to be there, so she couldn't be all that retiring. Probably Baltasar was painting a fictitious picture in order to keep Hortense at bay, and she could hardly blame him. But why then had she chosen to get involved with Hortense in the first place? Or hadn't he realized what he was getting into?

"I read about Lady Daphne's little brush with the law in the papers," Susan said to Hortense. "If she needs help posting bail, anything like that . . . ?"

"Sweet of you to offer, but she's out on bail already. Thousands have rallied to her side, and one of the top women lawyers in the city has volunteered her services. We're going to make a cause out of this. First, ban the bicycle; then, the bomb."

Susan would have thought that Hortense, as a fitness buff, would be pro-bicycle. Perhaps she had been, before the invasion of the bicycle monsters had turned the city into a three-way battlefield, with the pedestrian losing out to both bicycle and automobile. "They accused her of using excessive force," Hortense said, "as if you could use too much force against a rogue bicyclist." Susan nodded.

Baltasar looked dismayed. "Violence, violence, is there no getting away from it! I thought a health club would be so quiet, so peaceful."

Obviously he didn't understand about health clubs. "After all," Susan pointed out, "Lady Daphne does teach unarmed combat. You could look on this in the light of a testimonial to her expertise."

"Hear, hear," Hortense said.

Baltasar looked ill.

"Wasn't it rather a sudden decision to turn the gallery into a health club?" Susan asked Baltasar.

"Do you think so? I suppose it does appear that way. But I was

interested in the club from the moment I read the brochure. I had
been looking for some sound local investments. It is so important
for a businessman to diversify these days, you know. And the idea
of a health club for ladies of a certain age seemed so right, so
American, so attuned to your national passion for physical fitness.
It seemed to me it could not fail to succeed."

"And it will succeed," Hortense beamed.

"And so I telephoned Miss Pomeroy—"

"Hortense."

"—Hortense, later that day. When I spoke to her, she happened
to mention that she had not as yet found a suitable location."

"Everything was either too expensive or too awful. Sometimes
both."

But what could be more expensive than this place? Unless Baltasar was giving Hortense a spectacular break on the rent. And
why should he do that, even if he was taking a piece of the action?
Was he so anxious to get rid of the place to anyone who had no
connection with the art world that he was willing to lose money on
it?

"Last evening," he explained, almost as if he had been able to
read her mind—not that it was difficult to know what she or what
any intelligent person must be thinking, "after I had been told
what had happened to poor Roland, I found I could not bear the
thought of having another art gallery take the place of this one. It
would always remind me of him."

"Great pals, were you?" Hortense asked sympathetically.

"Merely professional associates," he said, moving just enough so
that her meaty hand missed his shoulder. "Still . . . well . . . I suppose we Spaniards are more . . . sentimental—is that the right
word?—than you Americans."

Hortense murmured something to the effect that it did them
credit.

"Then I had my inspiration. Why should we not turn this place
into a health club? It would be perfect. All the ladies who come to
make themselves beautiful will want beautiful gowns."

The idea was ridiculous. All those middle-aged pink berets

trooping in and out were hardly likely to enhance the couturier image. And what about the T-shirts and the bag-lady scholarships? The scholarships had probably been just a come-on to draw Susan into the fold, but Hortense would never give up her T-shirts, at least not without a fight.

Well, Susan told herself, it was none of her business what Baltasar decided to do with his gallery. Whatever arrangement he might have had with Roland, it was unquestionably his gallery now.

"I suppose you phoned me last night to find out if I'd heard from Lupe?"

He looked a little embarrassed. "Well, yes, that, too, of course. But the principal reason I called concerned my little Esmeralda."

He picked the animal up and stroked her. She purred and wriggled languorously in his arms, shedding hairs all over his sleeves. "I did not like to leave her here alone at night and I certainly did not want to put her in a kennel. It would be like—like putting her in prison."

Hortense nodded. "Lady Daphne feels the same about her hounds."

"I thought I might prevail upon you to take her for a few days. But then Damian and Paul kindly agreed to stay in Roland's apartment; and they said they would be happy to look after her, so it seems I will not have to impose on you after all."

Not that you would have stood a chance, Susan thought, making a mental note never to accept a free dress from a couturier again —never to accept a free anything from anyone again, or she might wind up with a zoo in her apartment. Not that that would stop people, even those without any real or imagined claim on her gratitude, from asking favors. Hadn't Lupe, a complete stranger, tried to park Rover and Fido on her? However, she had sensed, even at the time, that hadn't been Lupe's real reason for seeking her and Jill out. People didn't come to New York with wolves unless they had already made provision for them.

Had Lupe been asking for some other kind of help, and had

Susan been too obtuse to realize it at the time? No reason to feel guilty, Susan told herself; she does have my telephone number. She can get in touch with me if she wants to. And maybe she had tried. Maybe there was a message from Lupe on the tape waiting for her, along with all the other messages she hadn't picked up.

A phone rang somewhere in the back of the gallery. Damian's winsome face appeared between the two halves of the glitter curtain. "It's for you, Baltasar."

"Tell whoever it is that I am busy, and I will get back to him later."

"I know that must seem rude," he said to his visitors, "but it has been nothing but one call after the other all morning—the police, the press, the plumbers." He sighed. "I suppose life must go on, but must it go on in such niggling detail?"

"It's that detective who was here yesterday," Damian elucidated. "He seemed rather anxious to talk to you right away."

"Again!" Baltasar paled. "Such a nuisance. I suppose I had better speak to him, though. One must keep in good standing with the police."

He vanished behind the curtain.

"Such a charming man," Hortense said. "Don't you agree?"

Susan agreed.

There was nothing to keep her in the gallery any longer. She made a gesture in the direction of the front door. "Well, now that I know what he wanted, I must be on my way. I know you two have business to discuss."

"Nothing private. I'd be happy to have you stick around. In fact, why don't you come look over the place with me, give me your ideas on what should be done with it? Certainly can't be left the way it is. You should see the apartment that man who was killed had upstairs. I hope I'm not a prude, and I know it's all very artistic, but, oh, my dear!" She rolled her eyes.

"Of course I don't mean the room in the basement where the body was found. That's still sealed off and there's a policeman on guard outside. I will have to see it eventually, because it's part of the space the club will occupy. I understand it's quite gruesome," she added with relish, "all those antique torture instruments. Well, we're going to put in our own instruments of torture."

She whinnied melodiously. "On the other hand, you should see Baltasar's own place at the top of the building. Such a contrast, so tasteful, so elegant."

Susan was surprised. "I thought it wasn't finished. Why is he staying at the Plaza then?"

"I didn't know he was staying at the Plaza, but it certainly looked as if somebody had been living on the top floor here. Cat hairs all over and whatnot."

"That doesn't mean anyone's been living there. Esmeralda sheds all over the place."

"Not just cat hairs. It looked as if a person had been staying there. Of course I only had a glimpse. I'm only supposed to be looking at the gallery floors, but when Baltasar was called to the phone, I couldn't resist dashing upstairs and having a peep."

She giggled. "I'm sure you'll think it was very naughty of me."

Susan did. She also knew she would have been tempted to do the same thing herself. Under normal circumstances, she would have liked to look over the place, even in Hortense's company, but she knew that even at that moment Lieutenant Bracco might be saying to Baltasar, "I've been trying to get in touch with Susan Melville all morning," and Baltasar might be saying, "Why, she's right here. I'll go get her for you."

"Perhaps I could go over the place with you some other time. Afraid I must dash now. I'm late for an appointment."

And she practically ran out of the gallery.

The policeman was standing inside the areaway now, leaning over the gate, staring into the street with unfocussed belligerence. He paid no attention to her. Just the same, she strode purposefully down the street with the air of someone who has a definite destination.

XXIV

AFTER SHE had turned the corner, she slowed down. Why don't I just give up, call Lieutenant Bracco, and make an appointment to see him? she asked herself. All he wants is to ask me a few more questions. Just routine. He isn't suspicious of me; not that there's anything for him to be suspicious of. Might as well get it over with.

That was very sensible advice she had given herself, and she would act on it, she told herself—just as soon as she'd gone to the MAA and spoken to Hal Courtenay. There were several things that needed to be cleared up, and it would be better if they could be taken care of before, rather than after, she spoke to the lieutenant. Why, she didn't even try to explain to herself. It just seemed neater.

She felt a little uneasy about talking to Hal. It wasn't that she feared violence. Even if he were a violent man, he wouldn't be violent in his own museum.

Or would he? Especially since, the way things looked, there was a good chance it was not going to stay his museum much longer. It depended on how much time it would take for the information Andrew had given her about the Turkel Gallery to reach the public.

Hal might try to brazen it out, but what could he say? That he'd been young then? He'd been in his late thirties or early forties, old enough to know better, but that was absurd. No one is ever old enough to know better. He could say he hadn't been a museum curator at the time, so he'd had no responsible position to

betray. But he'd been a critic, an art authority, and a teacher—
sacred callings all three.

Perhaps he would be able to get away with saying he'd merely
tried to bring this neglected artist to the public attention, and had
reaped no financial rewards from the arrangement; but that would
be difficult to prove and impossible to believe. What a pity Darius
Moffatt wasn't Daria Moffatt. Then he could say the artist was his
mother and he had done it for her. His father? No, the American
public didn't feel the same about fathers. In any case, it wasn't the
public he'd have to worry about so much as the Museum's board
of trustees. They were a tough bunch, unlikely to be moved by
sentiment.

He wasn't likely to be left destitute. As Mimi had pointed out,
he couldn't live the way he did on his salary as director of the
Museum; he had to have other resources. Even if the settlement
he'd received almost thirty years before from Cissy Flicker had
been eroded by inflation and attenuated by extravagance, he still
had that island of his to which he could always retire. Alternati-
vely, he could sell it. On the other hand, if he had in some way
been concerned in the deaths of Roland, Rafael, and/or Darius
Moffatt, he might have to worry about more than the prospect of
reduced affluence.

She decided it would not be necessary to call for an appointment before she went to the Museum. If his secretary said he was
busy, she would simply say, "Tell him I know his secret." That
should get her into his office without delay. However, if his secret
fell among the more sinister of her speculations, she might not
find it so easy to get out again. As she recalled, his office and the
corridor outside were plentifully endowed with those old wooden
chests that always seem to be around in museums, and which
seem expressly designed to conceal bodies. She patted her handbag. The gun thumped reassuringly against her side.

The area around the museum was no longer the oasis of peace
and quiet she remembered from the days when she was a young
art student. Today the noise levels approached the threshold of

physical pain. Digging machines were at work in what had once been the museum's parking lot, crunching up rock and spitting it into dumpsters. They were excavating foundations for the Chomsky Addition to the museum. It had turned out the Museum had no choice. The exterior of the building could not be altered. Sometime during the past few years it had been landmarked when nobody was looking. As the only extant work of an architect who had (understandably) never been commissioned to do another public building, it had been designated by the Landmarks Commission as worthy of preservation.

In spite of the excavators' din, street musicians were valiantly playing on their instruments, sidewalk vendors were loudly hawking their wares, and the people whose social life seemed to be spent on the museum's front steps were shouting at each other. The fact that they were failing to communicate did not seem to bother them. They were not there to communicate; only to affirm their existence, apparently through the creation of as much noise as possible.

Not all the vendors were itinerant. A species of flea market had sprung up on either side of the steps. One entrepreneur had been so bold as to set his own (or an associate's) paintings against a wall of the building's projecting side wing. A sudden stop in the excavation process made the words he was bawling audible: "See the finest in contemporary American art at affordable prices, without an admission charge."

Susan wondered whether the Museum ever chose to add to its collections from this cheap and convenient source. The pictures seemed to her as good as (at least no worse than) some of the art inside. But she knew that before the Museum would even deign to acknowledge their existence, they would have to receive the cachet of a gallery exhibition. Otherwise they didn't exist.

A car was waiting outside the Museum. For a moment she thought it was a hearse. Then she saw it was a stretch limousine.

As she made her way toward the building through a gaggle of mimes on the sidewalk, Hal Courtenay came down the steps.

From a distance he looked the same confident, well-tailored figure as always, but as she drew near, she could see the tense, strained look on his face.

He was about to get into the limousine when he caught sight of her. His smile looked so forced it was painful. "Susan, have you come to see me or the Appalachian Exhibit?"

Today he was wearing horn-rimmed spectacles. Behind them his eyes weren't nearly as blue as they had been the last time she'd seen him. They were the paler blue she remembered from art school days. Not only contact lenses but tinted contact lenses. Sham clear through.

"I want to talk to you."

"There is nothing I would enjoy more," he said. But he didn't look gratified. He looked worried. "At the moment, though, I'm afraid I have to go see a Lieutenant Bracco at homicide. In connection with DeMarnay's death. He's questioning everyone who knew DeMarnay, even slightly. A nuisance, but one must cooperate."

He was taking the same tack as Baltasar, but Hal didn't have the excuse of being a foreigner. "I understand that first they're talking to people who knew Roland fairly well; anyhow, people who'd been associated with him, who'd had business dealings with him." There was no reason to suppose this was true, but it was a delicate way of making her point without hammering it in.

From the way he changed color she could see there would be no need to hammer; he took the point. He drew her aside, out of earshot of the driver, away from the curb. This brought them closer to a balloon seller, who seized the opportunity to try to interest them in a balloon bearing a picture of Whistler's Mother.

Hal turned on the balloon seller with a look of such fury that the man fled, balloons bobbing. Hal almost pushed her against the wall of the building. She could feel the barren ivy stems scratching against her hair. "How much did Jill tell you?"

"She didn't tell me anything," Susan said, moving sidewise so she could escape from the ivy's clutches without getting further into Hal's. "It was the police who told me about you."

Of course, according to those concerned, Andrew was not actually part of the police force, but there was no point cluttering her implications with technicalities.

"What did they tell you about me?" he demanded.

She was tempted to say "Everything," in the best melodramatic style. However, that might place her at a decided disadvantage in case there was more that she did not know but that he might think she did—and that might make him feel it necessary to eliminate her on the spot. Not that she was afraid of him. Even though he might possibly, improbably, be armed, she was sure she could outshoot any museum director in the western world. But, although she had not been dismayed by the possibility of having to draw on him in his office, the idea of a shootout in front of the Museum, at—she glanced at her watch—as near as high noon as made no difference, would be ridiculous and undignified.

The events of that morning and the evening preceding must have addled her brain. Why would he kill her to keep her from passing on information that the police had given her in the first place? Unless he then planned to take on the whole police department plus their computers. She couldn't see Hal as Sylvester Stallone. She couldn't see Sylvester Stallone as the director of an art museum.

"I know about the real ownership of the gallery," she said. "The Turkel Gallery, I mean, not the DeMarnay Gallery."

She knew about the real ownership of the DeMarnay Gallery, too, but that was beside the point. It was evident by this time that it had belonged to Baltasar all along, and Roland had been little more than a figurehead. However, as far as she could see, there was no connection between that gallery and Hal or Jill, except through the links of an old animosity.

Hal sighed. "I'd always been afraid that one day it might come out that I'd owned that gallery," he said. "It was a matter of public record. I kept telling myself that there wouldn't be any reason for anyone to look up the record, especially after so much time had passed."

"You took a big risk."

"I didn't realize how much of a risk until it was too late; I'd signed the papers. And, of course, I never really expected to become Director of the MAA then. Well, there goes my job, I suppose." It was no longer a "position."

He seemed to have resigned himself to the prospect. But as soon as he learned of Roland's death, he must have known Roland's past was bound to be investigated and he himself was likely to be found out. Which would seem to argue against his having killed Roland himself. He would hardly have done such a thing, knowing what its inevitable aftermath would be. That is, if he'd killed him in cold blood. If he'd killed Roland in a fit of temper ... That didn't seem like him, but then she didn't really know what he was like.

"You didn't go to Houston, did you?" she asked, trying to keep any accusatory note from her voice.

"No, there was a change in plans. I had to go up to my farm."

She didn't believe that he'd ever had any intention of going to Houston. All he'd wanted was to break his date with her and Jill, for some reason that was none of her concern. It was important to make it clear to him that she took no interest in his private life except insofar as it might be connected with Roland's very public death. "After she heard about Roland, Jill went into a panic. She's afraid somebody's going to kill her."

"Anybody in particular?"

"It looks as if it would have to be somebody who knew both her and Roland."

"There are a number of people who fall into that category, but I take it you're alluding to me." He smiled with what seemed like genuine if bitter amusement. "Believe me, there have been times when I was tempted to kill both of them, but that was long ago. And I assure you that I didn't break our date just so I could kill Roland, because, as I understand it, it would have been perfectly feasible to do both. Dinner first murder, afterward. However, I was up at Litchfield. I do have an alibi, in case you're interested. There was someone with me at the farm."

Since his alibi would have to cover the whole night in order to be valid, she presumed that his companion had been a woman. But it was none of her business, she reminded herself.

He looked at his watch. "Now, more than ever, I don't want to keep the police waiting, but I can see we do need to have a talk as soon as possible. There's something that needs to be straightened out. I'll get in touch with you as soon as the police get through with me."

"I think Jill should be in on this, too."

"I agree. If she is seriously afraid of me, tell her we can meet in my office and I can have one or more of the museum guards posted outside to protect her, in case I go berserk." The idea seemed to amuse him.

Susan just managed to restrain herself from informing him that she could provide all the protection Jill would need, from him at any rate. "I'd be happy to make the arrangements," she said, "but there's just one hitch. I can't find Jill."

"Oh, she'll turn up," he said. "She always does."

XXV

THE LIMOUSINE drove off. She stood there for a moment wondering what to do next. She might even go in and look at the Appalachian Exhibit. But she didn't feel like looking at pictures. She was sick of pictures. Nor did she want to look at statues, curios, architectural models, or period furniture. She'd promised herself to go see the lieutenant as soon as she'd spoken to Hal, but the lieutenant would be busy with Hal now. No sense going over there and having to sit kicking her heels in a waiting room.

Maybe I'll just go home, she thought. But before she had a chance to act on that decision, "Susan, Susan Melville!" a voice called. And Andrew Mackay came out of the Museum and pounded down the steps. Her first impulse was to run, which would be not only unseemly but irrational. Besides, he could probably outrun her.

"I left a message on your phone," he said reproachfully. "You never called me back."

"I haven't had a chance to pick up my messages," she explained.

"I thought you'd like to know I found Jill."

He seemed calm, even cheerful, so she gathered that he had found Jill alive and in reasonably good condition.

"That was quick work. I am impressed."

She was registered at the Hilton."

"Oh, it was that simple."

"Simple!" he repeated indignantly. "Do you have any idea of how many hotels there are in the city?"

She had never thought of looking for Jill at a hotel, not even after Hortense had suggested that that might be where Lupe was. Why then hadn't Jill gone to a hotel in the first place and saved her client a lot of grief? Because she'd been afraid to be alone? Because she was cheap? Perhaps cheapness entered into it, but last evening she had been genuinely afraid. And, unless something had happened that Susan didn't know about, she might still be afraid now.

"Did you tell her you knew that Hal had been the backer of her gallery?" she asked. But of course Jill must have realized that he'd known and had told Susan. Otherwise Jill wouldn't have behaved the way she had.

"I didn't get a chance to tell her anything. She hung up on me. But at least she's safe."

"She was safe when you spoke to her," Susan reminded him. "You don't know where she is now."

"I do know where she is now, and she's safe. I called the lieutenant, and he said he'd send someone to bring her in for questioning. She should be with him now. On her way there, anyhow. Depends on how long it takes her to dress. I don't know very much about her," he said sadly. "I know the bare facts, the kind of things you find in dossiers: social security number, birth date, place of birth, parents' names, school records—"

"She'll hate that," Susan said.

"—But not the important things, like her favorite color and what kind of music she likes and—"

"Did you look for Lupe Montoya in all the hotels, too?"

"I left that to the police," he said. "No reason I should do all their work for them."

"Did they find her?"

"Not so far, at least not under the name of Montoya or Hoffmann."

"Why would there be any reason for her to use another name?"

"I don't know why," he said. "I don't know anything about the woman except what you told me and Baltasar told the lieutenant.

But the people I meet in my line of work use false names as often as not. And the Australian authorities don't seem to have a record of anyone of that name having toured Australia with the kind of act you described."

"Not act, art. Performance art."

"Whatever."

"And I was only repeating what she told Jill and me. I never saw her perform."

"The Australians say there was an act something like that called Dolores and her Dingoes that was closed down. It's possible she was working under that name, except that she told you she couldn't bring any animals with her, and the name of Dolores's act seems to imply that she was working with animals."

"Maybe Lupe didn't want Rover and Fido to know she was working with some native animals and get jealous."

"Well, if we find them we won't tell them. Providing she is—or was—Dolores. And providing they exist."

They'd checked at the airports to see if they could get a line on Lupe through her wolves, but there was no record of any wolves having arrived at either Kennedy or Newark. "And that's the only way you could bring wolves in from the Coast unless you brought them in overland."

Susan thought back. "She didn't actually say she'd brought them with her. She said they'd been left with friends in San Francisco and she was trying to find a place for them here. They might still be in California."

"If they are," he said, "there'd be no way of tracking them down. In California people have all kinds of animals—lions, tigers, elephants. Nobody would notice a pair of wolves. Another funny thing, there's no record of anybody named either Lupe Montoya or Lupe Hoffmann having entered the United States. I know," he said, as she opened her mouth, "Lupe's a short form of something, but the computer's checked out all the possibilities."

"Maybe her passport is still in one of her former husbands' names," Susan suggested.

He frowned. "You didn't say anything about former husbands."

"For heavens' sake, I couldn't be expected to have total recall of every word the woman said, especially something as trivial as that."

"Who knows what name she entered the United States under," he said. "It could all be a perfectly innocent misunderstanding. And probably the reason we can't find her is that she read about DeMarnay's death in the papers and she's lying low. Foreigners tend to be leery of the law."

"That's what Baltasar said."

"He should know. He—" Andrew checked himself. "He seems to be the only one who knows her at all."

"What connection do Baltasar and Lupe have with Hal and Jill?"

"None that I know of. Jill is acquainted with Baltasar and, according to you, Lupe, the same way you are. As far as I know Hal Courtenay and Baltasar haven't met. But that doesn't mean there isn't some connection that we don't know about. Anything else you haven't told me?"

There was something on the edge of her mind, something she couldn't quite get hold of, something Lupe had said or done, which probably was of no importance, but that nagged at her. "Not that I can recall," she said.

It was beginning to get a little cold standing there. Susan thought she might as well go back to her apartment. Besides, as she informed Andrew, she was getting a little tired of being importuned by vendors to buy their wares. "Do you think Jill would like one of those?" he asked, indicating one of the Whistler's Mother balloons.

"I'm sure she wouldn't."

"I was afraid of that," he said sadly. "I don't even know her taste in balloons. Well, if you must go, you must go. By the way," he added, as she turned to leave, "there's something I forgot to tell you. I found out something interesting in connection with that first gallery, the one DeMarnay and Courtenay owned."

"And Jill," she said.

"And Jill," he agreed, "but she was really more of an employee.

Her financial interest was minute; not that DeMarnay's was much bigger. The gallery really belonged to your friend Courtenay."

Had Hal ever really been her friend, she wondered. Was it possible that Jill was still working for him and had been working for him all along, that she had just been a front for him, the same way she had been for the Turkel Gallery? Which would explain why she had seemed so parsimonious; Hal could have been taking the lion's share of the profits from both Melville and Moffatt, and only the IRS would know the truth.

All right, so that first rave review of her work had come before she'd met him and joined Jill, but maybe that had been a promotional venture. He knew he would be bound to meet her because of the Chomsky legacy to the museum and hoped to be in a position to influence her. All those glowing notices afterward, and the museum retrospectives he'd arranged for her, had to be suspect. Even his interest in her might have been merely proprietorial.

No matter that there had been favorable accounts of her work in the press while he had still been in Europe, hot on the trail of those Cassatts, unaware as yet of her existence, or that she might have been just as successful even if he hadn't written a line about her. Whatever he had written about her had all been part of the big hype. She felt like a living Darius Moffatt. *Susan Melville, Woman and Myth*. That wasn't as catchy. *Susan Melville, Woman and Wimp*, *Susan Melville, Painter and Patsy*—that was more like it.

"That's very interesting," she said. "Thank you for telling me, even though I already knew it. And now I really must be—"

"But I told you about that last night," he said. "This is about Darius Moffatt, the guy in that book you lent me."

She waited. "I'm starving. Care to join me for breakfast or—" he looked at his watch "—an early lunch, while I tell you what I found out?"

More bargains. Maybe that was all detective work consisted of, basically, bargains and deals. Still, all he was bargaining for was her company. At the moment she had nothing better to do.

"I could use a cup of coffee," she said.

"Great. How about the Museum cafeteria?"

"The food there always tastes as if it had been left over from an exhibit of something prehistoric."

"Do you have any suggestions? You know the neighborhood better than I do."

"There's a coffee shop over on Madison." They went there and settled on opposite sides of a booth. Suddenly she was very conscious of the weight of the handbag in her lap. I must be sure not to stand up suddenly, she thought; all I need is for it to fall to the ground with a thud.

Andrew ordered a hearty breakfast. "Got to keep up my strength," he said.

She ordered coffee and, since she didn't want to seem ungracious and it had been a long time since breakfast, a muffin. He ate as if he were indeed starving, not speaking until he had put away the better part of a plate of bacon and eggs. "In case you were wondering what I was doing at the Museum, I was there talking to Courtenay. I had to make a phone call and when I came out you were down there talking to him. I didn't like to interrupt, so I waited until you'd finished before I spoke to you. Did he have anything interesting to say?"

"He did say he wasn't the one who killed Roland."

Andrew looked surprised. "Had anybody accused him of killing Roland?"

"It occurred to me as a possibility," she admitted, "and I think it did to Jill, also. Do I take it the idea hadn't occurred to the police?"

"The police suspect everybody," he said. "But, really, Susan, you mustn't go around asking people if they're murderers. It could be dangerous."

"Why were you questioning him then?" she asked. "And why does Lieutenant Bracco want to talk to him now?"

"They're questioning everyone who had any connection with DeMarnay, but I don't think that he's among their prime suspects.

As far as that goes the field's wide open. Anyone could have killed DeMarnay." He grinned. "You, for instance."

Susan smiled and buttered her muffin. "My doorman will tell you I didn't leave my apartment all night."

"Ah, but would he have noticed if you never came in at all? You could have been lurking in the gallery, waited until everyone had gone, killed DeMarnay; then waited until morning and strolled out. Which anybody could have done. Or somebody could have come late at night and DeMarnay let him in. Nobody on the street would have been likely to notice. We both know that."

He took a sip of coffee. "But don't worry. I can assure you the lieutenant doesn't think you did it. That isn't why he wants to talk to you again, which he told me when I called him from the Museum. I'll take you down there as soon as we've finished eating."

Trapped! And no way of getting out of it. If only he'd told her before they'd gone to the coffee shop at least she could have seen to it that he went hungry for a good while longer. Of course, that was why he had waited until now to tell her.

But she didn't need to be escorted into the lieutenant's lair, like some sort of malefactor. "You don't have to come with me," she said.

"Oh, but I do. You're a very elusive lady. Don't worry, I won't put you in handcuffs, unless you start to get rough." He laughed merrily.

You wouldn't laugh if you knew I had a gun in my handbag, she thought. "I was under the impression that you don't have the authority for that," she said. "Or have you been lying to me all along?"

"You're right, I don't have the authority. I'll just phone the lieutenant and tell him to send a police car."

"The way you did with Jill?"

He winced. "I was afraid she'd get violent if I tried to take her down myself, and I didn't think she could be any madder at me than she is now." He waited, but she had no reassurance to offer. "I did suggest to Sergeant Collins that it might be a good idea to interview Courtenay before talking to Jill, if it could be managed. Courtenay's a bigwig at the Museum and the Board of Trustees has a lot of clout. It wouldn't be a good idea to keep him waiting. So we might run into Jill there."

Oh, we might, might we, she thought furiously. Upholding the law is one thing; using me as a cat's paw is another. I hope Jill never speaks to you again. But she knew Jill would. Young men who looked like toothpaste ads were not to be come by easily.

They had been beating about the bush long enough. "I suppose you said you'd found out something interesting about Darius Moffatt just so you could hold me here, while you stuff yourself like a pig."

"I never lie to a taxpayer," he said, pushing a butter-and-syrup-drenched forkful of pancake into his mouth. That clinched it. Even if he wasn't a policeman, he must have an official position of some kind. No private detective would have a qualm about lying to a taxpayer; and probably no public detective either, but he might have a qualm about saying so.

"Remember you said you thought his death might be tied to this whole thing somehow and I said I'd look into it?"

"You mean you found out something to indicate there was a connection?"

"Have another muffin. I plan to continue to stuff myself and it embarrasses me to have you staring at me. Besides, it might be a while before you get to have lunch. Not that the lieutenant is likely to take all that long with you," he added quickly, "but because it may be a while before you get to see him. He's talking to a lot of people today."

She was hungry, and the muffins were surprisingly good—much better than at far more costly establishments, as is so often the case. She ordered another. Some government agency was probably paying.

"About Darius Moffatt," she reminded him, as he took another sticky forkful of pancake. All that cholesterol, she thought. He would get fat and his arteries would harden and it would serve him right.

"I searched the records, went back . . . oh . . . fifteen years. Didn't get any sleep to speak of."

"You're young," she said. "You'll survive. Besides, I expect a computer did most of the work."

"I suppose it's useless to expect any sympathy from you. Well, here's the interesting part. There's no record during that time of anybody named Darius Moffatt dying of a drug overdose, or of anything else, anywhere in the five boroughs of New York City."

The revelation became less startling when she considered the facts. "You must have guessed the biography wasn't . . . er . . . strictly accurate. Even I guessed that and I'm not a detective."

"I just glanced through it," he said. "I assumed that since there was a whole book about him somebody must have done the appropriate research on his life."

"Unless that somebody had reason to alter the facts," she pointed out. "He could have died long before the date they gave. He could have died in another state, another country. He could have died under another name."

"I thought of all those possibilities," he said. "And none of them have been ruled out, of course. On the other hand, there's one that doesn't seem to have occurred to you, one I like a lot better because it explains a lot of things that none of the others does."

"What's that?"

"That he never died at all. In other words, that he's still alive."

XXVI

AFTER ALL her tergiversations and equivocations, her hedging, hemming, dodging, pussyfooting, and (she finally admitted to herself) just plain hiding, Susan's interview with Lieutenant Bracco turned out to be almost an anticlimax. He was kind. He understood perfectly, he said, why she hadn't responded right away to the message he had left on her machine. Of course it wasn't reasonable to expect her to pick up her messages from an outside phone. "I know a lot of ladies have trouble with these mechanical devices," he said, "especially if they haven't grown up with them, so to speak."

Why, you old goat, she thought, I suppose you grew up with them. But then it's only "ladies" who have trouble with "these mechanical devices."

He even forgave her for having neglected to mention Jill's connection with Roland and for not having mentioned Lupe at all. She must have been all shaken up on learning of Roland's grisly death; it was only natural for her to have overlooked such details. How could she, in the stress of the moment, have been expected to realize how important these details might be.

By and large it was the same explanation, rather, extenuation, she had prepared in her mind, but if it had come from her it would have been self-serving; from him it was patronizing, and she did not take kindly to being patronized. If there hadn't been a glass window in his office, through which they were visible to an assortment of police personnel, she wouldn't have put it past him to have patted her hand. And then, in spite of her determination to be amiable and placatory, she would have been arrested for attacking an officer of the law.

Either Andrew had succeeded in getting Jill's interview with the lieutenant postponed until after Hal's, or the fates had ordered it that way, for Susan ran into Jill as she was on her way into, and Jill on her way out of, the lieutenant's office. But that happened only after Susan had been waiting for nearly three-quarters of an hour in an anteroom, along with a number of very odd-looking people and no sign of Hal.

Andrew waited with her, to keep her company, he said, but she knew it was in the hope of getting a chance to speak to Jill. Susan would gladly have done without his company. There was a lot she wanted to think about. However, there didn't seem to be any civil way of getting rid of him—or uncivil, either, she suspected, though she was incapable of putting that to the test, for she could never bring herself to deliberate rudeness. In any case, she thought, after she'd gotten a good look at the somewhat outré individuals who shared the waiting room with them, she would probably have had no chance for solitary reflection. All, except the ones who were already carrying on animated conversations with themselves, looked disposed for a chat.

In fact there was one elderly man, garbed in a long black cape and with a bald head that ran up to a peak, who took a warm interest in her from the moment she entered the room. After she had ignored his winks and leers for some minutes, he finally interrupted the conversation she was holding with Andrew on matters of minor meteorological interest with, "Why don't you run off and play with somebody your own age, sonny? This lady looks like just my type."

"He can't leave me," she said, before Andrew was able to stop her. "He's a plainclothesman assigned to guard me because I'm very dangerous."

The uniformed policeman standing at the door raised an eyebrow. Andrew shrugged.

"Dangerous, eh? That's the way I like 'em," the old man cackled, moving his chair closer to hers. "How about it, baby?"

"Get lost, grandpop," Andrew snapped, "before I deck you. And I'm not a policeman, so don't start licking your lips over the idea of a police brutality charge. It'd just be a plain misdemeanor. And worth it."

"He's a private investigator," Susan said, not wanting to be publicly branded a liar even before a public such as this. "Very tough."

"You're not Magnum, are you?" a woman with chrome green hair and a face that was either masked or so heavily painted that the effect was the same asked.

"Don't be silly," a woman wearing a nun's habit said. "He's one of the Simon brothers, of course. The cute blond one."

They stared at him avidly.

"Ladies," Andrew said. "Magnum and the Simons are fictional. I'm real."

"Of course you are," the greenhead said. They cackled in unison with the pointy-headed old man.

Andrew got up and went over to the door. "Isn't there someplace else we could wait?" he asked the man in uniform.

"Are you asking for special privileges?"

"Yes," Andrew said.

"The answer is no."

At that point Sergeant Collins came along to escort Susan to the lieutenant's office, from which they met Jill emerging. Although there was an angry expression on her face, she seemed a lot less tense than she had the night before—almost relieved, as if a weight had been lifted from her. She must have unburdened herself to Lieutenant Bracco in some way, Susan deduced, and wondered whether there was any chance she could weasel out of the lieutenant what it was that Jill had told him.

Jill caught sight of her client and looked even angrier. "You had to go and sic the police on me," she snarled.

"Not the police," Susan said, "just him."

And she pointed to Andrew, who stood his ground, where a lesser man would have shrunk at the expression of utter loathing on his beloved's face.

"I was worried about you after you walked out like that," Susan explained.

"Well, he's a policeman."

"Not a policeman exactly," Andrew said. "Or even approximately. Just an *amicus curiae* or whatever it is when there is no actual court."

"Friend of the family?" Sergeant Collins suggested helpfully.

"And I went looking for you," Andrew said, "because I was worried about you, too."

"Oh, sure! You just wanted to rack up brownie points for fingering me."

"That's not true. I don't get credit of any kind. It's not my—my job."

"Then why did you tell the police where I was once you knew I was safe?"

"But I didn't know you were safe. Funny things have happened even in the best hotels. And I told the police about you because —well—because I had to," he admitted.

"In other words, he could not love thee dear so much, loved he not honor more," Sergeant Collins said. "Now would you please come this way, Miss Melville? The lieutenant is getting impatient."

Querulous noises from within appeared to support his claim.

"Just a minute, I'm sure the lieutenant won't mind," she said, ignoring the expression on the sergeant's face. "Jill, I have to have a talk with you as soon as possible. Where will I be able to reach you later?"

Jill thrust out her chin pugnaciously. "What do you want to talk to me about?"

As if she didn't know. "About you and me and Hal and our various interconnecting relationships."

Jill turned on Andrew. "Blabbermouth. All right, go and detect. I suppose you have to; someone has to clean the sewers. But did you have to tell her about Hal and me? It isn't any of her business. Or yours either."

He opened his mouth as if to deny the allegation; then seemed to think better of it, probably because I'm here to give him the lie, Susan thought. "I had to tell her," he said. "It is her business. She deserved to know."

"Oh, you're so fucking upright you make me sick."

"We can't have language like that in a police station, Miss," Sergeant Collins said reproachfully. "It'll give us a bad name."

"The whole thing was bound to come out sooner or later once Roland was killed," Susan told Jill. "Even Hal admits that. Don't you think it's better that I should hear it from Andrew instead of reading it in the papers?"

It would have been best of all if she could have heard it from Jill herself, but she supposed that would have been too much to expect.

The lieutenant appeared in the doorway of his office. He was in shirtsleeves and looked as though he were at the end of his tether. If he'd been dealing with friends and associates of Roland's all morning, Susan could understand it.

"What's going on here? Why is Miss Melville standing out there instead of coming in here?"

"My fault entirely," Susan said. "I stopped for a word with my representative." She indicated Jill.

"I can see how you would want to have a number of words with her," he said, glaring at Jill. She glared back. Apparently their meeting had not been devoid of acrimony. "You'll have to wait until later to deal with her, though. And what are *you* doing here?" he demanded, as he caught sight of Andrew. "Is this a police station or a lonely hearts bureau?"

Andrew paid no attention. "Look, Jill," he said, "please come have a drink with me. In fact, it's lunch time; let's have lunch."

After that breakfast he just ate, Susan thought, he's likely to swell up and burst; and she, for one, was not going to feel sorry for him.

"I can explain everything. Well, not everything but a lot. At least hear me out."

"Seems to me it's she who should do the explaining," the lieutenant observed. "Go with him, Jill," he ordered, "or I'll have you arrested for loitering."

Jill looked at Andrew. Andrew looked at Jill. Although she was obviously fighting to hold her stern expression, it softened. He was really a very personable young man.

"Well," Jill said, "I don't have anything planned, since you went and busted up my schedule, so I might as well hear what you have to say. Besides, I could use some police protection."

And, as Andrew opened his mouth, "Protection from the police, that is."

"And now, Miss Melville, if you would . . ." The lieutenant indicated the interior of his office.

"Susan," Jill called, as Susan started to go inside. Susan turned. The lieutenant emitted a hissing sound, like a kettle about to boil over.

"Gil Stratton didn't really ask you to be his client, did he? That was just a ploy to get my attention, wasn't it?"

"No, it was true. He's been after me to sign up with him for nearly a year."

"The bastard," Jill muttered. "You just can't trust anyone any more."

After that, Susan's interview with the lieutenant was short and comparatively sweet—except for her thoughts, which she kept to herself. He wouldn't tell her why he seemed so interested in Lupe or what Baltasar had done to make him look so black every time the man's name was mentioned. Was it simply because Baltasar hadn't informed him of Lupe's existence? No. From his expression, it had to be more than that.

He was more forthcoming about Hal and Jill. They had, to his knowledge, done nothing illegal, at least as far as his own area of operations was concerned. "I'm not even sure they could be accused of product misrepresentation," he said. "In any case that would be the concern of some other agency—Department of Consumer Affairs, maybe. Which doesn't mean they're the kind of people a nice lady like you should be associating with. If you'll take the advice of somebody who's maybe got a little more street smarts than you, you'll get yourself another agent. Maybe that girl isn't actually crooked, but she isn't straight either."

"What makes you think so?" Susan asked. "Did she tell you anything to give you that idea?"

"If she did I'm afraid it's privileged information," he said, smiling to show he was not reproaching her for what was, after all, natural female curiosity. "Now, I have a nephew—"

"I do have a contract with Jill," Susan pointed out.

"Speaking off the record and as a private citizen rather than a police officer, contracts were made to be broken."

"I'm going to have to consult a lawyer before I do anything about that."

"Let me tell you about lawyers. No matter what side they're supposed to be on, they're nothing but—"

He cut himself short. "I better be careful what I say. Even here the walls have ears."

Susan visualized a wallpaper patterned with ears of varying size. No, she was a fine artist; she did not do wallpaper. A mural, though, would be another matter—a pattern of ears growing on vines (which turned into telephone wires, perhaps), on which bugs were crawling. And then some designer could turn it into wallpaper and drapery patterns and she would reap royalties. I am developing a business sense, she thought, a little sadly.

As for Darius Moffatt, the lieutenant said, he had no interest in him whatsoever. "If he's dead and there's no reason to suspect he was murdered, it has nothing to do with me; and if he's alive, it has nothing to do with anybody."

She made a last desperate effort. "How about the Bureau of Missing Persons?"

"Nobody's reported him missing."

"I'm reporting him missing."

"You don't have the authority to report him missing, Miss Melville. You're not a relative or even a close friend. You've never even met him. Why," he said, working himself up to oratorical pitch, "you don't even know that he exists."

And suddenly she saw the answer. Where Darius Moffatt was and where the mysterious picture had come from and why Jill had kept on lying to her, even when there seemed to be no more need. What a fool she'd been not to see it before. True, the rest of the world had been fooled, too, but they had not had the advantage of her superior and peculiar insights.

"Goodby, lieutenant," she said. "You've given me a lot to think about."

And he had, indeed.

XXVII

IT WAS the middle of the afternoon by the time Susan got home; after stopping en route for a quick lunch she found she couldn't eat. She played back the messages on her tape. None from Lupe. She hadn't really expected to hear from Lupe, but it would have been reassuring to hear her voice.

She picked up the phone and dialed the number of the gallery. It was Damian who answered, fortunately. If Baltasar had picked up, she would have had to give an explanation for the request she was about to make. Undoubtedly she would be able to make up a plausible explanation, but it would be increasing the risks.

"Damian," she began, after identifying herself ("not that you need to tell me who you are, dear Miss Melville, I would recognize your voice anywhere"), "I don't want to bother Baltasar, but—"

"You couldn't bother him if you wanted to. He left an hour or so after you did, saying he wouldn't be back for a few days and Paul and I would be in full charge until he returned. Such an awesome responsibility."

"That must have been a sudden decision," she said. "He didn't say anything to me about going on a trip."

"It couldn't have been sudden, because he brought his bags with him already packed when he came in this morning."

"He did say something the other day about going back to Madrid, to see about replacements for the gowns that were damaged in the fire." Of course the lieutenant had told him not to leave the state, which would automatically imply that he should not leave the country, either, but perhaps Baltasar hadn't understood that.

"Oh, he couldn't be going to Spain," Damian said, "because an official-looking person came by soon after that phone call that came when you were just about to leave and took his passport. He was very angry. Baltasar, I mean, not the official-looking person, who preserved an Olympian calm. The things Baltasar said after the man had gone! He really added to my Spanish vocabulary. And then he told us we should take care of things, and he left."

He waited, as if inviting her to offer her comments on the situation, but she had nothing to say, at least not to him.

"Damian, I wonder whether you'd do me a favor?"

"Anything at all, Miss M. Your wish is my command."

"Could you get me the address and phone number of Baltasar's assistant, Mrs. Gutierrez? You remember, the lady who fitted my dress? I'd like to get in touch with her."

"Sanchia? Nothing easier. The police took Rollie's Rolodex—" he started to laugh, then choked a little before he could go on. "We've always done most of Baltasar's paperwork, though. He didn't have any staff here yet, except Sanchia, of course, and that weird husband of hers. Neither of them speaks much English; in fact, I don't think Diego speaks any. So we do have Baltasar's address file. It's upstairs. If you'll hold on, I'll be back in a jiffy."

As she waited for him, she found her nervousness increasing, her self-confidence ebbing. Should I be doing this on my own, she asked herself. Wouldn't it be better if I told the police or Andrew what I thought? But her suspicions were so nebulous she couldn't put them into words. If she did she was afraid they might turn out to be ridiculous. She had been able to put up with the lieutenant's attitude of lofty superiority, because she knew he was a male chauvinist fool. She did not want to appear before him as the "womanly woman"—i.e., the female fool—he took her to be.

She was not going ahead with this on her own, for the sake of her ego, she told herself. She was doing it to keep the possibly innocent from harassment. Not that she believed anyone of those involved was wholly innocent. Even Esmeralda had her secrets.

Damian picked up the phone. He was slightly out of breath. He gave her the address and telephone number, adding helpfully, "That's in Queens. Over the river, but not through the woods. Terra incognita."

"I know where Queens is."

"You're so well informed about such things. I suppose it comes from your . . . er . . . fiancé's being an anthropologist."

Of course Peter's existence was no secret, and she knew that people did gossip; it was an established form of recreation these days. Just the same she was annoyed. She thought of telling Damian that Peter was not her er . . . fiancé but her lover, and that they had no intention of getting married, but she was afraid she would embarrass the poor boy. Despite his inclinations, he was basically very conventional. Besides, the word *lover* had acquired such squalid connotations through years of misuse that it was not really appropriate.

She knew the safest course would be to approach Sanchia at phone's length. But it would be hard to get the information she wanted without causing alarm. Sanchia's English was, as Damian had pointed out, meager. It would be hard to convey delicate nuances of suspicion in Basic English. If there was anything to be learned in Jackson Heights, she would have to appear there unannounced and alone.

Perhaps she should tell someone where she was going just in case. But who? Alex? He would tell her to keep out of it, that it was none of her business. If she insisted, he might even insist on accompanying her. The same would hold true for Andrew, even if she could get hold of him. She had no idea where he and Jill might have gotten to.

Maybe I could leave a note with Alex's doorman, she thought, inscribed "To be opened only in case of my death or disappearance," but it might cause talk in case she didn't die or disappear. She remembered how embarrassing the results of her suicide note had been when she'd changed her mind and killed her landlord instead of herself.

Her phone rang. She let it deliver its message while she listened on the monitor without acknowledging her presence. The monitor was, she had often thought, the answering machine's one saving grace.

The caller was Mimi, full of news. Eloise Charpentier had finally gotten her divorce, after a great deal of unpleasantness on the part of her third (or was it her fourth?) husband who'd been trying to get more than his fair share of the Charpentier billions; Ariel Slocum—"

Susan turned down the sound without waiting to hear what Ariel Slocum had been up to. She let the tape run on for its two-minute maximum before the caller got cut off. At the end of the two minutes, the phone rang again. Susan turned up the sound. This time it was Hortense Pomeroy. Susan turned down the sound.

The third time the phone rang, she almost didn't bother to turn the sound up. She couldn't resist, however, and she was glad she had, because it was Jill. She wanted to talk to Jill.

She picked up the receiver.

"Oh, you are there," Jill said. "Why did you make me listen to all that rigmarole then?"

"Wasn't that just like Jill? All Susan's tape gave was her name and an invitation for the caller to leave a message if so inclined. Jill's recording, which included not only her name, but her current hopes, fears, and plans took up so much of the tape there was little time for the caller to do more than give his or her name and telephone number.

"I'm at the MAA," Jill said. "In Hal's office, as a matter of fact."

Susan was surprised. So Hal had gone ahead and made the arrangements by himself. Just as well, it would spare her the necessity of tracking Jill down. But it was Jill who must have approached Hal, because Hal wouldn't have known where to find her.

"I thought you'd still be with Andrew," she said. "Or didn't he

succeed in getting you to forgive him? Not that there was anything to forgive. He was only doing his duty, whatever that is."

"I know, I know. Don't you start in on me about that too. We
had lunch at Leatherstocking's, and he explained how he couldn't
help ratting on me, because it was part of his job."

"What is his job exactly?"

"He didn't say exactly, but I gather that either it's very hush-
hush or he's ashamed of it. I'll get it out of him sooner or later. I
don't suppose it pays a lot. He nearly fainted when he saw the
prices on the menu. He wouldn't let me pay for the lunch,
though; he's very old-fashioned about things like that; don't you
love it? So I had them put it on your account. You don't mind, do
you?"

"No," Susan said wearily, "I don't mind."

"I told him *everything*. As much as he needs to know, anyway. I
explained to him how the things he knew already weren't as bad
as they looked."

And the things he didn't know? Susan had a feeling they might
be worse, but who was she to put a blight on young love? Let
someone else do it.

"Andy said I ought to get things straightened out with you before I do anything else, and that's why I'm up in Hal's office now.
We're going to have a meeting. You and Hal and I, that is. Andy
doesn't want any part of it. Just keep things approximately legal,
he says."

Good Lord, Susan thought, he's going to try to make an honest
woman out of her. She wished him luck, but didn't think much of
his chances.

"You sound a lot different today than you did last night," Susan
told Jill. "You were practically hysterical then. What's happened to
calm you down?"

"I guess I was overreacting a little," Jill admitted. "People I
know don't get murdered very often, not even acquaintances. But
talking to that pig—" by which Susan presumed she meant Lieutenant Bracco "—helped me get things in perspective."

"I'm glad to hear it," Susan said. "What—?"

"So come over right now and we'll get this thing over with."

"I told you, I'm busy right now. How about tonight? Or would tomorrow be more convenient?"

"It's got to be right now!" Jill wailed. There was a thud on the other end of the wire that sounded as if she were stamping her foot. "Right away! I have a dinner date with Andy tonight and I've got to get through with this as soon as possible, so I can go downtown and buy a really smashing dress."

"He'll think you look lovely no matter what you wear."

"I do look lovely no matter what I wear. But this is an Occasion and an Occasion calls for a new dress." There was a dreamy quality in her voice. "I think this time it's the real thing."

Susan had heard her say the same thing before, in the same tone of voice. But I mustn't be cynical, she thought. Maybe this time it is real. Maybe the other times it was, too.

"Go buy your dress," she said. "I can meet you tomorrow. I have to go to Queens today."

"To Queens!" Jill shrilled. "What are you going to Queens for? You don't think you're going to Long Island City to get your paintings out of the warehouse, do you? Because, if you do—"

"I'm going to Jackson Heights. Nothing to do with you." Eventually, she was going to have to get the pictures out of Jill's clutches, but there was no hurry, especially since as yet she had no idea of whose clutches she was going to deliver them into.

"I'll bet you don't know how to get to Queens."

"I take a cab."

"All right, I lose my bet. But couldn't you stop over here before you go out to Queens? It wouldn't take long. Hal wants to talk to you before he writes his letter of resignation to the Board. I think he's crazy myself. I think he ought to hang tough until he's kicked out. It'll take time before the news gets around. Maybe it won't get out at all. After all, who's interested, really?"

The Board of Trustees would be interested, Susan thought, as well as every artist about whom Hal had written unkind things. Even if the general publications didn't pick it up or give it much space—since the masses might not understand what was so wrong in a critic's favorably reviewing the paintings shown in a gallery which he happened to own, or the curator of a museum not only representing an artist but writing glowing articles about him—*Connoisseur* would go for Hal's jugular, and then the art magazines would move in for the kill.

No, there was no way he could avoid scandal, but there was a way he might be able to turn it to his advantage. And, not being ill-disposed toward her old classmate, she did want to talk to him before he burned his bridges in the wrong direction.

"All right," she said. I'll come over right away. But it can't take too long."

"I told you, I have a date with Andy. We've got to keep it short."

XXVIII

HAL'S OFFICE had been designed to impress. Panelled in age-darkened wood, it was furnished with massive eighteenth- and early nineteenth-century pieces that had been not considered quite worthy of the Museum's collections, either because they had been restored by some vandal more interested in utility than in authenticity or because they were a trifle dubious to begin with. Hal was sitting behind his desk as Susan entered. He rose and came to meet her and would have taken her coat, but she refused saying, "No, thank you, I won't be staying long."

He was no longer wearing spectacles, but she knew now that the color of his eyes was not a true blue. "Susan, I can't tell you how sorry I am," he began.

"I'm sure you are," she cut him off. "We all are. But there's no point going into that now. I don't have much time, but Jill said it was important we meet now."

"Please sit down." He indicated a Chippendale wing chair. And, when she hesitated, "No matter how short a time you're staying, you'll be more comfortable sitting down. At least I'll be."

She looked at him. What made him think she cared whether he was comfortable or not?

"I won't take it as a sign of forgiveness if you sit down," he said, "although I hope you will forgive me—a little, anyway—when you hear the whole story."

"The whole story doesn't concern me," she said. "What does concern me is whether Jill was working for you or for me?"

"I was working for both of you," Jill piped up. "What's wrong with that? I never said you were my only client." She was already sitting down, in the most comfortable chair in the room, and looked her old perky self.

"But he's not your client," Susan pointed out. "He's your employer."

"Not any more," Jill said. But when had their relationship ended?

"If you'll just sit down and listen, Susan," Hal said, "I'll explain how it all came about."

Grudgingly she sat down. He started to sit behind his desk; then thought better of it and took another wing chair across from hers, not so close that he would encroach on her space.

"I started the gallery for a lark really. I'd always thought that if I couldn't be a painter, owning a gallery was what I'd like to do. And I couldn't own one in my own name. Jill and I were living together at the time. I'd met her at a course I was teaching at the New School. I forget its title, but the general idea was how to talk about contemporary art as if you understood it, even if you didn't. It was very popular."

He smiled reminiscently. He means he was very popular, Susan thought. She was willing to make a small bet that most of his students had been female.

"Jill had just finished college and had some kind of low-level job with a third-rate PR firm—"

"I was a trainee," Jill said indignantly, "and the firm might have been small but it was very prestigious. Everybody said I had a great career ahead of me."

"I thought it would be nice if I could set up something that would give her more meaningful work, and that would belong to both of us."

Jill snorted. "Belong to both of us! You needed a magnifying glass to see my percentage. Even Roland's was bigger."

There was good reason for that, Hal explained. Roland had been brought in because Hal had had no expertise as a dealer, and

Jill had no expertise at anything at all—at least that related to an art gallery. The gallery had been put in her name only because Roland had to be kept in the background.

Both of them had, according to Hal, received generous salaries (here Jill sniffed) in addition to their percentages.

"Since the gallery had been losing money up until the first Moffatt show, everything—salaries, overhead, running expenses—had come out of Hal's pocket.

The plan had been for the gallery to show the work of promising little-known or unknown artists, and for Hal to write enthusiastic reviews for some of their artists. "Not all," he said, "or it would look suspicious. I figured that would make the pictures sell, and in time the gallery would pay for itself, I didn't count on anything more than that."

"He thought all he had to do was write up an exhibit favorably," Jill said, "and buyers would come running, checkbooks in hand."

"Perhaps I did suffer from an excess of *hubris*," he acknowledged. "By the time we broke with Roland, we'd already had three exhibits. I'd written enthusiastic reviews for two of them and—" he smiled sadly "—nobody else paid the least attention. Nobody else wrote a review. Nobody bought the pictures."

Hal's pockets were not all that deep. As things stood, he couldn't afford to keep the gallery going. Then Roland came to him with a proposition. An acquaintance of his knew a Colombian artist who was anxious to have his work shown in New York, and was willing to pay for the privilege. "Roland showed me some of his work. Decent stuff in the traditional style: nothing to get excited about; nothing to be ashamed of. Something to be going on with until we could find a painter who would sell."

He swore that they had not known about the drug deal. When Customs found cocaine in the frames of the pictures, he had been genuinely shocked and angry. Jill was still angry. "Roland went and set up the whole thing without cutting us in on it!"

"That was because he knew we would never go along with such a thing, of course," Hal said smoothly.

Jill shot a glance at Susan. "Of course. We wouldn't have dreamed of it. But," she burst out, "he was a double-crossing weasel all the same."

They had gotten rid of Roland immediately. Which left them without a show. "And just then Old Mother Moffatt happened to turn up with the paintings?" Susan asked.

"Why are you using that tone of voice, Susan?" Hal asked. "Artists and their relatives were always coming around trying to get us to show their work. She just happened to come around at the right time. You're shaking your head, as if you didn't believe me."

"I don't believe you. There is no record of Darius Moffatt's ever having died of a drug overdose in the East Village or anywhere else. There's no record of his ever having died at all."

Hal and Jill looked at one another. "Uh—oh," Jill said. "I told you people would start asking questions about Moffatt once they got to know about your connection with my gallery. I still think of it as my gallery," she explained, "because it was in my name and everybody thought of it as mine."

"Spiritually it was your gallery, and always will be," he assured her.

"Thanks a lot," she said.

"I'd been beginning to wonder about Moffatt long before Andrew told me that Hal was the one who actually owned the gallery," Susan said.

It then had to be explained to Hal who Andrew was.

"That investigator who was up here before!" he said incredulously. "He's the man you're going out with tonight?"

"Yeah," Jill said. "Ain't love wonderful?"

"Well," Susan demanded, "is Darius Moffatt dead or alive?"

"He's dead, of course," Jill said crossly. "Don't you believe what you see in print? All right, so maybe he didn't die in the East Village, or even in New York. We wanted to hide the truth, that he was a—a sex fiend and murderer, and he died in jail. Under a false name. We didn't reveal the truth because we wanted to spare his family pain."

"And you made up the whole East Village story to spare the family pain?"

"Yes," Jill said.

"And his mother went along with that? The drug overdose and all? Didn't she find that painful? Or were you going by degree of pain?"

Jill tossed her head and was silent.

Hal cleared his throat. "Don't pay any attention to Jill; she's of a melodramatic turn. We kept the true story secret so as not to offend religious sensibilities."

Both Jill and Susan looked at him.

"Darius—only that wasn't his real name, of course—belonged to a religion which forbade the creation of graven images. His family was very orthodox; consequently he painted under the name of Darius Moffatt, so his relatives would never know what he was doing."

"So he travelled around the country leaving the paintings with them? Susan asked.

"That was the reform branch of the family," Hal said.

Jill snorted.

"And what did he die of?" Susan asked.

"Natural causes," Hal said. "A thunderbolt. Oh, what's the use. I can see you don't believe me."

"How could she?" Jill asked. "Any religion that forbids graven images wouldn't be the least bit bothered by the things Darius painted."

Hal looked keenly at Susan. "You've guessed the truth, haven't you? When I first met you again, after all those years, I was afraid you might. And then I realized I'd been suffering from *hubris* again. You didn't remember anything about me."

That wasn't strictly true, but the things she had remembered were the things he had probably himself forgotten, or wanted to forget.

"The truth didn't hit me until this afternoon," she told him, "while I was in Lieutenant Bracco's office. It was from something he said, but, don't worry, he didn't realize what he was saying. There never was a Darius Moffatt, was there? Except that, since it must have been you who painted the pictures, I suppose it could be said that you are Darius Moffatt."

"Nonsense," Hal said weakly.

"I should have known. Somebody who really wants to paint doesn't give up painting that easily. And, you're right, I should have remembered. I'm sorry."

It was coming back to her now—the student who had driven the teachers crazy by painting like Van Gogh one week, Braque the next, Matisse the third. It had made little impression on her at the time. Technical facility was not something the students at the Hudson were encouraged to set store by. The ability to express one's own personal inner vision was what counted. And Hal, so far as anyone could tell, had had no personal inner visions.

But he'd been so young then. There'd been no reason for him to give up. In time he could have developed a style of his own. And where would he have been then? Perhaps where Susan had been before she killed General Chomsky. Nowhere.

Jill wasn't ready to concede defeat. "Don't pay any attention to Hal, Susan. You've got it all wrong. Except the part about Darius being alive. He is alive, I admit. He didn't die in prison. He's serving a life sentence for—for unspeakable crimes. And he must have smuggled out that painting somehow and consigned it to Allardyce's—the skunk!" She glared at Hal.

"Give it up, Jill," Hal said. "She knows. The thing is, does anyone else know?"

"I haven't told anybody, if that's what you mean. And I don't intend to tell anybody, unless there's something more that I don't know that could make it necessary. But I feel I should mention as a matter of general interest that I have written a full account of my conjectures and deposited it in a safe place, where it will be opened in the event of my death."

"Susan," Hal said reproachfully, "you don't really think I . . . Or even Jill . . . ?"

"What do you mean 'or even Jill'?"

"Of course I don't think you'd . . . er . . . do anything to me. But it's always wise to take precautions."

"That was the real reason you set up the gallery, wasn't it, Hal?" Susan went on. "What you really planned to do was exhibit the Moffatt paintings, review them favorably, and clean up on them— at least make some money from them. The other exhibits were just window dressing. You didn't really expect them to go anywhere. They were just to establish the gallery as a legitimate showcase."

For some reason Jill laughed. Hal shook his head. "Now, there I can say in all honesty you're wrong. I'd never planned to show the Moffatt pieces. I just did them for fun. I'd always had the knack of being able to paint in any artist's style."

"I remember now," she said.

"It took you a long time," he said bitterly. "I remembered *you* clearly from the start. But who could forget having been a class-mate of Susan Melville, one of *the* Melvilles. Every student in the class was aware of you and determined not to be impressed, or at least to show it."

She was stunned. "I never realized. It never even occurred to me to think the other students might feel that I was anybody special."

"That was the worst part. You were different, and you didn't even have the grace to realize how different you were. When I picked Jill to be a front for the gallery, I tried to teach her a little about modern art. I amused myself by doing a series of paintings that combined all the most egregious elements of con-temporary art at once. She and I used to kid around about exhibiting them some day as the work of a real person. We even gave him a name. But we never seriously intended to show them. At least I didn't."

"Me either," Jill said. "My artistic tastes hadn't been refined yet and I thought they were terrible." She paused to reflect. "I still do."

* * *

"I know this is a silly question but who were the photographs .of?" Susan asked.

"They were of me. After I got divorced from Cissy, I spent a summer working with the Peace Corps—why, I don't know—to prove something to myself, maybe. That was when the pictures were taken. I was sure nobody would recognize them since I'd never looked like that before or since. It was a kind of private joke—not very funny, I suppose, but then private jokes seldom are funny."

XXIX

SOMETHING OCCURRED to Susan. "Hal, it didn't by any chance happen to be you who painted those forgeries that Roland sold General Chomsky? And that you then authenticated?"

"Of course not. How could you even suggest such a thing? That would be illegal, as well as most improper." There was a smile on his lips, not just a smile—a smirk, a self-satisfied smirk.

"Sorry. I'd forgotten you always operate within the bounds of propriety, as well as the strict letter of the law."

"Incidentally, it was only one forgery that caused the trouble."

"The one that made the General get rid of Roland, you mean?"

He nodded. "As I've said, I had nothing to do with it—or with any others still around that haven't been called into question."

He paused. For some reason he was looking pleased with himself. "However, it has sometimes occurred to me—in one of the wild flights of fancy to which I am occasionally given—how amusing it would be to think that Hal Courtenay might be represented in some of the major art collections of the world, not merely the Chomsky collection, although under a *nom de brosse,* as it were."

Using the name of another artist was not precisely a *nom de brosse,* Susan thought, but this was no time to quibble. "Speaking hypothetically, of course," she said, "I can't help wondering why, if Hal Courtenay had been so successful at forging the big names in art, he would have given it up? Of course I know he was doing it for the excitement. He didn't need the money. Still..."

"I don't know about Hypothetical Hal, but Real-Life Hal certainly did need the money. And continues to need it. I know people think I'm well off, but I'm not. To begin with, I never got as much money from Cissy Flicker as people thought I had. They always exaggerate. They seem to think the more money you get, the worse you are; and, of course, they always like to think the worst."

"Only human nature," Jill said. "Bad is more fun than good."

Hal ignored her and addressed himself to Susan. "I'd already begun to grow accustomed to a life style the earnings of an assistant curator and art critic couldn't support. I made some bad investments that left me worse off than before."

"But why didn't you—excuse me—Hypothetical Hal go on forging paintings?"

"He got cold feet after the General cut up so rough about that alleged Picasso. The General suspected that Hal had been working with Roland. He couldn't make any charges without some kind of proof, because Real-Life Hal held a respected position in the art world. If the General had been wrong, he could have been sued and taken for everything he had."

"So that's why Jill's name had to go on the gallery," Susan said.

"Exactly. The General was out to get me if he could. If he had the faintest suspicion that Roland had any connection with the gallery, he would have his people investigate. They would find out that I owned a majority interest and then . . ." He shook his head. "I don't know what he might have done."

Maybe Hal didn't know, but Susan had a pretty good idea. When Hal had said earlier that he hadn't realized the risks he was taking in starting the gallery with Roland, he didn't know the half of it.

"Then the pictures you discarded as forgeries after the MAA inherited the Chomsky collection—or some of them, anyway— were the ones you . . . that is, Hypothetical Hal had painted and then authenticated?"

"Isn't it a hoot!" Jill said.

Hal shrugged. "The merest few."

Did he mean there had been only a few of his own forgeries in the Chomsky collection, or had he deaccessioned only a few, leaving the rest as part of the permanent collection?

She didn't think she wanted to know the answer. "But what about Jill? Was she working for you or for me? I know what she said, but I also know Jill."

Jill made a face at her. Susan tried not to smile.

"As far as the Moffatts went, she was still working for me," he admitted. "What did she know about art at the beginning? One course at the New School, which she would have flunked if it had been given for credit."

"But you said—"

"I said a lot of things I didn't mean then," he told her. And, to Susan, "Jill kept on getting her percentage the same as if the gallery had stayed open; and she was getting a very good salary, too—almost as much as I was getting at the Museum, as a matter of fact."

Susan waited for Jill to deny this, but Jill remained silent. I must ask Mimi how much the director of the MAA makes, Susan thought. But of course he had been only a curator at the time. And, it was none of Susan's business.

"You were something else, though," he said. "By the time you signed up with her, she was an experienced rep. You were her entire responsibility. I had nothing to do with you—as Jill's client, that is."

He caught Jill's eye. "Well, maybe I did take a small percentage, a sort of finder's fee, for having introduced her to you. That's quite usual in art circles; you know that."

She did know that. Just as it was usual in medical and legal and financial circles. Just the same, it left a bitter taste in her mouth.

"That's not the whole story," Jill said. "For the first year you were with me, he made me split my commissions with him. Then I told him enough was enough. My name was on the contract. I was doing all the work. Since we had already decided Darius Moffatt was finished—we really couldn't keep on finding more pictures—we were each on our own. So he goes and paints another picture and consigns it to Allardyce's."

"I'm really sorry," Hal said. "I know it looks as if I were—"

"Double-crossing me. You bet it does."

"It so happens that I'm financially strapped."

"Down to your last yacht, you mean," Jill snapped. "Why don't you sell that stupid island of yours?"

"I don't know where the rumor got started that I own that wretched island," he said querulously. "Full of snakes and mosquitoes. A friend of mine happens to own it and lets me use it from time to time. When all this comes out, she'll probably never —" he sighed "—well, that's probably the least of my worries."

"Hal," Susan said, "since you did keep on painting, haven't you developed a style of your own by this time? Aren't there pictures you've painted just because you wanted to paint them?"

She took his grunt to be an affirmation. "Did it ever occur to you to exhibit your own paintings? I mean those that were really your own? Not fakes or jokes."

He was silent. Jill burst into hysterical laughter.

Hal got up, went to the window, and stood for a minute with his back to them, contemplating the excavating machines as they snarled and spit their way through what had once been the museum's parking lot.

He turned, but, instead of coming back to the armchair, he perched on the edge of his desk, his leg dangling. "You were right, in a way. The real reason I opened the gallery, even though I didn't admit it to myself, was that it seemed the only way I would be able to get my own paintings shown. Not the Moffatt paintings, the ones I painted . . . the way I wanted to paint. That was the first show we put on. If you thought the write-up I gave Moffatt was enthusiastic, you should have seen the write-up I gave this one. But, as I told you, nothing happened. Nobody else even bothered to review the show.

"I'm really very sorry," Susan said. And she was.

"I'm not," Jill said, getting up and starting to gather her things together. "It's what you deserve. And, now all that's cleared up, I have to go. The shops will be closing soon."

* * *

"You know," Susan said, "all this time we've been talking, we haven't once wondered who killed Roland—unless one of you did it after all?"

"If I had been so inclined," Hal said, "I would have done it nine years ago, not now. As for Jill, I really don't think she's a killer."

"Thanks for nothing," Jill said. She regarded her image in a fret-carved Chippendale mirror. "The glass is so wavery," she said, "I don't know whether my hair needs combing or not. But I guess it wouldn't hurt."

She started burrowing in her handbag. "Actually, I think it must have been Baltasar who killed Roland. Drug dealers are always doing each other in, aren't they? And he was the one who bought Rafael's pieces."

With a triumphant cry she produced a comb. "I wonder why they bothered to set the place on fire. Maybe as an extra precaution. Roland was always such a fusspot."

Either Hal was a very good actor, or he really was astounded. As for Susan herself, she was surprised, but not as surprised as she would have been, say, a week ago.

"I expect Roland must have been working for him all these years," Jill said, getting to work on her red curls. "He was the one who came into the gallery to see Roland a couple of times. My gallery, I mean."

"But how come you never said anything about it—to me, anyway?" Hal asked.

"I did tell you at the time that there was a man, a Spanish type, who came to the gallery, and I was pretty sure he was Roland's liaison with the Colombian artist. And you told me not to mention it to the police, that I should keep out of the whole thing as much as I could. Otherwise they'd have me down to headquarters to look at photographs and a lot of stuff like that."

"Yes," Hal agreed, "it seemed best then. What I meant was why didn't you say anything when he turned up this time?"

"At first I didn't recognize him. He's changed a lot, gone way upscale. And I was sure he didn't recognize me. I looked a lot different then."

"But your name didn't change, Jill," Susan reminded her. "And your name was on the gallery."

"He acted as if he didn't recognize me or my name, so I figured I'd leave it at that. I admit I did start getting a little nervous, after Lupe told us she thought Rafael had been murdered."

They explained to Hal who Lupe was.

"When Roland got killed I did get panicky," Jill went on. "But by that time you and I weren't exactly chummy. Besides, you could have been the killer just as easily as Baltasar. I was too upset to think straight. I should have known you'd never have had the guts."

For a moment Hal looked as if he would have liked to kill her or at least commit significant mayhem on her person; then he shrugged and turned away.

"Before all that happened, though, I thought live and let live. I mean, what's so wrong with dealing in drugs, anyway? Everybody uses them. It's like prohibition. Everbody drank alcohol in spite of the law. And so they repealed the law. It'll be the same with drugs. Why blame somebody for being in advance of their time?"

"But drugs are destroying people, Jill," Susan pointed out.

"So is alcohol. So is tobacco. So is candy. I mean, where do you draw the line?"

Susan couldn't think of an answer.

"It's okay now, though," Jill said. "I did tell Lieutenant Bracco that I thought I recognized Baltasar as the one who used to come into the gallery, although I was very careful to say that I couldn't stand up in court and swear to it, because I'm not going to. He didn't look surprised. I guess maybe he suspected him already."

Or Andrew did, Susan thought, and passed the information along. "Damian—one of the young men at the gallery—told me they picked up Baltasar's passport early this afternoon."

"There, you see, I'm safe." Jill put her comb back into her handbag and snapped it shut.

"They picked up his passport," Hal reminded her. "They didn't pick up the man himself."

Jill thought about this. "Susan, would you like to come shopping with me? You can go to Queens some other time."

This piece of information seemed to divert Hal from the question of Baltasar. "Queens? Why are you going to Queens, Susan?"

Why is everyone so surprised that I'm going to Queens, Susan wondered. What's wrong with Queens? Doesn't anybody ever visit the outer boroughs except under extraordinary circumstances?

"It's getting to be something of an art center," Jill observed.

"That's right, I'd forgotten. A number of artists have set up studios in Long Island City and even farther in. Are you thinking of doing something like that, Susan?"

The atmosphere in the office had changed, somehow. If I don't get out of here in a hurry, Susan thought, he's going to have tea sent in. "No, nothing like that. And I do have to get out there as soon as possible. I think you'd better forget the new dress, Jill."

"Well, if I must, I must. In fact, I don't think I'll bother to go home and change. I'll call Andy, from one of the phone booths downstairs, because I want some privacy—" here she looked severely at her companions "—and tell him to pick me up in the lobby. Unless you want him to come up, so you can meet him?"

"I've already met him," Hal said.

"Oh, well in that case, ta," Jill said.

"Ta?" Hal repeated.

"Surfeit of *Masterpiece Theatre*," Susan explained.

Jill left. Susan got ready to leave but she was still shaken. Not by the knowledge that Hal had done the Moffatt paintings—that did not touch her personally, except as a matter of non-academic interest—but of how the other students had felt toward her when they were in school. How insensitive she must have been! And, even at that early age, she had prided herself on her sensitivity. She wished she could make up for it somehow.

"Hal, are you absolutely determined to resign from the Museum?"

"It isn't a matter of choice. Unless you mean I should 'tough it out,' the way Jill suggested? No, leave me with a modicum of dignity. Better to resign now than be kicked out later."

"Then why don't you at least tell them the whole story? Tell them it was you who did the Darius Moffatt paintings. That way, even the rave review wouldn't look so bad. After all, didn't Walt Whitman write a glowing review of *Leaves of Grass* when he was an anonymous book reviewer? And nobody thinks the worse of him."

"Nobody thinks the worse of him now, because he's dead. They probably wouldn't have been as tolerant at the time. Besides, he didn't write books and articles about a fake self he'd invented. As far as I know, anyway."

"But these are different times, Hal. Today people would think it was clever and amusing, a—a very 'cool' thing to do. Hard to forgive in a museum director, perhaps, but you know artists are expected to misbehave. It confirms their genius in the public's eyes."

"I would rather cut off my earlobe," he muttered.

"That wouldn't do you any good. This will. Admit you're Darius Moffatt. Be Darius Moffatt. Keep on painting—and selling—as Darius Moffatt. Remember that Darius Moffatt is one of the greatest geniuses of the twentieth century; you said so, yourself."

He laughed and then looked as if he would have liked to cry. "But the paintings are so goddamn awful."

"What does that matter? You'll be giving the public not only what it wants, but what it deserves. They say living well is the best revenge. They're wrong. Painting bad pictures and selling them to an undiscriminating public is even better."

"You make it all sound so easy," he said.

"Think of the money, Hal. That picture at Allardyce's went for two hundred and fifty thousand dollars. Two hundred and fifty thousand dollars!"

She seemed to have gotten through at last.

"Prices are bound to drop once the word gets out I'm alive," he mused aloud. "But they might not drop that far, especially after I appear on talk shows. And then lecture tours... Maybe I will take your advice. I suppose I do have nothing to lose. If I have to leave in disgrace, I might as well go out in style."

"That's the spirit," she said.

My God, she thought, I'm beginning to sound like Hortense Pomeroy!

XXX

OUTSIDE THE Museum she hailed a taxi, but, when she gave the driver her destination, he refused to take her there. "My shift is almost up, lady, and I live in New Jersey. I'm not going to go all the way out to Jackson Heights."

She was about to hail another cab, then she changed her mind. Perhaps it would be better to take the subway. Certainly it would be faster and simpler—although, if she had realized what the ride was going to be like, she might have changed her mind again. For the next half hour, she felt as though she had been plunged into one of Breughel's more graphic depictions of hell. Some people do this every day, she told herself, twice a day even. How could they do it and remain human?

The answer was: they couldn't. Going through this ordeal twice a day was bound to deprive them of all humanity. She knew that at the end of this ride she herself would be a little less human.

Maybe she had been wrong about choices, she thought. If these people had a choice, they wouldn't be here, Later, when she emerged from the platform into the chilly evening air—for somewhere along the way the subway had managed to escape from the lower depths and made its way up to ramshackle tracks elevated above the streets—she realized that she had been temporarily bereft of the human gift of reason. Like all the rest of God's creatures, the subway riders did have a choice. They could have taken a bus.

* * *

It was almost dark by the time she came down the subway steps (for it was still called a subway even though it was no longer subterranean and had never been much of a way) and descended into a street crowded with people speaking a variety of languages, mostly at the top of their lungs, with Spanish predominant and English virtually nonexistent.

As she went from the business section to what appeared to be the residential area, the crowds thinned out, but the noise level did not abate. People were conversing at shriek level both inside and outside the buildings. TV sets and stereos played at full blast, dogs barked; somewhere someone was playing the drums.

Rich cooking odors floated out into the air. They dined at an early hour in Queens. She began to regret the lunch she had rejected earlier.

Because the streets of Queens are arranged more or less in a grid pattern, she found her way to the address Damian had given her without any need to ask for directions. She couldn't explain to herself why, but it seemed important to attract as little attention as possible, to pass through the streets of Queens as though she had never been there.

Her destination turned out to be one of a row of nearly identical two-story brick houses on a tree-lined street. Each house was separated from its neighbors by a driveway on one side and an alley on the other. Each had a neat little garden in front, some with birdbaths or sundials—impossible to tell one from the other in the growing darkness. Although every house had a light over or next to its front door, the wattage was too low for details to be made out. Those might be gnomes (plastic) she saw in one garden. It might equally well have been a group of short, quiet people.

In only one respect did the house to which she was going differ from its neighbors. The occupants of the others had not bothered to draw their blinds, so that each pair of front windows was like a stage set, with the people inside going about their lives with as little regard for their audience as actors performing before a paper house.

The windows of this one were heavily curtained, so passersby could not see inside. Only the light, shining through cracks at top and sides, indicated either that someone was at home or electricity was being wasted.

As she walked up the cement pathway to the front door, she began to feel a twinge of unease. Maybe she should have told someone where she was going, giving some explanation—say, that she wanted to talk to Sanchia about having some dresses made—that would sound plausible; yet that would have given a clue as to where to look for her, in case she did not come back.

But if she didn't come back, who would look for her tonight? Or even tomorrow? If anyone called and she did not return their messages, they would simply think she was immersed in her art, avoiding the phone. It would be a long time before they discovered she had never come back. Intellectually she had always realized that she might be walking into danger. Now she was beginning to feel it emotionally as well.

For a weak moment she was tempted to retrace her footsteps, leave the garden, leave the borough, leave the whole thing to somebody else; but she sensed eyes watching her from the upper floor and she could not bring herself to turn her back on them. I am armed; I have a gun, she told herself, without patting the bulk of her handbag, because that might have given too much away to the watchful eyes. The knowledge was not as comforting as it had been before. These people must have guns, too.

She lifted the knocker on the front door and let it fall. It made a soft thud. Nothing happened. Its function must be primarily ornamental.

She rang the doorbell. That made a good loud noise. She could hear it resonate throughout the house. Silence for a moment. Perhaps nobody is home, she thought. Perhaps there is nothing for me to do here after all.

She was about to turn and go when she heard the sound of

heavy footsteps descending the stairs. The door opened. A tall man stood there, silhouetted against the dim light inside. For a moment she thought it was Baltasar. Then she saw it was the man whom she had met briefly at Rafael's funeral—Sanchia Gutierrez's husband.

"Is Lupe here?" she asked. "Lupe Montoya?"

Say no, she asked silently. Say you never even heard of her. That's right; you don't speak English. Just shake your head then. I'll apologize for having disturbed you, and do what I should have done in the first place, tell someone of my suspicions. So what if that did involve the innocent? Let their innocence be their own safeguard.

Without speaking, he gestured her inside and shut the door behind her with a finality that, she told herself, was only in her imagination. She found herself standing in a small vestibule with a staircase to the left and a narrow passage just ahead. There was an archway to her right blocked by a heavy curtain. He held back the curtain and indicated that she was to enter.

Beyond lay the most nondescript room she had ever seen. The color scheme was a drab monotone. The furniture looked as if it had been chosen, possibly from a catalogue, so that it would nei- ther appeal to—nor offend—any taste. It was very tidy. So that's what they mean by a safe house, she thought. The street noises were hushed in here. The place must be soundproofed.

Reclining on the oatmeal-colored couch, looking exotic and slightly absurd in those motel-like surroundings, was Lupe. She wore a dull gold trouser suit of some silky stuff that clung to her magnificent body in a way that was wasted on a female audience. Esmeralda reclined on her shoulder, shedding black hairs all over the gold silk. As Susan came into the room, she opened eyes as green as the jewels from which she took her name, and uttered a crooning sound. Lupe stretched up a beringed hand and patted her.

So Baltasar was here, or had been here. Unless he had given Esmeralda to someone else to convey to her mistress. For it was clear from the animal's confident air of possession that it was Lupe to whom she belonged, to whom she had always belonged.

Hortense had been right. Somebody had been living up in Baltasar's apartment. Lupe. Lupe and her cat. And Lupe had left the cat behind when she had gone to Queens.

But when and how long had she been living in Baltasar's apartment? Had she been there before the fire, before the opening of the gallery? Had it been the fire that had caused her to leave? Or had she gone there to live later, after the fire? Had she already been living there when she pretended to have just arrived in the city? And why had she—and Roland and Baltasar—put on that little charade for Susan's benefit? And, of course, Jill's, too, but Susan knew that it had been planned for her.

"Lupe," Susan said with tinny vivacity, "I'm so glad to see you're all right. No one seemed to have any idea where you were, and I was worried about you."

Lupe smiled. "So kind of you to worry about me, Susan," she purred, "and so clever of you to have found me."

"But you yourself told me where you would be," Susan said, affecting a wide-eyed innocence that, she was well aware, did not suit her and did not fool Lupe. "When nobody could find you, I remembered your telling us about the house in Jackson Heights."

Lupe stopped smiling. "That was very stupid of me. But I did not know then that Roland was going to die."

Susan thought of saying something like, "In the midst of life," but decided against it.

"Please sit down, Susan," Lupe said. "The chairs are not attractive but they are not uncomfortable."

Susan sat, leaning far back in her beige Naugahyde armchair to give an impression of ease and relaxation. Not that she thought she could fool Lupe, but she hoped to fool herself.

"I am sorry I cannot offer you any refreshment," Lupe said, "but the place is downside up. We are planning to leave very shortly."

Leave the house? The city? The country? She didn't like to ask direct questions.

"Is Baltasar leaving with you? I know he must have been here," Susan explained, "because of Esmeralda."

Hearing her name, the cat opened sleepy eyes and gave a meow of acknowledgement.

"Yes, Baltasar was here," Lupe said, caressing the animal. "But he has already left. He will not return."

"You mean he's dead?"

Lupe's laugh seemed genuine, but how can I tell, Susan thought. "What a vivid imagination you have, Susan. But, of course, you are an artist. It is to be expected. No, he has left the country sooner than . . . he expected. That is all."

"But they took his passport," Susan blurted, before she could stop herself."

Lupe's eyes narrowed. "Ah, I see you are indeed well informed. But he has more than one house, more than one car. Why should he not have more than one passport?"

And more than one name, too, Susan thought, but she didn't say anything.

XXXI

THERE WERE thumping sounds on the stairs. "Diego is getting things ready," Lupe explained. "We are planning to leave within the hour. I know that your government will not be pleased that Baltasar has departed so . . . informally. However, since he is not planning to return to this country, it is not of great significance."

"Then he's giving up the idea of establishing a salon here?"

"It was a mistake to have tried to establish one here in the first place. I told him so from the start, but he would not listen to me. He does not have the temperament for New York. 'If you must have a salon in the United States, Baltasar,' I told him, 'why not Miami? All right, Palm Beach.' But, no, it had to be New York or nothing. Well, now it is nothing."

Susan wondered whether this simply meant that Baltasar was never going to have a United States establishment or whether he was never going to have another establishment anywhere, ever; whether his dead body might not at that moment be lying somewhere, perhaps even downstairs in the basement. There wouldn't have been time to dispose of it in a more permanent way.

Lupe had denied that he was dead, but Lupe did not seem to Susan like a woman whose word could be relied upon.

"I am sorry now that I mentioned this place to you," Lupe admitted, "but I wanted some way to account for my presence in case I was forced to continue staying here. I invented my wolves and, in a way, myself. I am acquainted with someone who puts on a performance much like the one I described, although not so artistic."

"Dolores and her Dingos," Susan said, before she could stop herself.

"I see you have indeed been working hand in mitt with the police. Yes, Dolores is an employee of ours, a very low-echelon employee."

Probably travels around Australia distributing drugs, Susan thought. And a good cover, too. The police, arresting Dolores for being herself, would think to look no further. By the time they got to her, there would be no further to look. Everything about Dolores, if Lupe's account had been substantially accurate with regard to the real performer, would be out in the open.

There's no point sitting here, waiting to find out what she's planning as far as I'm concerned, Susan thought. She made a move to get up. "Well, now that I know you're safe, I'd better be going. I was supposed to meet my brother as soon as I made sure you were all right. He'll be expecting me."

"Sit down," Lupe commanded.

Susan was about to protest, caught Lupe's eye, and thought better of it. She sank back in her chair.

"I appreciate the point that you are trying so subtly to make, that there are people who are aware that you are here."

"I wasn't trying to make any point," Susan lied. "It happens to be the truth. A number of people do know that I was planning to come out here."

"That may be true," Lupe acknowledged. "Only a fool would have come out here without telling people where she was going, and I do not think you are a fool."

How wrong she is, Susan thought.

"However, I do know that you came alone. Diego was watching from the windows. And I do not think you told your brother or anyone else that you suspected you might find me here, or they would not have let you come alone."

Should I tell her that I've been wired and I have a back-up team waiting around the corner? No, it would be too easy and unpleasant for her to find out the truth. Besides, if I had been wired, the last thing I would do would be to tell her. No, the thing to do is smile enigmatically and let her think I have hidden resources.

"In fact, I would not be surprised to find that, even though you must have told someone where you were going, you did not tell them why."

Lupe stared hard into Susan's eyes, as if trying to wrest the truth from them. "You probably made up some excuse about having to see Sanchia, something like that. Which would mean there is plenty of time before anyone will come looking for you, and by then it will not matter any more."

Her words had an unpleasantly final sound.

"But I told Alex I would be right back."

"If you do not return as soon as he expects you, he is hardly likely to come rushing out here. Who would come out here, unless it is an absolute necessity?"

Poor woman, Susan couldn't help thinking, how she must have hated having to live out here. But I'll bet she never rode on the subway, she thought, and she hardened her heart.

"No, your brother will wait and then he will telephone, and I will answer the phone and say I am Sanchia and that you have been delayed for some very good reason, which I will think of. We are in the middle of fitting a gown or I have sent my husband out to match some thread or—"

"But why do you want to keep me here?"

Lupe shook her head. "Do not pretend to be so innocent, Susita; it does not become you."

Susita, Susan thought indignantly. That's even worse than Susie.

"I cannot let you leave, because you have too many suspicions. Too many accurate suspicions."

"But I can't prove anything. I don't really know anything, except that you must have been the one who was staying up in Baltasar's penthouse."

For some reason this seemed to irritate Lupe. "How did you know somebody had been staying up there?" Lupe demanded. "Nobody was supposed to know, nobody at all."

"Hortense Pomeroy ran up to take a look when Baltasar was called to the phone. She is rather nosy, I'm afraid," Susan said apologetically. "She's not really a friend of mine, just somebody who used to teach in the same school I did."

"Hortense who? Oh, yes, that gymnastic woman."

Lupe shook her head again. "That Baltasar, he is such a *bobo*. When I said to him—with lightness, mind you—that he might just as well have established a health club as an art gallery in the building, what does he do now that Roland is dead but call in this Pomeroy woman and offer to turn the gallery into health club. *Madre de Dios!*" She rolled her eyes.

"It did seem a little odd," Susan said.

"Odd!" Lupe said. "The whole set-out—thank you, set-up—was *loco*. To begin with, he should have known better than to establish Roland in a gallery after what happened with that Turkey Gallery."

"Turkel Gallery," Susan said. "It was named after Jill."

"Turkel, Turkey, what does it matter? And did he tell me that this Jill was the same Turkel and she might have recognized him? Did Roland? No."

Luckily for Jill, Susan thought. And she wondered whether the two men had been protecting Jill or themselves.

"I know it is difficult to find good assistants these days. Just the same, he should have known Roland was not a man to depend on. And, worse yet, he established his own atelier in the same building where he established the gallery. It would be more convenient, he said, and it would save money."

Her voice rose. "Save a few hundred thousand dollars, when we were spending millions!"

"We?" Susan repeated, knowing the answer, stalling for time.

"Of course we. You must know that neither Baltasar nor Roland had the brains to head an *empresa* like this."

By this time Susan had realized that it was Lupe who was the narcotics queenpin, but affected ignorance in the hope that this might still save her. Obviously that hope was futile. At least she could have her curiosity satisfied.

"Why did Baltasar kill Rafael and Roland?" she asked.

"Baltasar kill them, pah!" Lupe sneered. "He has not the *co-jones* to kill a flea. Even when it was not a question of killing, merely of having somebody beaten down—an occasional necessity in our business, you understand—he would always delegate it to someone else. But I always say the only way to get something done, is to do it yourself. I was the one who killed Rafael and Roland."

She stopped. If she's waiting for approval, Susan thought, she's not going to get it from me. Not that she didn't approve of Lupe's method in principle; she didn't like the direction in which she was afraid the practice was taking Lupe.

"You know, Susan," she said, "all of this is your fault. None of it would have happened if it hadn't been for you."

"My fault!" Susan echoed indignantly.

"Roland assured us he would be able to get your work for our opening exhibit. Very impressive, very respectable, very open and overboard. But it turned out you thought you were too good for us."

"It wasn't like that at all. I had other commitments. I told Roland that when he first asked me."

Lupe shrugged. "Whatever the reason, we had to use Rafael's work, which we had planned for our second exhibit, one which was supposed to creep quietly into town with no *fanfarria*."

"I see," Susan said. That explained several things, not that explanations were going to be of much use to her at that moment.

"If Rafael had not received so much *alabanza* at the opening, to justify our selection of him for that honor, I do not think he would have become so full of himself. He read the press releases and he believed them, poor fool. He said he had decided that he wasn't going to let his 'beautiful works of art' be destroyed, no matter how much we had paid him to concoct them. He said if we tried, he would tell the authorities. It did not matter if he got put in prison; it would be good publicity. Naturally, I had to kill him. What else could I have done? We had a good deal of money wrapped up in those things. So you see it was all your fault, Susan."

Susan decided it was wiser not to debate the point.

"He was already drunk," Lupe went on, "so it was simple to give him a shot of heroin."

"But how could you? I mean, you weren't there; how could you manage to do it? Oh, that must have been while you were living upstairs."

And Susan realized something else. Even if Rafael had been working for Baltasar, Rafael's wife would hardly have been staying in Baltasar's penthouse. Baltasar would have been living there with his own wife. The exhibition catalogue had not made a mistake in neglecting to mention a wife. Rafael had not had a wife. But Baltasar had. How could I have been so stupid, Susan thought.

"I had been planning to make my entrance into New York society at the opening," Lupe explained. "I had been looking forward to it. But I could not, after Rafael's death. I have far too much sensibility."

Also too much caution, Susan thought.

"*Naturalmente* I could not stay in the apartment after that. Someone might see me and wonder why I had not come to the opening. So I came to stay here. Imagine me, living in a lower-middle-class suburb!"

"It must have offended all your aristocratic instincts, *condesa*," Susan said.

"So, you have guessed that too! I suppose it was obvious."

"By this time it is," Susan said, "although I really had no idea before."

Lupe looked happy. "I have often thought I could have been an actress but, of course, it would not have been suitable for someone of my category."

Lupe looked sad. "But after Rafael's death it looked as if I would never be able to make my entrance into New York society. I could not help feeling disappointed, but not very much. New York society is not such a big thing, after all. Not that I wish to offend you, Susan."

Susan assured her that she was not offended.

"But I did not wish to keep on staying in Queens [she pronounced it "Quins"] all the time I am in New York. I had a plan. We would arrange that I should arrive at the same time as some very respectable person came to the gallery, to establish the fact that I was Rafael's wife and that I had come because of the money. Then Baltasar—out of kindness toward a poor widow—" she laughed merrily "—was going to offer to permit me to stay in his apartment."

"Suppose afterward you ran into someone you knew in the street?" Susan said. "A lot of Spanish aristocrats seem to spend more time here than in Spain."

"That is true," she said. However, the kind of people I know do not walk about the streets. They are driven through them in long limousines. But if by misfortune such a thing should happen all I would need to say was that I am not I, but someone else who looks like me."

"You thought of everything," Susan said, trying to sound admiring without sliding over in obsequiousness.

"When you telephoned Roland, to tell him you had seen a person prowling outside, he thought this would be a fine opportunity for me to make my appearance. He would ask you to come over and show him exactly where you had seen this person, and I would arrive at a similar time."

Susan wasn't sure she liked the idea of being classified as a "very respectable person," but this was no time to quibble.

"However, the whole exercise turned out to be pointless. It became necessary to kill Roland that same evening, before I even had a chance to move my possessions back into the penthouse. After that, I thought it might be advisable for me to return here until I decided what must be done. You will ask me why it became necessary to kill Roland?"

Lupe's smile was apologetic. "It was almost an accident, can you believe it? If I have a fault, it is that I am too impulsive. All along, I must tell you, Roland had been disturbed because I had killed Rafael. He said he had not bargained on murder when he joined us. But what kind of organization did he think he was joining, *válgame Dios!* The Boy Scouts? Then, when I happened to mention to Baltasar that the man you saw outside the building had a dog with him, Baltasar became agitated. He said the man must be a detective and the place must have been under suspicion."

"He was a detective and the place had been under suspicion."

"I know that now, but I did not know it then. I had not been working—what is the expression?—in the field. It did not occur to me that the dog also was a detective, a drug-detective. I do not approve of using animals in such a way, and neither does Esmeralda, do you, *querida?*"

Esmeralda meowed without opening her eyes.

"He's a very nice young man," Susan said, "the dog's master, I mean—not that he owns the dog; he just borrowed him—and he seems quite taken with Jill."

"I am glad to think that perhaps something good will come out of this fiasco," Lupe said. "It is a pity that, if they should get married, I cannot come to the wedding. I love weddings. However, I shall send them a very handsome present from Spain, in your memory, Susan."

Susan didn't ask for an explanation of that last remark. It was, she was afraid, self-explanatory.

It seemed important to keep Lupe talking, although there was no logical reason for her to do so. Nobody was going to come save her. If she was going to be saved, she must save herself. "I still can't understand how you killed Roland by accident."

"Almost by accident. To begin with, Baltasar started making a scandal. He insisted that now that we were under suspicion we must give up our plans and leave right away. While I was trying to convince him that if we kept firm and behaved innocently, it would all blow away, Roland broke apart. He said that maybe, if he made a clean breast of affairs, the authorities would be lenient with him. After all, he had not killed anybody; he was not even a principal in this *empresa*, just a funky—is that the right word?"

"Flunky," Susan told her.

"Thank you. Flunky. He said he was going to consult with someone about it and perhaps go to a lawyer. I think it was you he was going to consult with, am I not right, Susita?"

Susan swallowed. "He did say he wanted to talk to me about something, but I hadn't the least idea of what he was going to say."

"That is as may be," Lupe said. "At any rate, he went on talking like that, thinking only of himself; no consideration for others who were also involved and might suffer. He made me very angry, so angry that I hit him with a paperweight—a very nice respectable paperweight cast in the shape of one of the towers of my ancestral castle that I had given to him as a house-heating gift. I had not intended to kill him. Not at least just then, although I am sure that upon reflection I would have killed him sometime. However, he was dead on the instant, so there was no need for reflection."

At that point, she said, Baltasar had lost his head and gotten hysterical but Lupe was made of sturdier stuff. Came of being born on the right side of the blanket, Susan thought.

"I decided we must make it look like a sex crime. Then nobody would suspect anything out of the ordinary, because such things happen all the time here, especially in artistic circles. I read your newspapers and I know."

She and Baltasar had carried the body down to "that obscene place in the basement," where, since Baltasar had apparently been too squeamish, she had "hit him some more with that disgusting object I found down there, keeping my eyes shut all the time. Such a nasty thing; I could hardly bear to touch it." And she shuddered.

"I felt *ensuciada*—soiled—afterwards, even though I had put on gloves and an *impermeable* beforehand, so I could keep myself neat and not leave any fingerprints. You see, I know all about fingerprints, from reading the works of Miss Agatha Christie, whom I much admire."

Subsequently they had thrown the paperweight, along with the gloves, the raincoat, and a small rug which had been somehow involved, into the East River.

"We should also have dropped Roland in the river. Well it is no use weeping over spilt wine, don't you agree?"

Susan refused to agree.

"After that I decided there was no use trying to carry on at this place, and so I told Baltasar we would do as he wished and terminate our business, at least for the time."

It seemed to Susan that she was doing the wisest thing possible under the circumstances. But where does that leave me, she wondered. She soon found out.

XXXII

"AND NOW I am sorry, but I am afraid I am going to have to kill you, Susan."

"I don't see why," Susan said, "since you're closing down anyhow."

"Because you know too much," Lupe said simply.

"But I wouldn't have known it if you hadn't told me."

Lupe looked abashed. "Well, I had to talk to somebody. You don't know what it is like to be alone in a strange country surrounded by idiots. Besides, you had already unravelled most of it, I am sure. Or you would have, given time. You are a very clever lady, Susan."

Susan felt the compliment was undeserved. A really clever lady would have kept as far away from this place as possible. "What use would killing me be?" she asked. "The authorities are bound to figure out the truth sooner or later. And I did leave a letter to be opened in the event of my death, that outlines all my theories about what I thought might have happened."

"You are lying," Lupe said, without conviction.

Susan resisted the temptation to say, "I am not, either," and contented herself with an enigmatic smile.

"In any case, you did not know that I was Baltasar's wife. So let them look for Lupe Montoya. They will never find her."

"But, if you entered the country under your own name," Susan pointed out, "which I assume you did, since you were planning to make your entrance into New York society, your arrival and departure will be on record. And, since you were—are—Baltasar's wife, they will eventually suspect that you have some connection with the whole thing."

"I do not think that your police are as efficient as all that. As I have said, I read your newspapers. But let them suspect me. Once I am back in my own country they cannot touch me, no matter if they do have suspicions, because I am far too well connected."

"Then why do you feel it's necessary to kill me?" Susan argued. "All you have to do is make sure that I can't go to the authorities with my story, until you've gone back to Spain."

Lupe thought this over; then shook her head. "I am afraid not, Susan. If the police merely had suspicions of their own accord, they would not be likely to try to bother me, but if you told them of your suspicions they would, because you are so very well connected yourself."

Susan thought of promising never to divulge Lupe's identity, but realized that it would be futile. Lupe would never believe her. In Lupe's position, she wouldn't have believed it either.

"You, of course, I will not hit with a paperweight," Lupe said. "First of all, because it is more difficult when the person to be hit is forewarned, but secondly, because I do not wish to cause you unnecessary pain. I am sorry to do this, Susan, because I like you and I am a great *aficionada* of your paintings. You might be interested to know that I have several of them in the collection at my castle. I am very proud of the family art collection, to which I have added many fine pieces, and I am sorry you will never be able to visit my castle and see them, Susan. I find you *muy simpática*. Under other circumstances, I think we could have been friends."

In a pig's eye, Susan thought inelegantly, but then the situation did not call for elegance.

"On the other hand, as soon as it becomes known that you are dead, the value of your paintings will go up, so at least I will have that to console me for what I am about to do."

Lupe removed Esmeralda from her shoulder and placed the

protesting animal on the back of the couch. Then she took out a gun, a pearl-handled revolver, for heaven's sake, Susan thought in disgust. How corny could you get!

"You will wonder why I am doing this myself, instead of having Diego do it? That is because I seem to have surrounded myself with nothing but weemps."

Susan had already noted that Lupe had been getting increasingly nervous. Now she was beginning to babble. Good, Susan thought.

"Now, if you will hold absolutely still without moving, Susan, I will kill you with one shot through the head. And you will feel nothing. But if you wriggle it might take more than one shot, and then you will feel pain, and I do not want that. I am a good shootist, you understand, but not an expert."

"But I am," Susan said. And, taking the gun out of her bag, she shot Lupe cleanly through the head. Esmeralda meowed and scuttled behind the couch.

Lupe probably did not feel any pain. Susan wouldn't have cared if she had.

And now, Susan thought, getting up, for Diego.

But he did not wait for her. *"Madre de Dios!"* a voice called beyond the curtain. She started toward it but he was ahead of her. Footsteps pelted down the hall. The front door slammed.

She opened the door and saw him running down the pathway and out into the street.

Nobody paid the least attention to him. It wasn't likely that they had heard the shot, but, if they had, no one seemed concerned.

There seemed to be no one else in the house. Susan did not investigate to make sure. She dropped the gun back into her bag. Since she had not taken off her gloves, there wouldn't be any fingerprints on it. Somewhere along the way she would drop it in a litter basket. It would be gone before the sanitation truck came.

Then she quietly left the house and took the subway to Manhattan. The ride back was much less disagreeable.

XXXIII

"THEY'RE BEAUTIFUL children, Alex," Susan said. "Beautiful." In actual fact they looked like blobs to her, but it was not the sort of thing you said to a proud young father. "And Baldwin is a fine name, but why did you have to call the other one Buckley?"

"The Pattersons expected it," Alex told her. "How could we have called one twin after one grandfather and not call the other twin after the other one? But don't worry. His middle name is Alexander. We'll call him by some variant of that."

"Tinsley is already calling him Bucky," Susan pointed out.

"Oh, is she? Well, I haven't heard him answer to it." He laughed. Susan didn't.

"What does it matter, after all, what they're called? If they had been girls, she probably would have insisted on naming one Susan. How would you have liked that?"

"You and Tinsley aren't planning to have any more children, are you?" Susan asked anxiously.

He smiled. "Too soon to be thinking about anything like that now. Come, you haven't toasted the babies' health yet."

He steered her through the crowds which had come to celebrate the christening of Baldwin Patterson and Buckley Alexander Tabor. The guests of honor, after a brief public appearance, were no longer on the scene, but, in spite of the fact that the season was over, virtually everyone else in New York seemed to be.

"Where's Peter?" Alex asked, after they had both acquired glasses of champagne and had solemnly toasted the infants. "I haven't had a real chance to talk to him since he got back. I hear he's no longer with the university."

"He ran into trouble with some Eskimos on a field trip," she admitted, "and the university decided not to renew his contract. He's so excited over his foundation, though, I don't think he even noticed."

They moved back into the living room, greeting and being greeted from all directions as they passed. "My teeth are beginning to stiffen," Alex said, "and I wouldn't be surprised to find that my face is permanently stretched. Let's find a quiet corner where I can stop smiling for a while."

Owing to his superior knowledge of his own premises, they were able to establish themselves behind a screen which partially blocked off an alternative entrance to the kitchen.

"Peter's at the foundation building now, driving all the workmen crazy," Susan said. "He says he'll be over later, but I'm sure you'll forgive him if he never makes it. You know how Peter is."

"I do, indeed," Alex said, "and I forgive him in advance. What kind of foundation is it, by the way?"

"We'll think of something," she said. "What I mean is that the final details haven't been worked out yet, of course."

"Of course," Alex said.

"Hortense Pomeroy isn't here either," she observed.

"Hortense Pomeroy? Oh, yes, that gym teacher who was planning to set up a health club in what used to be Roland's gallery. Was she invited?"

"I don't know, but that wouldn't have stopped her if she'd wanted to come. She's furious with me, and, by extension, my relatives, because the building went to Peter's foundation instead of to her. She said Baltasar had promised it to her—the two lower floors and the basement, anyway, which I suppose he had."

"But she must know that the government confiscated it, that the law says a drug dealer's property is forfeit."

"She does know that, but she says it's quite a coincidence that Peter got the building. She insists that strings were pulled and connections used." Susan and Alex looked at each other and smiled.

"Doesn't she realize that without Baltasar backing her, she'd never have been able to afford that building, anyway?" Alex asked.

"Apparently she doesn't. Or doesn't want to." Susan took a sip of champagne. "I'm sure that, once she's simmered down, she'll find a much more suitable place."

"You better hope she does," Alex said. "I understand that Lady Daphne Merriwether—" of whom he, like everyone else, had heard much of by this time "—has indicated publicly that she's out to get you." Again Alex laughed and she didn't.

Andrew Mackay came around the screen with a glass of champagne in either hand. Apparently his detecting instincts did not stop with crime. "Hi, Susan," he said, "you're looking great. Great party, Alex. Great-looking kids. Have you seen Jill? She seems to have disappeared while I was getting more champagne."

"I saw her in the dining room talking to—rather, yelling at— Gil Stratton. She's never forgiven him for trying to get me as a client."

"I'd better put a stop to that. Can't have her making scenes at your party." He went off dining-roomward.

"He seems to have her well in hand," Alex said. I still can't understand, though, why you kept her on after everything that happened."

"Well, if Hal thought she was good enough to represent him, I decided she was good enough for me."

"Quite a surprise, his turning out to be the painter of those Moffatt pictures," Alex said. "I must admit I did have suspicions about his . . . er . . . integrity, but I would never have suspected that, and I know you couldn't have either, or you wouldn't have been so surprised to discover he was the real owner of Jill's gallery."

"No, I never guessed," Susan said. "That's one of the reasons I didn't fire Jill. If I had, it would have made me look like a fool—or, even worse, a victim. People would have felt sorry for me. This way—"

"This way, even though you deny it, it'll look as if you might have known about the whole thing all along," Alex agreed. "Much more dignified, or should I say 'cool?' And what's the other reason—or reasons—you didn't fire Jill?"

"She seems to be doing a perfectly good job," Susan explained. "Hal's prices have come down a little, because he's still alive, but his pictures are selling very well. And my prices have gone up. I've broken the six-figure barrier...I notice you seem to have acquired a Moffatt," she said, looking at the adjacent wall, trying to keep a chilly note out of her voice.

Alex looked abashed. "I like to keep up with current trends," he said. "Besides, I got it at a discount because I'm family, so to speak."

"I'm surprised you didn't hang it in your office to impress your clients."

"The other one's in my office. Jill gave me not only a family discount but a reduction for quantity."

Alex looked around. "Where is Hal? He certainly was invited."

"He must still be on his honeymoon," Susan said. "They're on that Greek island the bride owns—you know, the one everyone always thought belonged to him."

"I don't envy him the fair Eloise," Alex said, "in spite of the Charpentier billions. Not," he added hastily, "that I would envy any man his wife when I'm married to the most wonderful woman in the world."

It appeared that Hal and Eloise had been involved with each other for some time; but, because of the vindictiveness of her most recent ex-husband, they had been forced to keep their affair under wraps until her divorce was final. Had Hal been making up to Susan just as a blind? Obviously it could not have been Susan's modest millions he was after in the light of Eloise's billions. Susan got the idea that, billions or no billions, Hal wasn't altogether happy about having to marry Eloise, but it might have been her fancy. Or her conceit.

"More champagne?" Alex asked.

"I'd better get something to eat first," she said, "or I'll get tipsy."

"And we couldn't have that," he said, "not at a christening. It would set a bad example."

They made their way toward the buffet. "I wonder what happened to Baltasar after he murdered his wife," Alex said, as he heaped his plate. "Such a surprise to find out the woman you knew as Lupe was really the *condesa*. I'm sorry I never had a chance to meet her. I wonder why he killed her."

"I suppose we'll never know," Susan said, keeping her eyes on the food as she made her modest selection. "And nobody knows for sure that he was the one who did it," she added conscientiously.

"Well, when a drug dealer disappears and his wife is found murdered, it seems a logical assumption that he killed her. It might have been self-defense, though. She did have a gun, although it hadn't been fired."

"I know," Susan said.

He looked at her.

"I read about it in the papers," Susan said quickly. "And Andy filled me in on some of the details. Apparently, she didn't get a chance to fire it. But it still could have been self-defense, if she drew her gun first."

"Baltasar beat her to the draw, eh? Well, I don't suppose we'll ever know. He must have gone to earth in Colombia. He wouldn't dare go back to Spain now."

"It seems likely," Susan said. She wondered whether that was true, or whether Baltasar had already been dead when she confronted Lupe. There hadn't been any sign of a body in the Jackson Heights house, Andy'd told her, or any other indication of violence, so there was a good chance he was still alive.

* * *

"It's lucky you decided not to go out to Jackson Heights after all," Alex said, "or you would have walked right into the middle of things."

"I didn't actually *decide* not to go. It was just that I couldn't get a cab to take me to Queens. I actually went so far as to go down into the subway, but when I saw what it was like I found I simply couldn't face it."

Alex nodded sympathetically. "Andy tells me that if you'd told him about the house as soon as it occurred to you, that Lupe— whatever her name was—might be there, they would have been able to catch the gang red-handed."

"Of course he'd say that."

But it wouldn't have been the gang that they would have caught red-handed. Her escape—not from Lupe but from Andrew—had been narrower than she had realized. While Jill and Andrew had been having pre-dinner drinks, Jill had happened to mention that Susan was going to Jackson Heights, of all places! That had alarmed Andrew. He'd called first Alex and then Baltasar to see if either had any idea where Susan might have gone. Damian had answered the phone at the gallery and, after giving him the address, had offered the information that Baltasar had already departed with his luggage and his cat.

Andrew had rushed out to Jackson Heights, doing Jill out of still another dinner. He'd found an empty house and a dead *condesa*. Of course he hadn't known then that she was Baltasar's wife. He had simply assumed that, since she fit the description, she was Lupe Montoya. It was only later, after her photograph had been published in the papers, that her true identity had been discovered and a scandal of major proportions unleashed.

If the Spanish nobility had been popular in New York's social circles before, now they became the reigning social lions. A tribute to the *condesa's* memory was being planned at Mimi's Grand Ball and Gala against Drug Abuse.

"But don't they understand she was the one who was behind it all?" Susan asked Alex.

"It wouldn't make any difference," he said. "But what makes you think she was the one who was behind it all?"

"She—Andy told me that Baltasar and the rest of the gang seemed to have left the place in such a hurry that they left most of their stuff behind. There was enough there to convict them of drug dealing ten times over. They even left Esmeralda behind. The cat. Andrew took possession of her and gave her to Jill."

"I wouldn't have taken Jill for an animal lover."

"She loves Andrew," Susan said.

Alex put down his empty plate. "Do you think they'll make a match of it?"

"I don't know," Susan said. "It would be nice to think so."

And Esmeralda's collar could take the place of the wedding present Lupe had been planning to send the couple. Susan wondered whether they knew the emeralds were real. Maybe she ought to point it out to them. No, just to Jill. Andrew was just righteous enough to turn the collar over to the government if he knew its value.

Everything was not necessarily over, she knew. Diego had gotten away and he knew it was Susan who had killed Lupe. But, if he tried to tell anyone, she doubted that he would be believed. Perhaps Baltasar, if he was still alive, would believe, but she did not think he would blame her. Besides, she didn't think he would ever dare come back to the United States.

Actually, Susan thought, I'm in much more danger from Lady Daphne. Of course she wasn't afraid of her, but she felt she owed it to Hortense to make a substantial investment in the health club. After all, she said to herself, it is a worthy cause.